Mr Lynch's Holiday

Catherine O'Flynn was born in 1970 and raised in Birmingham, the youngest of six children. Her parents ran a sweet shop. Prior to the publication of her first novel she did a variety of jobs, including journalist, web editor, record shop manager, postwoman, teacher and mystery shopper. She won the Costa First Novel Award for *What Was Lost* in 2008. Her second novel, *The News Where You Are*, was published by Viking in 2010.

By the same author

What Was Lost

The News Where You Are

Mr Lynch's Holiday

CATHERINE O'FLYNN

VIKING

an imprint of

PENGUIN BOOKS

VIKING

Published by the Penguin Group
Penguin Books Ltd, 80 Strand, London wc2r orl, England
Penguin Group (USA) Inc., 375 Hudson Street, New York, New York 10014, USA
Penguin Group (Canada), 90 Eglinton Avenue East, Suite 700, Toronto, Ontario, Canada m4p 2y3
(a division of Pearson Penguin Canada Inc.)
Penguin Ireland, 25 St Stephen's Green, Dublin 2, Ireland
(a division of Penguin Books Ltd)
Penguin Group (Australia), 707 Collins Street, Melbourne, Victoria 3008, Australia
(a division of Pearson Australia Group Pty Ltd)
Penguin Books India Pvt Ltd, 11 Community Centre,
Panchsheel Park, New Delhi – 110 017, India
Penguin Group (NZ), 67 Apollo Drive, Rosedale, Auckland 0632, New Zealand
(a division of Pearson New Zealand Ltd)
Penguin Books (South Africa) (Pty) Ltd, Block D, Rosebank Office Park,
181 Jan Smuts Avenue, Parktown North, Gauteng 2193, South Africa

Penguin Books Ltd, Registered Offices: 80 Strand, London wc2r orl, England

www.penguin.com

First published 2013
001

Copyright © Catherine O'Flynn, 2013

The moral right of the author has been asserted

Typeset in 12/14.75 pt Dante MT Std by Palimpsest Book Production Ltd, Falkirk, Stirlingshire
Printed in Great Britain by Clays Ltd, St Ives plc

A CIP catalogue record for this book is available from the British Library

Hardback isbn: 978-0-670-91856-0
Trade Paperback isbn: 978-0-670-92332-8

www.greenpenguin.co.uk

ALWAYS LEARNING   PEARSON

Written for Peter and Edie
Dedicated to the memory of Donal and Ellen

I

2008

He arrived on a cloudless day. As he stepped on to the tarmac, he looked up at the sky and saw nothing but blue and the traces left by other planes.

The terminal was deserted. He wandered along polished floors with a handful of other passengers. Music was playing somewhere. An old tune, he couldn't remember the name. It was not how he'd imagined airports. It seemed more like a ballroom to him. Something grand and sad about the place.

Walking through a sliding door he found himself in the arrivals hall, confronted by a crowd of people crushed up against the rail waving pieces of paper and looking at him expectantly. Scanning the faces and signs, he smiled apologetically for not being their man. He looked beyond them to others who hung back and leaned against walls, but saw no trace of Eamonn. He had never assumed that he would be able to meet him. It wasn't always possible to just drop what you were doing.

———

Eamonn wasn't sure how long he'd been awake, or if what had passed before had been sleep. He seemed to have been conscious for hours, lying inert in a kind of trance. He rolled on to Laura's empty side of the bed and picked up the barely there scent of her perfume, citric and uncertain. He sat on the edge of the bed for a moment, waiting to recover.

He sidled over to the window, opening the shutters an inch before slamming them closed again. He tried once more, pulling back slowly, keeping his gaze downcast, watching colour flood the floor tiles. His feet retained their mortuary hue, luminously pale on the terracotta slabs.

When he thought his eyes could stand it, he looked out of the window. It was just as he'd known. Another day, dazzling and merciless.

He found the payphones and pulled an address book out of his bag. The book was ancient, a faded lady with a parasol on the cover, the Sellotape holding it together dried out and yellow. The pages bulged with various additions and amendments on old letters, birthday cards and torn scraps of tea-bag box. Looking for Eamonn's details he came across the phone numbers of various friends and family long dead or forgotten. It was strange to think that by pressing a few buttons he might hear some of their voices again. The book contained his and Kathleen's entire life, and the information it held was almost all obsolete.

When he found the number he realized he'd need coins and suddenly it was all too much bother and messing about when he could be off and on the road already. He was happy to make his own way. He thought there were few places you couldn't reach with a decent map and public transport.

He found the buses easily enough at the airport. He boarded one with the name of what looked a fairly large town, in the general direction of Eamonn's place. The woman driver gave a small nod when he attempted his pronunciation of the place. Receiving change was the first thing that really struck him as foreign. He wondered if she appreciated how much aggro she avoided by not insisting on exact fares.

Eamonn was hungry. He rooted listlessly in the kitchen cupboards, conscious that he had done the same thing the previous day, and maybe the day before that too. He found the madeleine cake hitherto rejected for the dark stain of mould on its underside. He cut away the exterior, leaving a cubic inch of untainted yellow sponge, which he put on a plate and took out on to the balcony along with a cup of stale mint tea.

He sat on the terrace, looking over at the shared swimming pool. It had been empty for almost a year, the chlorinated water replaced with a thin layer of pine needles. He noticed that a family of cats had moved in overnight, locating themselves in the deep end on a discarded Cheetos box. Lomaverde had proven to be a popular destination for hardworking cats and their families. The legion of them snaking in the shadows around the bins had steadily grown. It was hard to tell if fresh residents were continuing to flood in or if the original settlers were simply reproducing rapidly in the promised land.

He was startled by the door buzzer – a strange skip to his heart as he pressed the button, thinking: 'I have become a dog.' He was greeted with the klaxon voice of the postwoman. She made occasional trips out to the development, seemingly as and when she felt it worth her while. He didn't know what happened to the mail between being sent and being delivered, if it languished in a sorting office somewhere or if the postwoman herself kept it all in her flat. He imagined her rooms filled with crates of mail, sacks of other people's special offers and exclusive opportunities stuffed under her bed.

There was never anything much in the post that he wanted anyway. He shuffled down to the lobby for something to do and collected the pile from his mailbox, dropping each envelope after a cursory glance: Vodafone bill, Endesa bill, Santander statement, and then he stopped. He examined the pale blue envelope closely before opening it.

Dear Eamonn,

How are you? I hope well. All is fine here. Anne came over last week to help clear the last of your mother's things. I'm glad now that it's done, I'd been putting it off for too long.

You're no doubt wondering what spirit has moved me to write, so I will get down to brass tacks. I'm not getting any younger and I have to accept that I could follow your mother any day now and it's high time I crossed off some of those things on the 'to do' list.

I don't know if you remember John Nolan (son of Eugene), but he works in Harp Travel now and has sorted out flights and tickets for me. I'll be arriving at the airport in Almería at nine in the morning on 7 June.

Please don't be going to any bother on my account, I'm well used to taking care of myself. I'm looking forward to seeing you and Laura and getting my first taste of 'abroad'.

Best wishes,
Your dad

The bright sun on the pale paper was blinding. His father's looping blue words floated up off the page into the air around him like dust motes. He moved away from the window and read it again. He found himself fixing on irrelevancies like who John Nolan might be, or how Harp Travel could still be in business. He would phone his father later and tell him to cancel the trip. He started thinking of gentle excuses.

Dermot sat near the front of the bus and studied the passing landscape. Near the airport everything was huge. He saw elevated advertising hoardings and vast storage facilities, all on the scale of the airport itself, as if aeroplanes, not cars, might be passing along the road. Further on, the landscape broke down into a cluttered mishmash that he found hard to process. Small, scrappy agricultural plots with shacks made of plastic crates and tarpaulin huddled in the shadow of mirrored-glass buildings and their empty car parks. He looked at the graffiti under every flyover – colourful images as complicated and jumbled as the landscape around them – huge letters with teeth and eyes spelling strange words and names. He saw the same poster for a circus over and over again and later passed the circus itself in the middle of a parched field. The word 'Alegría' was written in lights above the entrance.

At the terminus he asked if the driver spoke English and she said a little. Eamonn's place was unmarked on the map. A new town. Purpose built. There was just a small cross in biro that Eamonn had made for his mother before he left. Dermot tried the name of it anyway on the driver and when she looked blank he was unsure if it was his pronunciation or the obscurity of the place. He pointed on the map to where he was heading and she shook her head and blew air as if trying to whistle. She opened her window and called to the driver of a bus parked across the street. She turned back to Dermot.

'Is very far. Difficult.'

'Right.'

'Bus T-237 to here.' She indicated a point on the map a little distance from Eamonn's cross. '*Después* . . .' she blew air through her lips again and shrugged. 'Taxi?'

'Right. Thank you very much.' He hesitated and then said,

'*Gracias.*' The driver smiled and showed him where to get the bus.

He took his time walking through the town, looking in the windows of the shops he passed. He saw one that seemed to sell only slippers and another one just pyjamas. At the baker's he paused and studied the display before deciding to enter. Inside he found he was a good foot and a half taller than any of the other customers. Some of the women turned to look at him and he gave each a brief nod of his head. There was no queue that he could discern, but the two women behind the counter seemed to know in which order to serve everyone. When it came to his turn, he pointed at a stick of bread filled with ham and cheese, and bought some kind of milkshake as well. He took them out into the street and ate them waiting for the bus, enjoying the warmth of the sun seeping through his clothes.

Time: 43:08; Moves: 579. Two kings were trapped behind the seven of clubs. He shifted cards from the ace piles and back again, treading water while the clock ticked on. Just visible on the screen, above the top-right corner of the simulated green baize, a folder of students' work sat unmarked. He glanced at it periodically and then back at the cards. There were different ways to traverse the vast floes of time.

He found himself staring at the blinking cursor, unsure how long he had been doing so. His body had become synced with the cursor's rhythm: the ebb and flow of his blood, the throb of his heart, the pulse of his headache. When his eyes finally refocused, it was upon the date display. He stared at it for some time, finding it distantly familiar, before reaching for his father's letter.

He stood up quickly, feeling dizzy, thrashing about in search of the car keys before running into the street. The hot breath of the Toyota threatened to suffocate him as he climbed inside. He turned the key and the engine clicked. He did it again and again, as if the act of turning the key could somehow recharge the battery. He got out to breathe and kick the car like a child and then he was still.

On the second leg of the journey the landscape was unvaried. He saw nothing for miles but great expanses of polytunnels, the entire countryside hidden behind wrapping. Occasionally he'd glimpse a field apparently abandoned, its plastic covering ripped open and hanging in sheets as if the crops inside had escaped during the night. For a long time he could detect no evidence of humanity, but gradually his eyes adjusted to the rhythm of the landscape and he began to spot makeshift shacks huddled next to the vast plastic tunnels, T-shirts and jeans hanging from washing lines, plastic garden furniture, a solitary young black man crouching in the shade.

The bus dropped him near the junction to the road that led to Eamonn's village. From the map it looked to be about four miles by that road, but he saw there was a more direct route over the hills. He had always been a walker, often finding himself walking his bus routes on days off, investigating more closely things he had been able only to glimpse from the driver's cab. As he climbed the main slope now, even with the footing a little tricky in parts, he realized how much he had missed decent hills like these and the feeling of his blood moving quickly around his body.

Eamonn's apartment was in the upper reaches of Lomaverde, at the rear of the development, or the 'urbanization', as some of the other expats called it in a strange mangling of the

Spanish. His block was at the end of the street; beyond its side-wall lay nothing but steep-rising, bare scrubland, optimistically described as 'impressive mountain scenery' in the sales particulars. Now, leaning against the car, paralysed by indecision, he glimpsed something in the distance on the hillside. He looked again and saw that it was a human figure. Nobody approached Lomaverde from the hill. Visitors, such as they were, came along the winding road from the town. The burglaries had stopped but they all remained suspicious of strangers. He shielded his eyes with his hands and looked up towards the black shape.

Dermot had grown used to the sparseness of the landscape on the climb: slopes of arid, white soil, broken up with wild rosemary. When he reached the top he saw the broad expanse of the Mediterranean stretched out before him. The deep blue seemed to rinse his eyes of the grittiness they'd had since boarding the plane that morning. The water appeared completely still and he stood, equally still, his breathing slowing, fully absorbed by the colour below him. He thought of the spray as you walked along the promenade in Lahinch and remembered, for the first time in many years, the taste of seaweed from a bag.

It was only now that he noticed the development below, between him and the sea. He wasn't sure at first what it was. The gleaming white cubes looked somehow scientific in purpose, a collection of laboratories or observatories perhaps. It was a few moments before he realized that what he was looking at was Eamonn's village. The neat, white boxes, curving black roads and lush green lawns stood out sharply against the dusty ridge. From where he stood, the sun bouncing off the

8

sea, a heat haze shimmering around its edges, Lomaverde
looked like a mirage.

———————————

The man was carrying something and shouting. All Eamonn
could catch was a single repeated word that sounded like
'*Llover*' and he wondered if this was some strange, wandering
weatherman come to warn them all of rain. It was Eamonn's
legs that recognized him first. They started moving, seemingly
independent of his will, up the slope, his ears finally unscram-
bling the words correctly:

'Hello there! Eamonn!'

He had just a moment to register the incongruity of his
father's presence there on the blazing hillside, dressed in a light
woollen jacket, carrying his Aston Villa holdall, before they
were standing facing each other, Dermot smiling shyly and
saying, as if it were the most normal thing in the world:

'And how are you, son?'

2

He lurked in the kitchen, making coffee, peering through the serving hatch at his father, still in his jacket, drinking water, the glass tiny in his hand. Dermot only ever looked in scale with his surroundings when sat in the driver's cab of a bus, the enormous steering wheel a perfect fit for his outsize paws. He was six foot four, with a lantern jaw and an epic chest. Reminiscent, Eamonn often thought as a child, of popular cartoon rooster Foghorn Leghorn. Eamonn had inherited his father's eyes, almost all of his height and about half of his width.

'I'm sorry if I gave you a shock,' Dermot called through to the kitchen. 'I thought you'd have got the letter sooner. I didn't know now the post was so bad.'

Eamonn saw that the arrival had a certain inevitability about it, being just the latest in a long line of unheralded appearances. There were the annual holidays to Ireland where his father would, on a whim, call in on some childhood friend. Though always delighted, those long-ago acquaintances would nevertheless take some time to recover from the sudden appearance at their window of someone they'd last set eyes on forty years previously.

There was a well-worn family anecdote related by his Uncle Joe at any opportunity. Not long after Dermot had moved to England, he took a train up to Liverpool to visit his older brother. Joe's lot had a flat above a shop back then and he, Tessie and the kids were gathered around the telly when they heard a gentle tapping at the window. Joe drew back the curtain, expecting a bird or a twig, and instead came face to face with his brother. Dermot had tried knocking downstairs, but on getting no answer had gone off scouting for a ladder in nearby entries and back gardens. Tessie had screamed and screamed, even when she saw it was just Dermot. It took several measures of Jameson's before they could calm her.

Eamonn brought the coffee through to the lounge and sat on a hard chair facing his father.

'Journey OK, was it?'

'It was.'

There followed a few minutes' silence.

'No hold-ups?'

'No. Nothing like that.'

Eamonn nodded. 'That's good.' He wanted nothing more than to crawl back into his bed, to finally fall asleep and on waking discover that his father's arrival had been an unsettling dream. 'So . . .' he was still nodding, 'is this a holiday, then?'

Dermot seemed surprised at the notion. 'Maybe it is. I'm not sure. I just thought I'd get away for a while.'

This said as if it were something he had often done. As if he were the type of man who regularly skipped off for foreign mini-breaks.

'In your letter, you didn't mention . . . I mean, you're welcome to stay as long as you like, but I was just wondering . . .'

'What?'

'The return flight.'

'What about it?'

Eamonn rubbed the side of his face. 'When are you going back?'

'Oh. A fortnight. I thought that was long enough.'

Eamonn let this sink in.

'I never imagined you travelling abroad.'

Dermot nodded as if agreeing and then said, 'Spain's a

fascinating place. The different regions and cultures, the separate histories, even separate languages. Of course the Generalisimo tried to do away with all that.' He paused to take a drink before adding: '"Extremadura – Home of the Conquistadores."'

Eamonn looked at him, waiting to see if there was to be any expansion on this chapter heading, but his father had fallen silent again.

He found his gaze returning to the Aston Villa holdall on the floor between them. Its provenance was mysterious given that his father had no interest at all in football and yet Eamonn had no memory of life before the bag. It had travelled with Dermot every day to the garage, filled with a Thermos of tea, sandwiches, a jumper and whatever library book he happened to be reading. In latter years, when his mother's health had grown too bad, it had served as his father's shopping bag. Somehow, despite its many years of service, it was in pristine condition. It was his father's emblem, the essence of him distilled.

'And Laura? How's she now?'

'She's OK.'

'At the shops, is she?'

'She's gone away for a few days. A research trip.'

'Oh. She'll be back before I leave though, will she?'

'Maybe. Depends on how the research is going, I suppose.'

'What is it she's studying?'

'Oh . . . no . . . she's not studying. She's writing. A novel. Historical fiction.'

This last he said in a voice not quite his own, as if he were uncomfortable with the words.

'A novel! Well that's something, isn't it? Why not? They're all at it. Look at that one. She's done well out of it, hasn't she?'

Eamonn nodded, waiting for the inevitable.

'J. K. Potter, is it? I'd say she has a bob or two by now.'

'Yes.'

Dermot smiled. 'You know, your mother used to think you might be a writer? Some idea she had in her head, back when you were young, like. Wrote some story about a dog, I think it was, do you remember?'

'No.'

'Ah, you do. A dog that could talk. What was he called?'

'I've no idea.'

'Patch or Spark. Something like that.'

Eamonn closed his eyes. 'Flash.'

'Flash! That was it. Flash the talking dog. The teacher said you had talent too. Your mother thought you'd be the next big thing.'

Eamonn said nothing. He noticed Dermot looking at the array of unwashed dishes lined up along the floor by the patio door. 'Don't mind those.' He stood and started piling them up. 'Just about to clear up when you came. You know how it is.'

Dermot leaned slightly to the left to see how far the dirty plates extended. 'Will she mind me being here? You didn't have any warning.'

'Laura?' He dumped the plates on the hatch. 'She won't mind at all.' And it was true, he knew she'd have been delighted to see Dermot.

There was a long silence before his father spoke again.

'I like to have eggs in the fridge. Your mother liked an egg every day and I can't eat them like that, but I like to have them handy for the odd occasion when I fancy one. I can go weeks between them.'

Eamonn felt something settle upon him: the discomfiting notion that he was now responsible for his father. Given Dermot's conversational halts and leaps Eamonn wondered how he could ever hope to distinguish between oblique verbal gambits and full-blown dementia.

'The thing is, they have the dates, don't they?'

'Sorry?'

'The expiry. So the box will sit there with five eggs in for weeks and then one morning I'll notice that I have two days left to eat the lot of them and I do it. Scrambled, poached, fried, whatever you like. I get through them all!'

Eamonn thought the sermon on the egg had come to an end, but after a few moments' silence Dermot turned to him and concluded:

'The expiry dates. They're great things.'

3

He looked back at Eamonn's block, identical to all the others around it. 'Do you have many there in the maisonette with you?'

'It's not a maisonette. It's not Castle Vale.'

'What do you call it, then?'

'I don't know. Apartment block. It doesn't matter.'

He remembered this habit of Eamonn's: correcting what you said, but irritated when you asked for the right way to say it. 'So, are there many others in there with you?'

Eamonn mumbled an answer he couldn't catch.

As they walked down the road he thought that Lomaverde didn't in fact look that different to the low-rise parts of the Castle Vale estate. Or at least Castle Vale when it first went up in the 60s. All very spick and span and modern. Eamonn, he was sure, wouldn't appreciate the comparison. He could be very grand at times. After university he'd come back to live with them for a few months, rising at eleven, taking a good hour over his breakfast, his newspaper spread out all over the table, the radio switched from Jimmy Young to Radio 4. Kathleen would wait on him attentively, spending a fortune on the inedible-looking muesli he favoured. 'The English Gentleman,' Dermot would say to Kathleen. 'To the manor born.'

They walked in silence, keeping to the pavement, though there were no cars to be seen or heard. Junk mail was visible sticking out from every letter box, flyers for mobile phones and estate agents lay inert, here and there, on the street, unhurried by any breeze. He stopped to appreciate the heat of the day.

He stretched out his fingers as if in the bath. It was bad for you apparently. That was the latest thing. Even the sun. He considered taking his jacket off.

He cast a sideways glance at Eamonn. A ghost in a cap. An unearthly glow around him where the sunlight bounced off his white skin. He'd inherited the pallor from his mother, a soft, milky tone apparently impervious to the strongest sun. Dermot's own skin was a complex mottling of red and brown. He had a flash of his hand, dark and covered in hair, resting on Kathleen's white brow. He heard again the muted pipe music, felt the carpeted hush of the funeral parlour all around him and turned his thoughts to something else.

'Work going well, is it?'

'Yeah . . . OK . . . you know. Up and down.'

Dermot couldn't ask more without revealing that he couldn't remember, or possibly never really knew, exactly what it was Eamonn did. It was enough anyway.

They followed the road as it wound its way down through the development, zigzagging lazily back and forth in wide swathes. He was used to the confusion and noise of Birmingham streets: UPVC porches, leaded plastic windows, swaying buddleia, stone cladding, paint-daubed wheelie bins, gnarled pigeons, dead cars, decorative pampas, monkey puzzles and feral privet.

Here all was hushed, planned, discreet. His eyes took time to adjust, to identify the basic features. It was a good ten minutes before he noticed that every window and door was shuttered. He thought at first that it was a way to block out the sun, but gradually he picked up on the general air of desertion. It put him in mind of the old Sunday-afternoon matinees on the telly, cowboys riding into empty Mexican towns. He and Eamonn used to watch them together. Squat men with big moustaches asleep under their sombreros, church bells clanging in the distance, heat haze blurring a stranger's approach.

Slowly he started to discern a difference between the houses that had never been occupied and the handful that had but were currently empty. A dead potted plant on a patio here and there, an occasional nameplate under the buzzer. He noticed that the ones showing some evidence of habitation also had signs on their gates or on their shutters. The signs were in different colours, but always the same two words. '*En Venta*,' he said aloud. He guessed at its meaning. He wondered if Eamonn had a destination in mind.

From a distance everything had looked pristine and controlled, but now, as they walked, he began to spot instances of disrepair and chaos. Cracks in pavements and fault lines along the road. An electric cable snaking along the street. Lawned verges overgrown and weeds at their perimeters. He saw the empty swimming pool, strewn with grit and pine needles, a stray cat curled up in the corner. He had already noticed plenty of jobs he could do at Eamonn's place. He thought again of Castle Vale. It had taken longer for the cracks to show there.

He knew something of the workings of places. The daily rhythms, the ebbs and flows. He was familiar with the different heartbeats of the suburbs, the inner ring, the outer ring, the windblown regeneration zones. All with their separate pulse points: the Asda, the job centre, the bookies, the daycare, the mosque, the cemetery, the school. Lomaverde appeared to have no such places. Neither had it, as far as Dermot could see, any people wishing to get to or from anywhere. Given the absence of passengers and destinations, the lack of bus stops at least seemed less surprising.

Towards the lower part of Lomaverde the development became more ragged. Six dwellings stood half completed. He took in the abandoned cement mixers, piles of breeze blocks and sacks of sand. The road continued down past them for a hundred or so yards before coming to an abrupt end. Beyond the final kerb the land reverted back to scrub, the hillside dropping away to the sea. They walked to the furthest point on the road and stood together, gazing out at the horizon.

It was a while before Eamonn spoke. 'So there you go. Lomaverde in all its glory.'

Dermot nodded. He got the picture. He'd read about places like it in Ireland. 'How many of you are there?'

He waited while Eamonn counted in his head. 'Fifteen. Permanently. All foreigners like us. Maybe another twenty or so Spanish owners. Second homes. They don't come much, only to dust and air them for potential buyers.'

'Are there any of those?'

'Not so many, I suppose.'

Dermot looked around at the half-finished houses. 'What's happening with these?'

'Hmmm . . .' Eamonn seemed intrigued by the question, as if he had never considered it himself. 'I'm not really sure.'

'Well, is any work being done on them?'

'No, not now. Not for a while really.'

'A while.' Dermot nodded. 'How long would that be, then?'

'I suppose . . . it must be about nine months. Last September – that's when we heard the developers had gone bust. And vanished.'

'Right.'

'Not really been much in the way of maintenance since then either. I hear the sprinklers at night sometimes still. I suppose someone forgot to turn them off. Sorry. You're not really seeing it at its best, been a while since anyone cut the grass. It used to be . . . you know . . . short. All that.'

'Is there any prospect of it ever being finished?'

'Well . . . I think . . . not currently, no.'

Dermot rubbed his face with his hand. 'Can I ask how much are you in for now?'

Eamonn screwed up his face. 'Pffffff – hard to say really.'

'Roughly, like.'

'Roughly . . . roughly – I'd say the mortgage is somewhere in the region of a hundred and two thousand euros now. We put down a big deposit.'

'Right.'

They were silent again for a while before Eamonn turned to Dermot and gave him a small smile. 'Ours was the third property to be bought. We got in early. Before the rush.' He paused. 'Mom always thought I was cleverer than I was.'

Dermot said nothing.

Eamonn kicked a stone out over the hillside. 'Still, it's not so bad. I mean, it's a nice place. Quiet. Plenty of time to think.'

Dermot looked back out at the horizon. A distant ship was heading towards Africa. He remembered something in his pocket and reached for it. He held a small paper bag out to Eamonn. 'Do you still like these fellas?'

Eamonn didn't seem to hear him.

'Coca-Cola bottles? Is that right? Do you still eat them?'

Eamonn turned slowly. 'Cola bottles?'

'That's right.'

He peered cautiously into the bag as if it contained spiders. 'I haven't eaten them since I was about ten.'

'Seemed to remember you eating them sometimes when you came out on the buses. Devil to find now, they are. Can't get them round the corner any more. I found these over in a place in Shard End the other day. Thought maybe you were missing them.' Eamonn just stared at him. 'Maybe you've gone off them. You don't have to have them if you don't like them any more.'

Eamonn reached out and took one. He held it up to examine it. 'No sugar on it.'

'No, had an idea you preferred the ones without the sugar on.'

Eamonn brought the sweet slowly to his lips. 'I do.'

Dermot nodded. 'Good. I'm glad I got them, then. That's something I got right.'

4

It was a large flat, not much furniture, tiled floors. The sound of his father busying himself had been filtering through his bedroom door for the past two hours. Footsteps this way and that, washing up, kitchen cupboards opening and closing. Before that he had heard him go to the toilet at midnight and again at three. Eamonn must have slept briefly, then, as he'd thought it was Laura in the bathroom, and he'd experienced a moment of peace before he woke fully and his thoughts became jagged and unmanageable once more.

He had dreamed he was holding a baby with shining eyes. The baby had spoken and he had called to Laura in amazement, but she had not come, and he could not tear his eyes away from the face of the infant to look for her. Awake he felt the ache of the baby's absence but now he saw that it had not been a baby in the dream at all, but a fluffy kitten, and the banality seemed only to compound the loss.

He had been willing himself for the past hour to get up and attend to any one of the things that needed attending to. The folder of unmarked work, the lack of food, the piles of laundry, his father. He turned in bed and tried to imagine once more that it was Laura, not his father, on the other side of the bedroom door. He pictured her clutter on the side table. The oversize and now filthy teddy-bear key ring, bought to help locate keys in her cavernous bag, staring up at him with an unjustified expression of self-satisfaction.

He had told his father a partial truth. Laura had gone away for a few days to research the novel. What he'd omitted to say was that she had returned from the trip five days before Dermot arrived. He'd omitted to say this because it was as yet unsayable. It was as yet unthinkable. It had happened, that was undeniable, but it had not yet resolved itself into any kind of comprehensible action. He had found her in the bedroom, moving from rucksack to wardrobe. She was wearing a top he hadn't recognized. There was a time when they'd known all of each other's clothes, had shopped together, had sought each other's advice and approval. He wasn't sure when that had stopped. As he watched her, he had tried to imagine what he would think if he was seeing her for the first time, walking towards him along the street. What would he make of her hair? Those sandals? That vest? And what might she make of him? He imagined them passing each other by. The thought of it made him want to touch her gently, to lay a hand on her arm. It was only then he noticed that she was putting clothes in – not taking them out of – the rucksack.

He had not seen it coming. He found himself repeating that phrase. Laura had disputed it. She said he was deceiving himself. If that was true, he'd told her, he was doing a good job of it. He felt that if he had seen it coming he might have said the right things. But he had not.

She needed time to think, she had said. She needed to get away from him. She was going back to her parents in England. She would be in touch. But she didn't answer her phone. She didn't reply to his emails or his texts. After eight years she had left him alone in a terrible, featureless limbo.

He wasn't sure if it was the lack of sleep, the lack of food or simply the lack of Laura that was causing the hallucinations. Several times since she had gone, lying in his bed, apparently awake, he had heard strange sounds at night. A heavy vehicle – a lorry or truck – chugging past on the road outside in the early hours. Such a vehicle would have a purpose and therefore no place on such a purposeless road. He wondered at the symbolism of it. What clumsy metaphor was his subconscious trying to deliver? One night he thought he heard footsteps and voices beneath his window, but when he looked there was nobody there. In the days since Laura's departure he'd been keenly aware of his isolation, the only occupant in an otherwise empty block, in an otherwise empty street.

A knock at the door made him jump.

'Eamonn?'

He closed his eyes tight.

'Eamonn. Are you awake yet?'

He said nothing.

'Would you like a cup of tea?'

A long pause. 'Yes. Please.'

'Right. There's no milk I'm afraid . . . or tea bags. Except some that smell like toothpaste.'

He lay still.

'I thought I'd walk down to the town and get a few things. You don't seem to have much in the way of food. I'm not sure what you normally have for your breakfast but all you have in is a jar of gherkins and a tin of grapes.' There was a pause. 'I didn't even know you could get grapes in a tin.'

Eamonn ran his hand over his face. 'You can't walk to the town, it's over four miles away. I need to get the car battery recharged.'

'I can walk that right enough.'

'Are you sure?' He sensed a reprieve. His father had always been a great walker. He'd enjoy it.

'I am, yes.'

'OK,' he called from beneath the cover, 'well, maybe I'll stay here. I can get on with some stuff while you're out.' He closed his eyes, but waiting for him behind his eyelids was an unwelcome vision of an elderly man in inappropriate clothing, struggling with bags of shopping in the blistering heat.

'Right-o. I'll be off, so.'

He saw him losing his footing on the hillside, collapsed by the roadside, snapping a bone.

'Bye.'

He listened to his father's footsteps move away from the bedroom and heard the jangle of keys in the front door, then silence. He threw the sheet off and ran.

'Dad!' He saw the front door close. There was a pause, then the sound of the key turning again, before his father's head poked back in.

'What is it, son?'

'Wait. I'll come with you.'

Dermot nodded. 'Good man. The air'll do you good.'

5

'It looks as if they're out.'

'I'd say so.'

They remained where they were, staring at the front door. Walnut veneer, matt finish, discreet brushed-steel escutcheon. Eamonn simmered on a low boil: irritated with Jean and David for their absence; irritated with himself for ever thinking they might be home. They would be out, of course. Walking purposelessly. Rambling. He saw them most days, David with his rucksack, his Berghaus map case; Jean in her dove greys, her outdoors sandals and floppy sunhat. He'd look up from his laptop and watch them through the window as they passed by, their faces betraying no particular joy at the prospect. Keeping busy, keeping active. Ever onwards.

He wondered what now to do with his father. He considered the eight-mile trek to and from the shop, the preparation of lunch, the eating of lunch and the protracted clearing up after lunch was more than enough activity for one day. But still the afternoon had stretched ahead of them. And still Dermot had sat on the futon, with apparently nothing to do. Every image he had of his father was of him busying himself at some task. If not actually out at work, he would be gardening, or washing the Astra, or rearranging tools in the garage, or doing something impenetrable with the gutters. Even his occasional moments of relaxation had an intent quality to them. A concerted decision to sit down and watch a television programme between certain times. A silent hour in the front room reading one of his library books. In retirement, with Kathleen virtually housebound, his industry had only increased, with shopping, cooking and cleaning added to the rest of his domestic duties. This sitting about, doing nothing, was unsettling. It made Eamonn think he should be providing activities.

Jean and David had been his best idea. It wasn't a match made in heaven. He didn't see that much common ground between his father and a couple of retired bookkeepers from Hampshire, but all three of them were polite and friendly and, more importantly, all were over sixty-five and thus possessors of the mysterious art of making lengthy conversation about absolutely nothing at all. Perhaps they'd offer to take Dermot on one of their rambles.

'Shall we call on someone else?' Dermot ventured and Eamonn wondered if he too was finding their time together passing slowly. With Jean and David away there were few obvious second choices. He considered Rosemary and Gill, also in their sixties, also very pleasant, but gay and therefore problematic. He wasn't sure what his father might make of them being a couple, or if he would even realize that they were and, if not, then Eamonn might have to explain that fact and perhaps even the whole concept of lesbianism to him. Eamonn's anxiety was even greater at the prospect of Dermot sitting in Raimund and Simon's lounge, staring at the various monochrome male nudes that covered their walls. There was Inga the Swedish woman, who lived on her own, but Eamonn knew little about her beyond her nationality and her fondness for painting. About Henri and Danielle he knew only that they came from Toulouse. That left Roger and Cheryl, who he was actively avoiding, and Ian and Becca, who he actively disliked.

He considered giving up on the idea altogether, but the thought of returning to the flat with Dermot stopped him. It was one thing to avoid work, to waste hours on YouTube, to moon about the flat and write pleading emails to Laura. It was another thing entirely to do that with your father sitting on the futon constantly saying, 'Don't mind me now, just get on with whatever it is you have to do.'

'I suppose we could give Ian and Becca a try.'

'You're the boss.'

Eamonn hesitated. 'They're just acquaintances. Not friends.'

Ian and Becca had moved in three months after he and Laura and it bothered him enormously that anyone might think the two couples, both in their thirties, both having emigrated to Spain, both having bought property in the same modern, purpose-built development, could have anything in common. Ian and Becca had been 'bitten by the property bug' in the 1990s, a phrase Becca actually used, leading Laura to later comment that it was a shame the property bug wasn't of the venomous Japanese Giant Hornet variety. They had been picked up and carried along in a giddy wave of property renovation and speculation at the very zenith of the laminate era. Eamonn would sometimes imagine them back then, sitting glassy-eyed and open-mouthed in front of a vast wall-mounted flat-screened television, watching any one of the seemingly identical programmes featuring spivvy presenters and an endless procession of minutely differentiated couples buying, decorating and then selling houses, over and over again.

Assuming a curiosity that was not there, Ian would often give Eamonn his earnest advice and insights into the vagaries of the property market. It was apparently a tricky game, hard to second guess. Logic might dictate that a cheap area adjacent to a more sought-after neighbourhood would inevitably improve and increase in value, but some stubbornly refused to do so, retaining their high crime levels, their underperforming schools and, worst of all, their native populations. You had to have enough of the right kind of people moving in and enough of the wrong sort of people moving out.

Ian and Becca thought that the only people who lived in poor housing in deprived areas were people who had failed to watch enough Channel 4 programmes. Eamonn had watched Laura's doomed attempts to find any trace of awareness or responsibility in Ian and Becca with some amusement.

'So do you think you're helping to improve those run-down areas?'

'Definitely. We buy a house, do it up, nice people move in, you get better shops, better schools – it all starts to happen.'

'But haven't you just shifted the problem somewhere else?'

Becca would nod enthusiastically. 'Exactly.'

Ian and Becca were hurt and bewildered by their fall from grace. Like the innocent victims of a fairy tale they had simply followed the trail of breadcrumbs, never suspecting that it might lead to disaster. They had seen great opportunities in Spain. Who hadn't? Many Britons were at an arrested stage of development, locked for ever in adolescent crushes on another country. They watched TV shows about it, bought magazines about it and dreamed for fifty weeks of the year of escaping their loveless marriages with Maidenhead, Sutton Coldfield and Altrincham for fresh starts with Mojácar, La Manga and Nerja. Ian and Becca bought the house in Lomaverde as a home and base for their new business; from there they would scout out and buy new investment opportunities in the ever-expanding Spanish property market to sell on to other Brits. They were stuck now, with three half-built apartments on the Costa del Sol and their home in Lomaverde, unable to sell up and leave and having to live off their dwindling remaining capital. They had been the last to move into Lomaverde, which made them, in Eamonn's eyes, reprehensibly dumb. He thought that they of all people should have

28

seen that the cruise liner they were boarding was already beginning to list.

'Hello, Becca.'

She took a step back from the door.

'Eamonn! We've not seen you for ages.'

'Yeah, I've been tied up with work, that kind of stuff. This is my dad. He's popped over for a visit, so I'm just showing him around.'

'Ahhhhhhhh,' said Becca, putting her head on one side and looking at Dermot as if he were a kitten. She glanced back at Eamonn. 'Funny. Never imagined you having a dad.'

Dermot cleared his throat and put out his hand. 'Hello there, Dermot Lynch.'

'Ooh. You have an accent! Wait till the others meet you.'

Eamonn started to retreat, realizing his mistake. 'Oh, look, if you've got company, we'll come back another time.'

'What do you mean, "company"? It's only Roger and Cheryl. Who else is it going to be? Come in! We're just having a barbe-cue, tons too much food as usual. Roger was saying earlier that he'd not seen you for ages. Where's Laura, she not with you?'

'We shouldn't have just dropped in like this . . . ' but it was too late, Roger's voice came echoing down the hallway.

'Is that Lynch I hear? Get in here, you insufferable streak of piss!'

'With his father!' Becca called out in warning as she ushered Eamonn and Dermot into the lounge.

Roger was standing in the middle of the room with his hands on his hips – a peculiarly disconcerting way he had of greeting people. Part-King of Siam, part-Matalan billboard.

'Eamonn's father, eh? Well, this is interesting.'

Roger was somewhere in his early fifties. His features had a kind of Le Bon-like swollen-bully quality to them. Handsome to some, perhaps, in the past, but chubbed-up now. Fleshy in an affluent kind of way. His accent hovered between the south-east of England and the west coast of America. He spoke with a somewhat sardonic inflection, making him sound like a jaded commentator on all he saw.

Dermot held out his hand: 'Dermot Lynch.'

Roger squeezed and shook: 'Ah – a proper Paddy at last. Very good to meet you.'

'Roger!' said Becca.

'What? Jesus, don't you start. Normally it's PC Lynch there policing my every comment. Paddy? Paddy? Really? I can say "Paddy", can't I? "Paddy!" There. It sounds affectionate to me.'

Ian came in from the terrace where the barbecue was smoking, and after further introductions were made, asked, 'Can I get you a beer, Dermot?'

'I'm grand, thanks.'

Roger feigned shock. 'What? A good Irishman refusing a drink?'

Dermot smiled, but Eamonn detected the note in his voice. 'It's a little early in the day for me.'

Becca steered the conversation on to safer ground, asking Dermot about his journey, which led to a lengthy discussion about different possible routes from the airport, rip-off taxi drivers and public transport in the region. Dermot mentioned his bus-driving days and Becca clapped her hands, both delighted and amazed that the conversation appeared to have some cohesion.

Eamonn watched Roger and Ian back at the barbecue. He and Laura thought there was something slightly vampiric about Roger and Cheryl's need for 'young blood'. The older couple exerted a certain pull, having been the first settlers in Lomaverde, and had positioned themselves at the very heart of the small community. In their first three months there he and Laura had spent a lot of time with them. On the surface all was great bonhomie, endless beer and barbecues, but underneath there seemed to be something darker. Initially, they interpreted the older couple's constant invitations as an uncomplicated desire for company, but over time they came to feel that Roger and Cheryl needed the presence of spectators in order to be able to function. They each had the habit of appealing to their guests to support whatever aspersion they were making about the other; their relationship at times taking on an almost pantomime quality, demanding audience participation. Roger and Cheryl seemed to assume a greater intimacy between the four of them than either Laura or Eamonn felt comfortable with, the younger couple often finding themselves fending off prying questions, pretending not to notice heavy-handed innuendo. They had tried to extricate themselves from the friendship, but it hadn't been easy. Finding your hosts indefinably creepy was not an acceptable reason to give for declining an invitation; instead they had to fabricate excuses, an exercise made very difficult by their close physical proximity and the stark absence of other people or things to do. They longed for the day that the development would be fully populated and they could melt away unnoticed in the crowd, and, while that day hadn't (and was unlikely ever to) come, Ian and Becca's arrival had provided some respite, as they became the prime object of Roger and Cheryl's attentions. Eamonn and Laura engaged in fierce and scandalous speculation as to what went on between the four of them.

Becca was still talking to his father. 'That's absolutely right, Mr Lynch – you of all people will understand that, transport-wise, we're completely stranded.'

Roger came in carrying a tray of ribs: 'Why stop at transport? We're stranded whatever way you cut it.'

Roger had earned his money running various tech companies with nebulous names like SysPop and ROKware. Eamonn
had no idea what they made or did or sold or traded. They
morphed into each other in Roger's stories – as one called in
the receivers a new one was spawned. The fact that he
appeared to have left a trail of collapsed companies and
unpaid creditors behind him didn't seem to impinge on
Roger's view of himself as a straight-talking, clear-headed
businessman of the world. The reason for his move to Spain
was never made explicit. It was possible that he was retiring
early, or equally possible that he was simply sitting out a ban
before returning to the UK, to launch yet another flawed
business enterprise.

Dermot turned to him. 'Are you trying to sell your property,
then?'

'No point doing that. No point at all. You can send yourself
mental asking who's to blame. Thieving developers? Corrupt
town councils? A useless government? A mismanaged global
economy? That fucking android Gordon Brown? It's every-
body and nobody. But what you have gathered here before
you, Dermot, are the mugs who have to pay the price for all of
that. The survivors of a shipwreck. All of us washed up here
on the same little island.'

Eamonn wanted to squeeze Laura's hand, to give her a
secret smile. She had always enjoyed Roger's shipwreck analo-
gies. Soon he'd move on to the shark-infested waters and start
lamenting Ian and Becca's lost life-savings. Eamonn privately
doubted that Ian and Becca had saved a penny in their lives. But
Laura was no longer there to share the joke with, to make it all
easier to bear. She had left him alone with these people. He felt
a sudden urge to weep.

Roger's mention of shipwrecks had prompted Becca to
interrupt.

'Oh God, Eamonn, isn't it terrible? Did you see it? We were just talking about it before you came.'

'What?'

'It's started again. Bodies down on San Pedro beach.'

'Eight of them,' Ian added. 'Africans, of course.'

'What? Murdered?' asked Dermot.

Roger looked grave. 'Illegal immigrants, Dermot. Trying to reach Europe on nothing much more than a raft. They die of thirst or hunger or hypothermia, or they drown. Happened all the time a few years back, but most of them seem to have got the message now. No bloody jobs here either. Evidently some-one forgot to tell this lot.'

Becca turned to Eamonn. 'It was just vile. They showed the pictures on the telly. Covered-up bodies on the beach. Can you imagine it? There were families and kiddies right there when they got washed up. How awful for them. I said to Ian, "Imag-ine seeing that." How would you explain that to your kids?'

At that moment Cheryl emerged from the kitchen carrying a tray of salad.

'Is the dressing out there, Rebecca?' She stopped when she saw Eamonn. She looked at him and he gave a small smile. Becca brightened.

'Thank God for Cheryl! Perfect timing. We were getting ever so depressing. Look, you'll never guess who this is?'

Cheryl moved her eyes slowly from Eamonn to Dermot. 'I'd imagine it's Eamonn's father. The resemblance is quite strong.'

Eamonn felt the heat in the back of his neck.

'It's a pleasure to meet you, Mr Lynch. What brings you here?'

'Dermot, please.'

'Dermot. What a lovely name.'

'I thought I'd come and see what this one was up to.' He gestured towards Eamonn.

'And have you found out?'

'I'm sorry?'

'Have you found out what he's been up to? We'd all love to know.'

Eamonn squirmed and Dermot laughed. 'Ah, I think he's a good lad, on the whole. Well, we did our best with him anyway.'

'I'm sure you did.'

Eamonn was relieved when Roger shouted from the terrace: 'There she goes. Lunatic!'

'Who's that, darling?' said Cheryl, her eyes still on Eamonn.

'The Swedish one. Thingy.'

'Inga.'

'Yeah. Her.' He rejoined them in the lounge, walking over to Eamonn. 'Have you seen what she's gone and done?'

'Er . . . no.'

'Bloody cats' bowls! Cats' bowls on her terrace, at the front door, out on the street. What does she think she's doing?'

Eamonn thought for a moment. 'Is she feeding the cats?'

'Course she's feeding the fucking cats! The question is: is she mental? Haven't we got enough problems here without luring more feral cats to come and settle? Why don't we start advertising for squatters too – I mean, there's enough empty accommodation, why not invite them all in? Gypsies, squatters, burglars, cats, maybe we could let cattle graze on the lawned areas too.'

Eamonn shrugged. 'I suppose at least the cats prevent an infestation of rats.'

'And what would be the bloody difference?'

They managed to escape after a couple of sausages. In contrast to his earlier feelings, Eamonn now found the prospect of time alone with his father to be quite bearable. It was Dermot that broke the silence between them.

'I'd say you're in a bad way if you can't see a difference between cats and rats.'

'Yes.'

'He seems to get very worked up, that fella.'

'Yes he does.'

'Is he a good friend of yours?'

'Not really. You just end up spending time with them because it's hard not to. You get sucked in.' For some reason he found himself wanting to say something positive about Roger. 'He's very hospitable.'

'Well, yes, there's that.'

'He just goes on a bit.'

'Maybe the sun doesn't suit him.'

'Maybe.'

They rested on a bench on one of the overgrown grass verges.

'It never suited your mother. I remember we went to Weston once, before you were born. A beautiful weekend and she got terribly burned and sick. Awful journey home it was.'

'Dad, he doesn't have sunstroke.'

Dermot nodded. 'Well. You know what they say.'

'What?'

'Mad dogs and Englishmen.'

'What does that make you, then?'

Dermot shrugged. 'A "proper Paddy", I believe.'

6

On his first morning in Birmingham he sweated his way along Digbeth in a heavy woollen suit, dragging a suitcase behind him. He asked a man leaning against the wall outside a pub for directions. The man glanced at the scrap of paper and said in a Dublin accent, 'Aggie Kelly's?'

'Do you know her?' replied Dermot.

'She's Michael's missus. Everyone knows Michael Kelly.'

'Good lodgings, is it?'

'It'll do you.' He pulled a short pencil from behind his ear and sketched a map on the back of Dermot's paper. He looked at Dermot as he handed it back. 'Box?'

Dermot hesitated. 'I think I'm grand with the suitcase.'

The Dubliner hissed. 'I'm not here giving you luggage recommendations. I was asking if you box. Do you spar? Are ye a pugilist?'

Dermot shook his head, embarrassed. 'I never have, no.'

Someone called out 'Jack' and the Dubliner walked towards the voice. He glanced back at Dermot. 'You should go see John Joe Riley.'

When Dermot got to Kelly's the landlady gave him a mug of tea and a narrow bed in a tiny room shared with a boy from Sligo called Matty Keegan. Matty was a big lad like Dermot and a few months older than him at nineteen. On their first evening together Dermot questioned him about the Kellys, their fellow lodgers, Brummies, and the English in general and received nothing much more than 'yes', 'no' or a shrug. He was inclined to think Matty simple. It took him a while to appreciate his care with words and his shyness.

In time he learned that Matty had been in England for a year, starting off in London before coming up to Birmingham. While Dermot had got his Corporation job at the recruitment office back in Dublin, Matty had emigrated with no arrangements in place. He ended up labouring, picking up work in the pubs and getting paid there too. It turned out that he boxed at the place the Dubliner had mentioned. Dermot would tag along sometimes to Riley's, but while he was powerful he lacked Matty's agility.

Kelly's house was a three-storey terrace with a lingering smell of bacon. The other lodgers were older men: Devlin from Cork, who was a know-all; Aloysius Dempsey, who shook and smelled of TCP; a man named Liam Corgan, who had a budgerigar he had trained to peck crumbs from his lips; Aggie's own brother Eddie, and countless unnamed others who stayed only days or weeks before moving on to the promise of better opportunities or lodgings elsewhere. One bed on the first floor was shared between Bernard Feeney, who worked a night shift at Lucas, and Gerry Byrne, who was a labourer.

Some nights a group of them would play cards down in the kitchen with Aggie's husband, Michael. They played hand after hand of Twenty-Five. The stakes, at Aggie's insistence, were just matchsticks, but Michael took it deadly seriously, lambasting anyone he felt had played poorly, blaming them for his losses. 'You gave me a bad lead!' he'd shout and rage, employing all manner of theatrics. No one paid much attention, except, Dermot noticed, Matty. He saw how his room-mate jumped when Michael banged the table, and caught him trembling sometimes when Michael was giving out, despite the fact he could have flattened the landlord with one lazy swipe.

Other times Dermot would go out with Matty and some of

his gang to the local pubs in Sparkhill. The following day Dermot's memories of the night before were always fragmentary, stray images lacking context – Mick Conroy with a lampshade on his head, Tim Murphy reciting a poem to nobody, someone singing a song about a lost dog, Matty sitting quietly and smiling at it all.

Dermot persuaded Matty out to a dance at St Catherine's once, the two of them dressed up in their best clothes. They stood by the bar and looked at the women.

'There's a conductor I know, Brummie fella, name of Garrett. You should hear the lines he comes out with to the girls on the buses. He's got all the chat.'

'A loudmouth, is he?' asked Matty.

'A smooth talker I suppose you'd call him. Very confident, like. He'd come to a place like this on his own, wouldn't bother him at all, he'd pick a girl he liked the look of and walk straight up to her.'

'And what would he say?'

'He has a line. He goes up to the girl and he says: "Would you mind pretending you know me for a moment? I have an old flame here tonight looking for me and the only way she'll leave me alone is if I'm with a pretty girl like you."'

Matty looked at him. 'What about when the old flame catches up with him?'

'There is no old flame. It's a just a line to get the girl's attention, make her think another girl's interested in him.'

'So it's a lie.'

'It's a line, Matty. Just to meet someone.'

They were silent for a long time, sipping their pints.

'So the idea is that this girl believes him and likes him?'

Dermot sighed. 'Ah, forget about it. It was just a story about a fella from work.'

'I know, I know, but I don't understand.'

'What don't you understand?'

'So the girl likes him and he likes the girl and they start going together, is that the idea?'

'I suppose so, yes.'

'And say then they get engaged and get married and maybe they go on and have six kids and grandkids and they have a long old life together and one day, the girl's an old woman now, and she's lying on her deathbed and she turns to the fella, this conductor, though he's retired now too, and she says: "Whatever happened to that old flame?" What does he say to her then? How does he answer her? Does he lie again, as she's there about to meet God?'

Dermot stared at him. Matty shook his head and returned to his pint. 'He sounds a gobshite to me.'

Dermot was made a driver soon enough. He was teamed up with a conductor from St Kitts called Leonard Blythe. They worked the 43 route.

'But it's an ugly town,' said Leonard quite frequently. 'The people are nice enough, but the setting is inelegant. Grimy and besmirched,' he'd gesture at the industry around them. 'What must Mother Nature, in all her majesty, think of such abominations?'

But Dermot thought there was something wonderful about it all. The hissing and clanking of the GKN factory, the rise and fall of the gasometers, the silhouetted towers of the coke works. He'd sit at the terminus each evening, watching the sun set behind the power station. He'd think about Saturday's dance at St Catherine's, the next coach trip with the Irish Citizens League, the new suit he was saving for and other things beyond as he watched the white plumes above the cooling towers billow and rise up into the orange sky.

7

They had worked for the same company back in England. Laura edited Web-design manuals with pretensions to being coffee-table books. She spent her days clarifying the meaning of words written by men who wore shorts to work, most of whom, she discovered, collected dolls of one sort or another. Eamonn worked on computer-programming titles with astonishingly ugly covers. He once queried a jacket design and learned that the move from restrained typographic covers to large, brutal, greyscale portraits of the author's face had single-handedly driven up sales by 200 per cent. Programmers were reassured by the faces of other programmers.

He and Laura used to debate whether programmers or designers had the more abysmal prose style. They would email each other passages of clogged, impenetrable text, a competition between them. Laura began to suspect that her own literacy was being eroded by spending each day laboriously disentangling knotted jumbles of words and punctuation marks. She worried the shattered sentences, orphaned sub-clauses and teetering conjunctions would start to colonize her brain and a viscous fog descend over all meaning.

As time went on there was less and less need for either of them to go in to the office, until eventually they realized that they could work remotely and live wherever they chose. They were not tempted by the quaint seaside towns of Suffolk that seemed to attract many of their colleagues, or the self-regarding buzz of Shoreditch or Brighton. Laura was drawn to the sun. Her ideal scenario was their existing life minus the nine interminable months of greyness and damp. For his part, Eamonn had no qualms about leaving England – overfamiliar and cloying, unsurprising and pleased with itself. He felt the lure of somewhere different, the promise of renewal.

Their original plan had been for one of the big cities – Barcelona or Madrid or Bilbao. They had no interest in joining the hordes of expats clustered along the Costas in vast apartment complexes and chintzy hillside developments. Eamonn saw the majority of British settlers in Spain as an amorphous mass of *Daily Express* readers riddled with hypocrisy: railing against benefit cheats at home while happy to avoid Spanish tax; indignant at immigration levels in the UK, but oblivious to their own immigrant status. These were people for whom Spain's greatest cultural achievement was its tireless dedication to polished floors and gleaming kitchen worktops.

But escape was more difficult than they had anticipated. The competition for decent apartments in the overcrowded cities was fierce, and as a couple of clueless *guiris*, with barely any Spanish, they had no contacts or resources to call upon. It soon became clear that buying or even renting an apartment in such places was far more complicated and expensive than they had imagined. They spent a depressing two weeks in Barcelona looking at a succession of tiny apartments, with increasingly inventive layouts. Mildewed shower cubicles in the corner of bedrooms, toilets on balconies, a mezzanine bed platform suspended above the kitchen, and everywhere perky Ikea accents to mask the squalor.

Laura first saw Lomaverde mentioned in an article in the kind of decor magazine that Eamonn insisted he hated but surreptitiously read nonetheless. The houses and apartments were described as minimalist cube-structures with a nod to the principles and aesthetics of Bauhaus. Lomaverde claimed to offer all of the style and sophistication of city living but without the bureaucratic wranglings and complexity. Where Barcelona had been difficult and impenetrable, Lomaverde was easy and welcoming.

Nieves, the sales manager, spoke perfect English and carefully explained every step of the purchasing process. She understood what they'd been through trying to deal with private landlords and vendors, she knew how baffling the red tape could be and, true to her word, she shouldered the burden of much of the paperwork herself. In her startling zebra-print glasses, she painted a picture of Lomaverde as a creative and vibrant community – a haven for designers, artists, writers and programmers sick of city life in Spain and abroad. Her description sounded somewhat hellish to Eamonn and Laura, but they liked Lomaverde in spite of it. They knew the location, in Almería, was remote, far from the bars and culture they had thought were their target, but it was easy to devalue such attractions, to imagine themselves self-sufficient: working from home, free to travel to cities when they chose, masters of their own destinies with a spacious apartment and sea view for the same amount as a dingy, interior box in Barcelona.

They moved in the March of 2007. For the first few weeks their only neighbours were Roger and Cheryl and Raimund and Simon. The vacancy then had a certain other-worldly charm, rendering everyday life somewhat ethereal. They used to imagine themselves on a different planet – the buzzing of the electricity substation, the tinny echoes of the empty streets, the sci-fi sunsets. They feigned indignation at the idea of other buyers moving in and spoiling it all.

They quickly settled into a routine, working from early morning until mid-afternoon and then over to the pool. Their budget hadn't stretched to a private pool, but their terrace overlooked the communal one and they found this made it curiously difficult to relax. Even when they had no urge to swim or lounge it was impossible to simply look upon it all; the desire to be in the view too seductive to resist.

It was called an infinity pool, but they never really understood why. It was like a normal pool, but instead of a visible wall at the far end, the water fell away to a smaller, lower pool. This didn't, as far as they could see, make the length of the pool appear infinite. It made it appear like a fifteen-metre pool with no rear wall. Laura started to refer to any short distance as 'infinity' and anything longer as 'beyond infinity'. They would lean against the wall of the shallow end and see only blue: the surface of the pool, the distant sea beyond it and the sky above.

Lying on a lounger, sipping a beer, one of them would look at their watch and ask: 'What are the workers doing now?' And they'd try to outdo each other in their lurid imaginings of friends and colleagues. Rob dying on his feet as he pitched a book to the sales team in the US. Tony Daly standing on a chair just to be seen, shouting insanely about eating competitors' breakfasts. Endless grotesque fantasies about the mysterious yachting accident that had left Viv Crawford with a bald spot above his right ear and an inability to pronounce, though a compulsion to employ, the word 'segmentation'. They laughed, giddy at the improbability of their life, feeling as if they had pulled off a great victory.

Over a year on and Eamonn still experienced a small shock every time he opened the door or looked out from his terrace. A sense of disbelief that he lived in such a place. He used to imagine that it was a good thing, this palpable sense of 'wow' each time he stepped outside and was confronted by deep blue sky, gleaming white cubes and glistening sea. Now though he felt that a permanent state of wonder was not right, that a more profound or complicated relationship with the environment should have evolved over time.

It was a stark contrast to the cluttered, choked environment they had left behind in England. They'd lived in a Victorian terrace on a tiny road with constant friction over parking. The compensations were an apparently nuclear-powered central-heating system that meant the house was never cold or damp, and an incomprehensible rear garden, stretching sixty feet back before turning a corner and running another fifty behind the other houses. Twice a year they would run howling into the long grass, crazed survivors of a forgotten jungle war, wielding machetes and hacking back bindweed and laurel, but largely they let it be, their L-shaped wilderness. It was much loved by their limping cat, Werner. Eamonn would stalk him through the long grass, mimicking his every move, attempting to infuriate the implacable animal with a bad German accent. In summer they had barbecues with Laura's caipirinhas and their friend Dave's boxes of charity-shop vinyl. In winter they curled up inside with boxsets and books, Eamonn terrorizing Laura with his frozen feet.

He wondered now if maybe there had never been anything wrong with any of it.

Dwelling on the past was perilous but still his mind went back. The more he tried to fight them, the harder the memories pressed in. He thought back to the early days, his caution with Laura in the beginning. It had seemed too easy and perhaps it was some vestige of Catholicism that made him believe that suffering had to be involved. He thought there must be a virtue in the customary awkwardness, the minor misunderstandings and endless adjustments normally necessary to get aligned with another human being. The ease and instantaneity of their attraction made him suspicious; he thought of catchy songs whose appeal proved thin and short-lived.

A chance remark about a particularly egregious type of trouser briefly popular in 1988 led to the discovery that they had attended many of the same parties as teenagers. When she realized this, Laura suggested that they had simply worn each other down, that their attraction was subliminal and attritional. Her friend had gone to a nearby girls' school and Laura had apparently formed part of the haze of hairspray, Thunderbird and Impulse that he had seen huddled in corners of darkened suburban sitting rooms over several years. Neither of them remembered the other, though when he first visited her parents' house, he had a distinct sense that he had been there before.

She had honey-blonde hair, green eyes and a faded tan even in winter. He was gangly and pale with black hair and pale blue eyes. Even in his early twenties he had a tendency towards misanthropy, as opposed to Laura's generally sunny disposition. She thought him smart and funny and honest, and found the difficulty he experienced enjoying himself endearing. For his part he loved her openness, her generosity of spirit. He mocked her for it, labelled it as confidence born of privilege, but he marvelled at it. In his darker moments he would characterize their relationship as one long failed attempt by him to contaminate her good nature.

If they went to a restaurant, Laura would blithely eat her food and enjoy the change of scenery. Eamonn though would look at the people around them, people superficially just like themselves, and he would have bad thoughts about them, their hats, their haircuts, their shoes, their conversations, an itchy kind of contempt spreading over his skin like a rash. It seemed to him that the key achievement of his education had been to alienate him from both the people he had mixed with as a child and the people he went on to mix with as an adult. In both worlds he felt adrift, bobbing erratically between feelings of inadequacy and contempt.

By the time he reached thirty, comfortable in his job and in his life, he was bored by his own incessant commentary, sick of beating himself up about every lifestyle choice he made. That was at the heart of his willingness to move abroad: to live in a place where he was unaware of the secret signs, for such things to be invisible or unreadable to him, where he might imagine the best of everyone. He hadn't been lured to Spain by the sand and the sea and endless re-runs of *A Place in the Sun* on daytime television, but rather by the promise of sitting in a bar and not being able to extrapolate an entire way of life from someone's choice of shoe.

One afternoon, settled in Lomaverde, leaning back against the wall of the shallow end of the pool, he had squinted at the horizon. A transformation had taken place. The beauty had become invisible. Blue sky, blue sea, blue tiles. What once was sublime had become banal. He knew he'd made a mistake. A few weeks later the pool was empty and he knew then too that there was nothing he could do about it.

8

Dermot searched high and low and still there was no sign of it. He wondered if Laura could possibly have taken it with her. He tried to picture her struggling with it down the road. It seemed only marginally less likely than the fact that his son, at the age of thirty-three, did not own an ironing board. Based on Eamonn's appearance, he shouldn't have been surprised, but he was.

He laid his shirt out on a towel on the dining table and did the best job he could. Afterwards he sat on the futon and tried to read his book. It was a history of Spain he'd ordered from the library. On the flight over he had been absorbed by its accounts of Los Reyes Catolicos and their efforts to drive out the Moors. He had been particularly taken with the tale of Boabdil the Unlucky, picturing him sighing as he looked back over the Granada he had surrendered. He thought now of the poor souls he'd heard about the other day, washed up on the beach, never even getting a glimpse of their lost land. The book kept championing the great gains made by Ferdinand and Isabella, but Dermot found them an unsympathetic pair. Intolerant, you'd have to say, by anyone's standards.

He looked at the clock and strained his ears for any signs of life from beyond Eamonn's door. He'd begun to think of it more as a crypt than a room. He imagined his son lying in state on his bier, the shutters closed tight to keep out the sun's rays. He thought Eamonn may as well have stayed in Birmingham for all he ventured out or appeared to care about the world outside. The only thing he seemed to do was look at his computer. He said he was working, but his face showed no sign of concentration or thought, just blank-eyed absorption in whatever it was he saw in the glow of the screen. The flat mirrored his lifelessness. He had never been handy. Kathleen always said Eamonn had been graced with brains, not brawn, but Dermot couldn't see that it took much brawn to put a line of sealant around a bath, nor any evidence of brains in not doing so. There was scant furniture and what there was seemed placed without any particular thought or care. It felt a makeshift rather than a homely place, the desire to leave evident in every corner.

And then there was Laura, the invisible woman. He wondered when Eamonn might reveal what in God's name he had done with her. There was nothing of hers that Dermot could see around the flat.

Eamonn had lost things often as a boy. Maybe all children did, Dermot didn't know. Jumpers, pumps, Matchbox cars, marbles, all of them vanished into the chaos of his days. It was a great mystery to Dermot where they went. He remembered being careful as a boy, cherishing the things he had, jealously guarding any small space he could call his own in the house. Perhaps because Eamonn was an only child he could afford to be careless and leave things lying around. Maybe they had spoiled him and not taught him the value of his belongings. Whatever the reason, his absent-mindedness was remarkable. It was made worse by his inability to conduct a logical search. He could not grasp the connection between a missing item and his own previous whereabouts. He would waste hours searching in places he had not been. Climbing a tree to search for a guitar. Looking in his wardrobe for a bike. The physical location of things seemed entirely mysterious to him, unrelated to any action of his own. Had his missing Action Man turned up on the top deck of the 43 bus, Dermot imagined

48

Eamonn simply shrugging and putting it down to the unknowable shiftings of the world and its contents.

He read another line and then closed the book. He did not enjoy unpunctuality. Sometimes, as a driver, with circumstances beyond his control – six inches of snow, a motorbike gone under a lorry, stuck behind Slow Joe McEvoy – he was late. But not often. With very few exceptions, unpunctuality was a choice, and Dermot chose to be on time. He walked over and knocked on Eamonn's door. 'Are you awake in there?'

Indistinct murmuring.

'Eamonn. Are you awake? It's quarter to one.'

He heard the clatter of something falling to the floor, followed by swearing. 'I'm awake. I'm awake.'

'They're expecting us at one.'

'Who?'

'For goodness' sake, Eamonn. Are you not up?'

'Oh . . . Is it lunchtime already?'

'It's quarter to one. They're expecting us at one. I don't want to be late.'

'Are you not ready?'

'Of course I'm ready. I've been sat here ready for the past thirty minutes. I've been waiting for you!'

A pause. 'Look . . . you go. It's you they invited really. They could see me any time. They wanted to meet you.'

'Eamonn. I don't know them. They invited both of us.'

They had bumped into them on the way back from the barbecue the previous evening. An English couple. Friendly. Polite. Nice people. The kind who, like him, would consider lateness as ill-mannered.

There was more noise from behind the door and then it opened. Dermot recoiled a little at the sight of his son stood in nothing but a pair of boxer shorts, white as a sheet, hair sticking up in the air, eyes screwed up.

'Dad, they'll be delighted to have you. They just want to make you feel welcome. I've got a load of work to catch up with anyway. They won't miss me. I'm not sure they were even expecting me to go along.'

Dermot looked at his son and then at his watch. He turned and left without saying another word.

As he walked along the street he couldn't think of another time he had gone to a stranger's house for lunch. He couldn't think of a time he had gone to a friend's house for lunch. He didn't, until Eamonn had introduced the word, even eat lunch. He ate dinner in the middle of the day, and dinner was a sandwich, a cup of tea and a look at the *Mirror* or the *Evening Mail*. Back when he was working he might have chatted to some of the other lads, maybe played a hand of cards afterwards in the canteen, but only because they were there, it was never an arrangement. Socializing was done in the evenings at the houses of friends, or at the social, or in the pub. You drank and you chatted and you had some laughs. He didn't know what you were supposed to do in the middle of the day. Kathleen would have known what to expect. She would have read about it in a magazine. She'd be briefing him now at the doorstep, picking at imaginary stray fibres on his shoulder.

'Hello, Dermot! It's so lovely to meet you.'

A woman with short, bobbed, silver-grey hair was smiling at him.

'Hello again, Jean.' He stood on the step, awkward. 'I'm very sorry now, but I'm afraid Eamonn can't come. He has a terrible amount of work to do and . . .'

Jean laughed. 'Oh, don't worry at all. I'm sure he has better things to do than sit and listen to us going on. Come in, come in.'

Jean and David lived in a large detached house with views towards the sea. It had more furnishings than Eamonn's

<50>50</50>

apartment – pictures on the walls, sofas, a few ornaments on shelves and cabinets – but something about it still felt empty and new.

David emerged from the kitchen, shook Dermot's hand and offered him a drink. Dermot asked for a cup of tea, realizing too late that Jean and David were both drinking wine.

They sat out on the patio, where a table was laid. It was David who served the food. Some sort of salad. Dermot noticed David was wearing an apron and that he didn't take it off. Dermot had worked alongside people from all over the world, all ages and levels of education, but he did not know people like Jean and David. People like Jean and David neither used nor worked on the buses. The English middle classes, like Emperor Penguins, Dermot knew only from the television.

'So how long have you been free from the shackles, Dermot?' asked David

'I'm sorry?'

'When did you retire?'

'Oh, right. Well, I clung on as late as I could. They let you stay on a bit on the buses, so I was there till I was seventy, but then Kathleen – my wife – her health was getting worse, so I gave up and looked after her. I was doing that till the end of last year. Five years in total it was. She passed away in November.'

'Yes, Eamonn told us. I'm sorry, it must be hard for you on your own,' said Jean.

'I'm not as badly off as I might have been. I'm not like some fellas my age who can't even cook a bit of toast.'

'Eamonn must be a comfort to you as well.'

The thought had never really occurred to Dermot, but he nodded and smiled. 'I think you two had the right idea though. This is the way to retire. A lovely place like this.'

'Oh, we're always reminding ourselves how lucky we are.'

'Luck has nothing to do with it. You made a decision. The rest of us are too stuck in our ways.'

Jean smiled. 'Well, we both retired in 2006 and we just felt we'd served our time. It had always been a dream of ours to live out here. We loved the country, had been coming every year to different parts. We just thought: "You only live once and life is for living." You know how it is.'

She must have been around the same age as Kathleen but they seemed worlds apart. Life wasn't about living for Kathleen, life was about striving and sacrifice and offering things up to God. She'd believed a reward was waiting for her.

'Well, you did the right thing, it's a very nice spot here.'

'It is, yes,' said David, 'beautiful coastal walks. The hills stretch for some miles. Really spectacular views.'

'And the food,' said Jean, 'is just wonderful. You can buy such a range of fresh produce all year round. Everything just seems to taste so much better. I mean, we miss having local shops. Sadly they haven't materialized, but we enjoy the walk down to San Pedro.'

'Yes, it's a day out! Tell him about the swordfish, Jean.'

'Oh, yes, Dermot, you must get Eamonn to take you to the market in Agua Blanca. The swordfish there is to die for. Absolutely mouth-watering. And the market itself is just delightful. The ladies all in their white aprons – spotlessly clean. Everything so immaculate.'

He thought he might have heard conversations like this before. Jean and David reminded him of the people he saw in the kind of slow detective programmes they showed on a Sunday night. Nice people, sitting around dinner tables, discussing fish and drinking wine. He always dozed off before Del Boy got his man.

They were eating a fancy fruit salad when he saw something

move out of the corner of his eye. He had noticed it earlier and assumed it was a bird, but this time he turned to look and saw instead a small security camera mounted on the back wall of the house.

'Did that come with the house?'

David followed the direction of his gaze. 'Oh, that. No.'

Dermot watched the camera swivel once more. 'It's a good one, I'd say – looks very professional. Better than the ones we had on the buses anyway. You fitted it yourself, did you?' But when he looked back David was disappearing into the house with a pile of plates.

Jean seemed embarrassed. 'Sorry, David finds it a little difficult to talk about.'

'Sure, I've no idea about them, I wasn't meaning to sound like an expert.'

'No, not the camera, the burglaries. Twice now. Just twice, I suppose you could say, but it's enough.' She paused. 'They waited till we'd replaced our original belongings and then they took them all again.'

'I'm sorry.'

She gave a tight smile. 'As you can see, we've replaced everything again. You can't let them win.'

'Did the police never catch them?'

'They did in fact. A long time after. Professionals apparently. Been doing it up and down the coast. I'm glad they were caught, though of course that's not to say someone else won't have the same idea and do it again.' She fell silent for a while, before saying, 'There's that unpleasant sense of being observed. Someone keeping tabs on our comings and goings. Watching us. Preying upon us. You can't help worrying it will happen again. It plays on your mind.'

David returned with coffee. 'Here we are! Sorry that took longer than I thought. I hope Jean wasn't subjecting you to tales of the grandkids. Once she gets a captive audience she can be merciless.'

Dermot smiled. 'She didn't mention them once.'

David pulled a face. 'Well, you're in for it now, then.'

Jean flapped her hand at him. 'Oh, ignore him, Dermot. Do you have any grandchildren?'

'I don't, no. Eamonn's our only child.'

'Oh, I'd always assumed he came from a big family.'

Dermot said nothing.

'Well, you need to tell Laura and him to get a move on and make you a granddad. David is pretending to be cool about it, but he's as besotted with our grandchildren as I am.'

'How many do you have?'

'Just two. Our daughter Rachel has two little ones – George and Olivia.'

David sat down beside her and put his hand on hers. 'Careful, love.'

'David's worried I'll get upset.' As soon as she spoke, tears filled her eyes. 'Oh, goodness, I'm sorry, Dermot. What a fool. It's just we do miss them so very much.'

David patted her hand. 'The plan was for them to come out every school holiday, and of course we'd be popping back often too, but it hasn't worked out that way. Unfortunately Jonathan, Rachel's husband, was made redundant shortly after we came out here. A terrible shock – but you know how it is – it's the same all over. So – well, with one thing and another, everything is a little stretched all round.'

Jean turned to him. 'We're hoping to get back for Christmas though, aren't we?'

David chose not to answer and said instead, 'It's not so bad though, is it? Have you told Dermot about the Skype?'

Jean brightened. 'Do you use Skype to call Eamonn?'

Dermot had no idea what she meant and shook his head.

'Oh, you must, it's free, you can chat as long as you like and it doesn't matter. Better still, it's on the Internet, so you can see each other. We see the kids on our computer screen and they can see us on theirs.'

'Oh?'

David nodded. 'Actually, Dermot, it's virtually the same as being there. Isn't it, love?'

'Oh, it's funny. We Skype them all the time now, often we haven't any news for each other, but it's just nice to see them, to be there . . . almost.'

'That's right,' said David, 'it's not a big deal any more, we do it so often. No need for everyone to gather around the computer and have a big, formal conversation. Now it's often just a quick "Hi" to Rachel or Jonathan, and then they take the laptop and put it in the room where the kids are.'

Jean laughed. 'George, he's the little one, only four, he might trundle over and say, "Hello, Granny and Grandpa," and tell us what new toy he has, or what he did that day at nursery, and then Olivia will come and chat for a minute or two, but then they just get on with whatever they were doing and we can just sit and watch them as if we're in the room with them. It's so lovely, just natural and relaxed, sometimes they completely forget we're there.'

'Yes!' said David. 'Last week they went out and didn't even say goodbye, just left us there in the playroom, wondering where they all were.' He laughed.

Jean shook her head. 'Well, we're no better, we sometimes fall asleep in front of the screen. It's just so soothing, hearing their voices. You know, sometimes, when we've felt a bit anxious about things here, we can just open the computer and straight away you feel that sadness lift. If we've had difficulty sleeping at night, we'll find we nod off the next day when we're there listening to them. It's odd though, isn't it,

David, waking up an hour or two later and seeing the empty room?'

'Yes, it can be. If they see we're asleep, they don't wake us, they just leave us and go off doing whatever it is they need to do.'

She nodded. 'You see the empty room and you say, "Is anybody there?" and it's a bit like a seance. I'm not sure who the ghosts are, them or us.' She was quiet for a moment. 'I suppose it must be odd for the kids.'

They sat in silence for a while, Dermot looking at his hands. Eventually Jean turned to him and smiled.

'And do you like word searches, Dermot?'

9

The same faces at every funeral. The same but fewer. It reminded Dermot of the game Eamonn and the other kids used to play at birthday parties. When the music stopped – the desperate craning of necks to see who didn't have a seat, who had been banished from the contest. It was the same thing now. Every few months a phone call and then a funeral, each of them wondering whose turn was next. Some deaths were shocking, others expected, others still felt long overdue. The florid, thickset ones were the first to go – stomachs pushing out their shirts, bacon every morning, beer every night, yellow spots in their eyes, they knew well themselves they would never live to see their kids married. Mick Fitzsimmons went at forty-two, collapsed in the car park of the Cash & Carry, a massive coronary. Others clung on despite all the odds. Nell Gahan, with her pills and her sticks and half her life spent in the doctor's waiting room, was still scuttling about like a Dannimaced cockroach, whispering prayers at every graveside.

Their promises to keep in touch and plans for future get-togethers 'in happier circumstances' never came to anything. There was an acceptance: they saw each other only when someone died. Long, bitter-sweet afternoons, sitting in the orange sunlight of a back lounge or function room. Recalling faded capers and well-worn one-liners. Half-hearted gossip still about long-ago scandals and comeuppances. Confiding small tragedies of estranged siblings and nervous illnesses. Endless ham sandwiches and double measures of Jameson's. Joe Fahey still failing to get his round in, Jim Scanlon as full of it as ever.

At funerals, sitting with old friends, they felt their true selves, but later, in living rooms with televisions on and grandkids racing around the sofa, they would be tired and irritable and wonder why they'd wasted the afternoon with a bunch of relics.

Once Dermot turned sixty-five the funerals started coming as thick and fast as the weddings had done in his twenties. He had attended both wedding and funeral of more friends than he cared to remember. It seemed to him now that a wedding was an IOU, a funeral the debt collected. Hidden amid the high spirits and cheers of the wedding day was the sobering truth buried in the heart of the vows: 'Until death do us part.'

Standing at the graveside looking at the newly widowed, Dermot would remember the newlywed. Glancing around he'd see others who had crowded into group shots in front of the church doors a lifetime ago. At least two of the old crowd – Paddy Mahoney and Johnny Begley – were still wearing the suits they got married in to the funerals of friends fifty years later.

He did not find the comfort in religion that Kathleen had. He mouthed the liturgy but it struck no chord within him. He found himself empty of any great insights or thoughts. As he attended one requiem mass after another, he felt like a man standing on a beach, paralysed in thought and action as the tidal wave approached.

He had always known that one day it would be Kathleen's funeral he was attending. Save an accident of some kind, it was never really in doubt that she would go first. He would make himself remember this sometimes when they were short with each other, the atmosphere curdled. But those good intentions were short-lived. Perhaps in the end it wasn't right to keep someone's eventual death constantly in mind, to frame each remark in the context of the graveside. Life had to be lived in denial of death, and with the right to be sometimes aggrieved, sometimes ill-tempered, sometimes disappointed.

When Kathleen's turn came, there were all the usual crowd and more. Some faces Dermot hadn't seen in over fifty years. Old girlfriends of hers: giggling, teasing mouths and darting eyes last seen in dance halls and crowded bars, now old grannies with thick ankles squeezed into patent-leather shoes.

'Do you not remember me, Dermot? You asked me out to the cinema and, when I turned you down, you asked Kathleen instead.'

Dermot remembered her well enough. He remembered too that it was she who had made a play for him, not the other way around, even though everyone had known by then that he was going with Kathleen. He recalled a red two-piece she used to wear. Kathleen said it made her look like a pillar box. He couldn't wait to tell Kathleen what she'd said, knowing how much it would tickle her. The realization that Kathleen wasn't around to tell came with weary acceptance. This, he knew, was only the first of many such lapses.

He had yet to feel the sustained impact of grief. At the hospital bedside, he had seen her face change at the point of death. A transition at once almost imperceptible and yet unmistakable. In that moment he had felt a pure blast of horror, calling out to the God he did not believe in and causing the nurse to hurriedly return. Since then, though, he had been busy with arrangements and phone calls and visits to the bank and other places. He felt only a strange lightness. He ate as much as he ever had, but feared a sudden gust of wind could blow him away.

He disliked the priest. He knew this was in part to do with Kathleen's devotion to the Church, but he couldn't help it. He tried to listen to his words about Kathleen's life without rancour. The priest banged on about her great faith, the consolation she had found in the Church, her struggle with ill health. He seemed gleeful to Dermot. His lips wet, his face shiny and pink, flushed with victory. It felt as if a long unspoken battle had come to an end and the priest had won. They had claimed her as their prize.

He was still there in the function room afterwards, sipping his pint of shandy. Dermot avoided the priest's corner of the room. He made his way around everyone else, thanking them for coming, accepting their condolences, listening to stories of Kathleen, some familiar, some new. Some cousin of hers from Cork waxing lyrical about Kathleen's abilities with a violin as a ten-year-old. Nurses from the General reminiscing about her sense of humour. Cronies from the church on her flower-arranging skills. He nodded and smiled and kept moving, his head jangling with faces and snatches of conversation. He had a powerful longing to be home, in the back room, gas fire on, glass of beer in one hand, cheese sandwich in the other, watching *University Challenge*. The thought of the programme, the banks of enviably clever and assured young people, always brought Eamonn to mind and Dermot realized he had forgotten all about him in the confusion of the gathering.

He cast about the room and eventually saw him hovering with an empty plate in hand at the end of the buffet table. Laura sat with a group of Eamonn's cousins at a nearby table, drinking and chatting with an ease Eamonn had never possessed. Eamonn stood on his own peering suspiciously at some chicken wings and Dermot wondered what crime they had committed. His son had been home for three days and it had been odd to have him back in the house, sleeping in his old room. He'd offered to help with arrangements but Dermot had preferred to do it all himself. In the end, purely to give him something to do, he asked him to sort through all the old photos. He'd only wanted them gathered together neatly in a box, but Eamonn had covered the living-room floor to sort them in some kind of order and driven Dermot half-mad, getting under his feet, spreading the job over two days and insisting on laboriously explaining the different piles to Dermot as he was hurrying to get dressed for the funeral that morning.

Eamonn had now reached the end of the buffet table, having taken nothing, as far as Dermot could see, but a tomato and a bread roll. He hesitated, plate in hand, deciding where to sit. He looked vulnerable and uncertain and Dermot saw him for a moment as a little boy again, waiting for him at the entrance to the garage. Eamonn looked across the room and met his father's eyes. Standing on opposite sides of the crowded room, they raised a hand at one another and then each went off to find somewhere to be.

IO

Eamonn paused in the doorway for a moment to watch him, registering as he did the familiarity of the posture. It was almost matronly – back straight, arms folded on chest, feet tucked under and crossed. This curiously attentive pose was how his father relaxed, whether in a pub or in front of the television, leaning slightly forward, head inclined to one side. As a gentle snoring struck up, Eamonn realized with some surprise that it was also how he took his naps. He moved quietly to the other side of the room to check Dermot was actually asleep. He frowned at the image – his father sleeping like a budgerigar. There was a strange novelty in the sight. He had very rarely seen him asleep. Occasionally, when sharing a room with his parents on holidays, he had woken in the night and listened to the intricate counterpoint of their snoring. His father's high and wheezy, his mother's deep and rumbling. The longer he listened the harder he found it to connect the sounds – simultaneously animal and mechanical – to the people. He would sneak over to their bed to look at their faces, to reassure himself that they were still his parents and that he should not be scared.

The intimacy of sharing a space with his father once more was unsettling. He found his gaze constantly zooming in and refocusing on certain details at once both mysterious and mundane. He was assailed by things that as a boy were so everyday as to be invisible, and as an adult he had not been around to see. The way his father read a newspaper, folded up into a neat square and held close to his face. The manner in which he ate:

a bit of everything on the fork, peas carefully halved to avoid imbalance. The sound of his razor scraping his chin, the smell of his soap. All these things Eamonn had forgotten and each one triggered a complex mix of recognition and distance, a nostalgia for something still there. His father both alive and dead.

He couldn't recall Dermot ever taking a nap before. He had noticed a few small signs of age since his arrival. Nocturnal trips to the toilet, the occasional effortful noise when standing or sitting. He remained, Eamonn was sure, fitter and healthier than himself, but there was a change nonetheless. Eamonn didn't know whether his father had aged a little in the months since his mother had died, or whether he had just seemed younger and more vital next to her.

He would one day become authentically frail and need someone to care for him, and, as his only child, it would be Eamonn's responsibility. This was something he had known for many years, but still he found it impossible to believe. Strength was one of his father's defining features, never something he had made a show of, but his sheer physical presence made it clear. There was a power within him, a manifest capability. At Kathleen's funeral Eamonn had offered to return from Spain, to rent out the apartment when such a thing was remotely possible, and to live nearby, but the offer was gestural. He didn't believe that his father needed or wanted him around and he knew moreover that he would never accept such an offer.

Beyond an assumption of some kind of standardized grief, he had not considered how the loss of his mother had affected his father. In some ways, neither had he considered how her loss had affected him. Living in Lomaverde, at such a remove, he was not confronted by her absence every day. It wasn't that he pictured her still alive, but neither did he always remember that she was gone, or consider the reality of Dermot's day-to-day life on his own. It was easy to not think too much about it, to half-imagine things essentially unchanged.

Laura had encouraged him to ring home more often, but Eamonn felt she didn't understand how self-sufficient his father was, didn't really get the nature of his relationship with his father at all. 'We don't live in each other's pockets,' he'd say. 'We don't need to be talking to one another all the time.' Besides, Dermot was surrounded by Kathleen's relatives back in Birmingham. That was part of it, though Eamonn tried not to admit it, even to himself. A long-held suspicion that his dad was easier in the company of some of his nephews than his son. Eamonn's cousin Brendan, for example. A man of few words who knew how to strip an engine and place an accumulator bet. Dermot saw him a lot. They seemed able to communicate in a language Eamonn had never learned.

The snoring built slowly to a peak with the loud finale inevitably rousing the sleeper.

'Oh . . .' His eyes opened and focused on Eamonn. Dermot smiled, embarrassed. 'I was asleep.'

Eamonn nodded.

'I wasn't the driver.'

'Sorry?'

'I was dreaming I was stuck in traffic on College Road, but I wasn't the driver. I was sat upstairs with all the bloody kids.'

'You must have been glad to wake up.'

'I don't know who was driving the bus.' He said this as if he should have known.

'Maybe there was no driver.'

Dermot looked at him as if he were an idiot. 'Someone was driving the bus, son. They don't drive themselves.'

Eamonn scratched his head. 'Went OK at Jean and David's, did it?'

'Yes. Very nice. They were advocating being a grandparent.'

'Right.'

'Did I tell you about Keiron, Brendan's eldest?'

'What about him?'

'He's gone and got his girlfriend pregnant. Fifteen years old, the pair of them. At the same school. So Brendan's going to be a granddad.'

'Christ.' Eamonn felt the familiar mixture of awe and horror. He remembered seeing his cousin nonchalantly smoking in the park when they were children. Brendan seemed grown up when he was eight. He had left school at sixteen while Eamonn went on to university, the only one in the family to do so. He imagined that, to Brendan, his other cousins and perhaps his own father, he would forever be thought of as a student – a pejorative label meaning someone daft, lazy and essentially childish.

'He was asking me the other day what you did out here, job-wise. And to be honest I couldn't tell him. Was it something to do with computers? I can't remember now what your mother said.'

'It was the same job I had back home.'

'Oh,' said Dermot uncertainly, 'they have an office out here, do they?'

'I didn't need an office, I was editing computer books. I worked from home.'

'Oh, right. So that's going well, is it?'

Eamonn hesitated. 'Well, no, I was doing it for the first few months, but the company went bust.' It pained him to admit this. He could imagine his father thinking there was something fundamentally unreal about the idea of working so remotely, so abstractly. He would assume the collapse of the company was a consequence of the intangibility of the work involved.

Dermot, however, looked merely concerned. 'So are you having to look for work?'

'No, it's fine. I'm sorted. I got a new job teaching English.'

'Oh, teaching. Well, Eamonn, your mother would be very proud. I had the impression that teaching wasn't your cup of tea.'

The impression was correct, but Eamonn shrugged it off.

'Well, now, I'd say your Spanish must be tip-top to be able to teach.'

Eamonn found it irksome that people assumed that living abroad somehow magically endowed you with a facility for language-learning. As if rewiring your brain and having to say a different word to the word you naturally wanted to say every time you wanted to speak wasn't incredibly, almost impossibly, hard, regardless of where you happened to live or what words the people nearby happened to be hurling around, with near-violent rapidity. The assumption was no less irritating for being one that he himself had held, and one that made his apparent inability to rise above the *bajo-intermedio* standard of Spanish very hard to accept.

'I'm teaching them English, Dad.'

'Sure I know that, but obviously you need to explain the grammar and so on in Spanish. You need to provide the translation.'

'That's not how it's done. It's all done in English. It's immersive. They pick it up.'

Dermot considered this. 'Immersive. I suppose you can communicate a lot with what they call "body language", can you? Hand signals and so on?'

Eamonn rubbed his face. 'I don't use hand signals, Dad. They can't see me, for one thing.'

Dermot looked at him, an expression of dawning realization on his face.

'Oh . . . but, that's great work to be doing. I'm sorry now – I didn't get you at all at first. What do they call them these days? "Visually impaired", is it? "Sight-challenged"?'

Eamonn found himself doing something that he hated. It was a noise he made only when talking to one or both of his parents. A kind of impatient sigh, bordering on a grunt. An adolescent habit that he knew was ridiculous in a thirty-three-year-old man.

'I'm not teaching blind kids. I'm teaching civil servants. It's all done online or over the phone.' He paused and then added: 'No hand signals!'

Dermot was quiet for a few moments and then said: '"*Er bekommt keine Luft.*"'

Eamonn looked around the room.

'Oh, yes, I remember that one all right. Linguaphone it was. Like you're doing. On the tape.'

Eamonn was minded to explain that what he was doing was nothing like Linguaphone, but his father continued.

'"*Er bekommt keine Luft.*" "He can't breathe." I took the tapes out of the library, thought I could listen to them on the job, but it never really worked. You'd get very absorbed in that stuff. I remember sailing past a stop full of passengers. I saw them there, but just forgot I was supposed to pull in. Raging they were, but I was listening to a conversation in a restaurant. Can't remember any of it now.' He shook his head. 'Only bit of German I have is, "He can't breathe." Funny to remember just that.'

He fell silent again for a few moments before adding, 'I'm not sure you'd ever really need to say it. You'd think the facial coloration would tell the story well enough.'

II

When he awoke from the dream he had forgotten where he was. The room was pitch black and for a moment Dermot thought he was back in the bed he'd slept in as a boy. He reached out instinctively for a lamp he hadn't thought of in over sixty years and as his hand flailed in the dark he remembered everything. He lay there still, trying to control his breathing and contain his sense of loss.

Finding the door eventually, he walked through the darkened apartment to the kitchen. He had gone for a glass of water, but found himself getting instead a beer from the fridge.

He slid open the door to the terrace and sat on a plastic chair. The air was warm and filled with the sound of night creatures vibrating invisibly in the bushes around him. He turned his gaze upwards. He'd become accustomed to city night skies, a meagre scattering of greyish pinpricks in the strip of hazy orange above the streetlights. Here he felt himself pushed back in his chair by the spectacle of the limitless stars and constellations covering every part of the sky above him. He remembered another night, lying on his back in Hamilton's field, his younger brother by his side. Dominic had woken up scared by noises coming from the kitchen and Dermot had taken him downstairs to show him there were no ghosts or banshees and told him that even if there were, they would certainly flee at the sight of such brave boys. Afterwards Dominic wanted to go out to the field. They lay on their backs, Dominic taking Dermot's hand and pointing up at the sky. He told Dermot the names of the stars, or at least the names he had given them, which were their own names and those of people and places and things they knew – their whole world mirrored in the night sky above them. He pointed out Sam the cat and old Hamilton's mad dog Blackie, he pointed out the constellations of their father, their brothers and their sisters, of the biscuit tin and the bar of chocolate hidden in Peggy's pillow, he pointed out their father's wife, Teresa, and somewhere further back in the sky at some infinite depth of space and time he showed Dermot the star that was their mother. Dermot scoured the sky now for any trace of these things, but found they had gone.

He was roused from his reminiscences by a low moan. He looked over the balcony in time to see a black shape darting along the side of the pool, realizing then it had just been a dispute between cats, a territorial confrontation in the deep end. He watched the vanquished tabby retreat and take cover in shrubbery and then looked up once more at the stars. It was a sure sign of old age, this constant picking over the past, a growing affliction since Kathleen's death. He made his way quietly back to his room, sitting on the bed and rubbing his face. He looked at the clock. Another two hours before dawn.

12

They had been caught. If he ever read the emails, or picked up the seemingly endless 'Dates for your Diary' slips that fluttered from his mailbox each time he passed, or took any notice of the forlorn printed reminders stuck on lamp posts all over Lomaverde, he would have known that it was not safe to leave the apartment that day. But he did none of those things and as a result, while he and his father were setting off for a stroll, Jean had spotted them.

'Oh, Eamonn, lovely! You're bringing Dermot too.'

He saw the folder under her arm and realized his error. At the same moment he had a flicker of hope that Dermot could be his salvation.

'Hi, Jean. Can't make the meeting today unfortunately. You know . . . Dad's on holiday. Doing my tour-guide bit.'

'Oh, of course I understand. Are you off somewhere nice?'

Dermot spoke. 'We had no plans at all.'

'Oh.' Jean looked confused and Eamonn laughed.

'No, that's not quite right. I was going to take Dad for a walk, show him around.'

Dermot frowned. 'Sure I think I know the way around myself now. It's not what you'd call a metropolis. I can't imagine I'd get lost.'

Eamonn looked at him. 'You don't want to go off on your own. What would you do with yourself?'

'Plenty of nice spots to sit and read a book. You don't want me in your hair all the time. You carry on.'

Eamonn noticed his father grinning broadly, delighted at this little manoeuvre.

'Oh, are you sure, Dermot? I don't want to ruin your plans. It would be good though if Eamonn could come along as he had to miss the last one too.'

'Well, there's no question, then. Go on, son, you go along and enjoy your meeting. I'm sure I'll find something to occupy me.'

But with that touch of pathos he had gone too far. Jean was concerned.

'Oh dear, I don't like the idea of you sitting on a bench on your own. Here's an idea: why don't you come along too? I mean, if you haven't anything special planned. It's just . . . it would be lovely to have an outside perspective. You know, sometimes we all get a bit of tunnel vision.'

'No, no, I'd just be in the way.'

'Not at all. Would he, Eamonn?'

Eamonn shook his head fervently and smiled at his father, who was no longer grinning.

'Right, so. I'll come along.'

'Oh, that's wonderful. To think we almost had neither of you and now we have both!'

Eamonn looked at Dermot and repeated: 'To think.'

It was Ian and Becca's turn to host the meeting and Becca was relishing the role, introducing Dermot to everyone.

'You know Roger and Cheryl, and Jean and David. That's Gill and Rosemary at the table. Gill's our chair today.'

Gill raised a hand, looking far from thrilled at the honour.

'That's Simon there, who lives with Raimund, who, incidentally is German. And over there, on her ownsome, is Inga, who's come all the way from Sweden!' She put her head to one side and wrinkled her nose at Inga. 'You all right, love?'

'Yes, I'm fine, thanks.'

'You let me know if you need anything.'

'Thank you.'

She gestured at the other corner. 'And finally, Henri and Danielle.' She turned to Dermot and mouthed, 'French.'

Eamonn led his father to a couple of chairs in the corner of the room behind Inga. Gill started the meeting.

'So, first up, back in December we said we'd review the security situation after another six months and that time is now up. How effective is the current solution, etc., etc. Would anyone like to start us off?'

David raised his hand. David loved meetings. 'Madam Chair' – Eamonn put his head in his hands. Sometimes it was hard not to scream – 'I'll start if I may. I think on the whole the results have been mixed. On the one hand I'd say we're all pleased and relieved to see that the burglaries have stopped, touch wood. And, while the gang in question have now been arrested, I think we'd all agree that it's probably Esteban's part-time presence that prevents others from thinking we are easy pickings. But there have been other incidents that signal to me at least that we need a greater security presence.'

Gill looked up. 'What other incidents?'

'Well, there was the unpleasantness with the red paint, that of course we all know about.' There was general murmuring at this and Dermot turned to Eamonn with a questioning look. Eamonn remembered the sight of the empty house, livid in the morning sun. Red paint running down the walls in thick rivulets. The door covered in crimson handprints. It was really too weird and inexplicable to take in let alone describe to his father. He shrugged.

'Just some vandalism.'

David raised his voice to speak again. 'Since then there has been the defacing of the sign at the entrance and the dumping of rubbish along the main approach road.'

There was some muttering at this between people who already knew and those who didn't.

'Disposable nappies!' Eamonn heard someone exclaim.

Cheryl looked bored and picked up a magazine.

Gill held up her hand. 'Can we have just one person at a time, please?'

Henri called out: 'What happened to the sign?'

Ian answered: 'The usual thing. Some local teenager with a spray can. "Look at me, look at me. I'm cool. I can write my name." Yeah, illegibly, you dick.'

'Actually, Ian,' Simon corrected him, 'that's not right. It's not kids writing their names. Someone has sprayed *"Ladrones"* all over the entrance sign. I think we can assume that both that graffiti and the rubbish being dumped near the entrance are because of local anger at the developers and their failure to pay off the contractors.'

Eamonn recalled the exodus the previous September. One morning he awoke to a different type of silence. He'd grown used to the absence of certain elements in the soundscape: traffic, commerce, workers, children. On that particular day though he noticed something else had dropped from the mix. It wasn't until lunchtime that he identified the difference as the lack of building noise. While the pace of finishing Lomaverde had never been frenetic, there was usually some activity: the buzz of a drill, slow hammering, the distant repetitions of Hit Radio. He had thought it was perhaps a local holiday, until he saw Hernán, one of the security guards, leaving the sentry cabin, wheeling an office chair loaded up with a computer tower and monitor. Between Hernán's basic English and his own poor Spanish he couldn't follow everything but he understood that *cabrones* were involved. That neither Hernán nor anyone else had been paid for some indefinite period and that Hernán was taking some crappy, low-quality office equipment as an unofficial compensation package.

Roger was speaking. 'Well, they can join the back of the queue. We've got our own issues with the bloody developers.'

'Exactly,' said Becca, 'and it doesn't bother Zadis if people paint all over their signs or dump rubbish, the only people it hurts is us, the people who live here. And I for one think we've suffered enough!'

Rosemary raised her hand and waited to speak. 'I think their anger is totally understandable and to be honest there is very little we can do about people dumping rubbish on the approach road. That's a matter for the local council.'

'Ha!' shouted Roger, mirthlessly. 'Well, don't expect them to do anything without a nice backhander. Same way this place got built in the first place! We know all about that now.'

Gill raised her voice. 'OK, let's save that for later.'

'And so' – Danielle had her hand in the air and spoke quietly – 'the red paint . . . that was someone angry at Zadis too? Yes? Is that what we are saying now?'

Raimund cleared his throat and stood up. Eamonn thought Raimund had an interesting aesthetic. It would be incorrect to say he looked like a Hell's Angel; what he looked like more precisely was someone playing a Hell's Angel in an 80s Hollywood movie. A generic barroom brawler with nightmarish tattoos and assorted ironware piercing his head and face. Laura liked to call him by his imagined film credit: 'Bad Guy One'. Eamonn saw Dermot staring at whatever it was Raimund had growing out of his forehead.

Gill gestured towards him. 'Raimund. You have something to say?'

And then came the voice – a sound that could not be more

at odds with his appearance, softly German-accented with a soothing, almost melancholy, ring to it.

'Oh, yes, I have something to relate that I think might have some bearing on this.' He stopped for a moment as if waiting for someone to grant him permission to continue, and then began again.

'I met a man in a bar last week in Mojácar. We got talking. When I told him I lived in Lomaverde he asked me if I'd happened to watch a programme recently made by a historian named Dr José Dominguez. Of course this then led on to a brief discussion about television and the difference between Spanish and German television news and he agreed with me about the intriguing differences in emphasis. I'm sure we all have our own examples.'

'Pringle?' Becca whispered loudly, holding out a bowl to Dermot. He shook his head and she continued around the room in a low crouch.

'It seems the programme in question was one of the kind so very popular here, you know the type, I'm sure: people sitting around a table discussing something: *la crisis* or immigration or lactose intolerance or whatever it might be. (I've never known a nation with such an appetite for watching other people discuss things.) Anyway, you are all familiar with such shows: the women with the little glasses and the men with the trimmed beards. I didn't see the programme, of course, but I was able to imagine it quite vividly from this man's description of it.' He paused thoughtfully and turned to Simon. 'I'm forgetting his name. Isn't that terrible?' Then he said something in German and they both laughed.

Gill cleared her throat and said gently, 'Raimund. The red paint.'

'Yes. Yes. The red paint. So. There is the programme, that I did not see, but which I hope I have given you some flavour of.

75

It seems the historian, Dr José Dominguez (I have googled him since and he is based at the University of Salamanca and is very respected) is doing a larger research piece about the latter part of the Civil War and in particular attempting to locate some of the graves of those who went missing.'

Becca whispered loudly again: 'What's he going on about?' And Ian shushed her.

'So, it seems that in November 1937, and no one disputes this, sixteen men were taken from Agua Blanca by Nationalist forces to be executed and the whereabouts of their bodies has never been discovered. Obviously all this was hushed up for years, but now there's this new investigation into all the executions and disappearances and Dr Dominguez has been active in this.'

Gill had given up on politeness. 'For God's sake, Raimund, get to the bloody point.'

Raimund looked put out. 'Very well. To cut a long story short, there is some justification to believe that there may be an unmarked mass grave under Lomaverde.'

General commotion broke out. Raimund held up his hand. 'That, anyway, is the contention of Dr Dominguez. Apparently another historian on the programme disputed it. The politician from the left said questions need to be asked about how much the local council knew and how permission was ever given to build here, and the politician from the right said there was no good to come from opening up old wounds.'

Jean held up her hand and gradually everyone quietened. 'Can I just ask Raimund, did you get from your acquaintance any sense of whether this information was going to be acted upon? I mean, are they planning to excavate?'

Simon answered for him. 'I've read up a bit about it in the meantime. There's a fierce debate raging on both sides. I don't think ultimately much will happen, but when we heard all this and read the news stories afterwards, we looked at one another, didn't we, Raimund?' – Raimund nodded – 'And we both said, "I bet that was what the red paint was about."'

Becca was tearful. 'This is awful. Awful. Just horrible.' She blew her nose. 'We will never, ever, ever be able to sell.'

Roger shook his head. 'Incredible, isn't it? Just when you thought things couldn't get any worse. Do you ever wonder what we've done to deserve all this?'

Rosemary stood up. 'With respect, Roger, I think it's in poor taste to portray ourselves as the victims here. We're talking about people being abducted and murdered. Families left not knowing what became of their loved ones for over seventy years. I think we should show a little compassion.'

Inga shifted slightly in her seat and Eamonn and Dermot were able to see the notebook she had been busily scribbling in. Instead of notes, the page was filled with a sketch of Roger. She had captured his likeness exactly, somehow rendering even the roll of his eyes. It was a faithful reproduction in every way except instead of sitting on a dining chair, he was shown sitting inside a glass case with a coin slot to operate.

Gill was speaking again. 'So, taking all this on board and returning to the original point, if we can, about the security situation. We're paying Esteban for three days a week. Is that enough?'

David spoke again. 'I think with all the potential uninvited guests we have to contend with, from outright criminals to locals with grievances and now to bereaved families, we might all feel safer with Esteban here full time.'

Ian nodded. 'And, quite frankly, the economic situation as it is, there's very little work down here in this part of the country. I don't know if you've been into Agua Blanca or San Pedro recently but they are slipping over the edge – shops closing down, delinquent kids necking Don Simon under the trees. And here we are, in what appear to be fancy houses; I don't like to be alarmist, but people will turn to crime and we're obvious targets.'

Eamonn remembered the not so subtle insinuations made by Ian in the wake of the burglaries about the community of Gypsies in the nearby town. The gang was in fact English, professional criminals from Essex targeting the many ghost towns and failed golf resorts of the Spanish Costas.

Becca joined in. 'He has a point. I mean, I don't think we're saying people who fall on hard times automatically become thieves, but envy is a terrible thing. Ian and I have plenty of tales of trying to establish up-and-coming pockets of housing in run-down, tatty areas. There can be a lot of resentment. Also, I'm not being racist but' – Eamonn braced himself – 'you have to consider the immigrants.'

Gill looked at her. 'What about the immigrants?'

'Well, there's more of them everywhere.'

'Like us, you mean?'

'No, I mean the ones from Romania, Morocco, places like that. The women with the babies begging for money. You ask any Spanish person who's responsible for most crime in this country and they'll tell you it's the Romanians. Or the Moroccans.'

Raimund said softly, 'I don't think that is the view of all Spanish people; I think that is the view of racist Spanish people.'

Ian called over: 'What did you say?'

Gill put up her hand. 'So, I'm taking my turn now. As far as I can see, we might all feel happier if Esteban was here more, but at the same time I don't suppose any of us can really afford that. The burglaries have stopped and that is the main thing. The other issues we face, it seems to me, can best be addressed not by increased security but by putting our message out there.'

'What do you mean?' asked Jean.

'I mean, something simple like approaching the local paper to do an article about us. Get active on community forums. Make it clear that we have suffered at the hands of the developers too. That we are sympathetic to others. That we are just normal people, struggling with the same economic situation as everyone else. It might achieve nothing, but I think the answer is to join forces with the local community, not barricade ourselves away from it. A siege mentality, this idea of "them and us", will not do us any good.'

She got a round of applause from some of the residents for that. Eamonn wondered if her words would do any good. No one wanted to be paranoid but the condition seemed endemic in Lomaverde. It was hard not to overreact to events that in less isolated places or for people with busier lives might have seemed minor. He remembered with some embarrassment his own fearfulness at times. The adolescent pranks of kids from neighbouring towns had occasionally felt truly menacing. He recalled one particularly inglorious afternoon after an argument with Laura. It was, he'd realized at some point, an argument with himself and he had used her as his proxy, something he had started doing more and more. Afterwards he'd been walking through the nearby woods to clear his head when a loud crack sounded in a tree above him. He had looked up and as he did so something hit him on the arm. He put his hand to where the pain was and saw a stone hit the back of his knuckle. He peered into the thicket of trees from where the stone had been thrown. Someone whistled, another made a monkey cry and then the air was thick with small stones, flying past his ears, pinging his face and body. It took him a moment to understand what was happening – bored kids, *guiri*-baiting. He knew he should be cool, be on their side, say something to show he understood. But he didn't understand. He found them unknowable and sinister. They weren't on his side, they were alien and hostile, like everything else in this place. He had fled in terror and shame, his heart pounding and a terrible anger burning his eyes.

He looked across at his father now and imagined what he would have done in similar circumstances. He pictured Dermot advancing towards the trees, unflinching as the stones bounced off him like bullets off a tank, shouting, 'Come here, you little devils!' as he chased the kids away. He had put up with far worse on the buses.

The meeting dragged on for another hour and a half, snagged for most of that time on some impenetrable point of Spanish law relevant to the planned legal proceedings against the local council and the developers. Eamonn looked around the room and felt almost overwhelmed by hopelessness.

Because Lomaverde was not in decline, because it had rather simply failed to take off, its death was more difficult to perceive. Awareness of its failure to thrive was slow and incremental, similar to Eamonn and Laura's own gradual realization, four months after arriving, that the pool was emptying. For the first few days neither of them mentioned it, each assuming that they were imagining it. But as the water level continued to sink there was no room for doubt. When they phoned Nieves they were assured the cause would be investigated and the problem fixed. It took an age for the pool to empty completely, the water seeping slowly through a tiny crack. It was peculiarly painful to watch.

It was after midday when Dermot and Eamonn were finally released from the meeting. They set off up the hill at a brisk pace as if trying to make up for the lost hours in captivity.

'Sorry. I don't know why I made you endure that.'

'You wanted me to suffer.'

'It seemed funny, fleetingly.'

'I suppose I've had worse.'

'When, for example?'

'Oh God, I remember some awful thing I had to sit through with your mother. Went on for hours.'

'At church?'

'No, some kids' show. Song after song after song.'

'Was I there?'

'You were in it.'

'Oh.'

'I'd hardly have gone otherwise. Something about Noah.'

Eamonn looked at him. 'That was a school production! I'm sorry if it was dull for you, seeing your only child perform.'

'It's no good getting huffy about it now. The fact was I didn't see you once. You spent the whole time lurking at the back.'

'Well, I didn't want to be in it. It was rubbish.'

'You don't have to tell me.'

'I don't know why Mom dragged you along.'

Dermot was quiet for a while before saying, 'I think it was the other way around. That was the worst of it.'

13

At the start of term Mrs O'Dwyer had given everyone in the class a folder to be used for the special instruction they would receive in preparation for the holy sacrament. Eamonn's folder was green. Mrs O'Dwyer had originally given him a pink one, but the moment she'd moved away from the table, he and Bernadette Keenan had swapped by mutual and wordless consent. On the front of the folder he had written 'My First Holy Communion', and decorated this, as Mrs O'Dwyer had said they could, with drawings of chalices, hosts, crosses and doves. Other pupils had struggled with the doves. He could see Mark Hurley's effort – some kind of winged dog – and Bernadette Keenan's flying fish. He had carefully copied his dove from the poster on the wall and Mrs O'Dwyer had said it was beautifully done.

He filled in that day's worksheet. A line had to be drawn to link matching words. He was carefully connecting 'Eucharistic Prayer' with 'A special prayer said during mass'. He had a suspicion about the worksheets, a feeling that they weren't quite right. The questions weren't like real questions, they didn't require him to be clever or to understand something complicated, they just required him to use and repeat certain words, like a baby learning to speak.

Bernadette nudged him, making the line wobble, and whispered, 'David Brennan thinks the bread and wine are Jesus's body and blood!'

Eamonn carefully rubbed out the crooked line. 'They are, aren't they?'

'No, I mean, *actually* the body and blood.'

'What? Real blood?'

'Yes!'

Eamonn looked in David Brennan's direction and pulled a face popular among his classmates, sticking his tongue under his lower lip and flapping his hands, implying an unspecified handicap.

'Is the priest Dracula, then, drinking blood?'

Bernadette grinned and said, 'Or a cannibal, eating a body?' She lowered her voice further: 'Mmmmm, could I have a nice piece of Jesus's arm, please?'

Eamonn twitched his eyebrows in Mrs O'Dwyer's direction: 'She likes the taste of his bottom best.'

To his distress, Bernadette emitted a high-pitched whoop and Mrs O'Dwyer swooped like a bat.

'Is there something amusing on the worksheet? Something funny about Our Lord Jesus's sacrifice?'

'No, miss.'

'You, Bernadette Keenan, are exactly the kind of washerwoman who would have happily watched Jesus drag his crucifix up the steep slopes of Calvary, laughing gaily at the spectacle. Madame Defarge, no less, knitting at the guillotine.'

Bernadette looked uneasily at the paper guillotine in the corner of the classroom, trying and failing to fathom its sinister role in Mrs O'Dwyer's anger.

'And you, Eamonn Lynch,' the teacher hesitated, seeing his worksheet neatly completed, 'you should know better than to get involved in her nonsense.'

Lunch was a bitter-sweet affair. The canteen staff had once again attempted to pass parsnips off as chips, and there was the gruesome matter of some cabbage to be disposed of, but this

was followed by the premium combination of chocolate concrete and custard.

Mark Houlihan plonked himself next to Eamonn: 'You
gonna watch me batter David Brennan after school?'

'Can't. I'm doing the whole of the Inner Circle.'

'What's that?'

'The 8.'

Mark still looked blank.

'The bus. The Inner Circle.'

Mark pulled a face. 'Oh yeah. The Inner Circle. I've done
that loads of times.'

'Where does it go, then?'

'London.'

Crumbs of concrete flew from Eamonn's mouth. 'London?
What are you talking about? It goes around the inner circle of
Birmingham. It goes up Newtown, Five Ways, Sparkbrook . . .'

'Sounds boring.'

'No. It's not boring. It's wicked and tonight I'll be the first
ever person, ever, to do the entire route who isn't a bus driver.
Plus I'll be stood up at the front the whole time, cos my dad
will be driving. Once, at the garage, he let me sit in the driver's
seat and steer the wheel.'

'So. I've driven loads of buses. And lorries. And motorbikes.'

'No you haven't.'

'Yes I have. Anyway, bus driving's a wog's job.'

'No it's not.'

'Yes it is. Your dad must be a wog. Are you a wog?'

'No.'

'You must be a Paki, then. They're the only other people
who drive buses. Are you a Paki?'

'No.'

Mark was doing some kind of accent now. 'Oh bloody hell!
Where's my turban! Oh bloody hell!'

Eamonn started to clear his tray. He didn't want to look as if he were running away, but he wanted to run away.

'Yeah, piss off, Paki, before I batter you too.'

In the afternoon Father Maguire paid one of his regular visits to the class. He had been talking for some time about something. Eamonn wasn't sure what. He remembered the priest had started by saying that God loved all little children, but that had been a long time ago and Eamonn didn't know what had happened since. Father Maguire had a sing-song voice, travelling up and down in pitch at perfectly regular intervals regardless of what he was saying or to whom he was saying it. The effect was similar to that of a hypnotist's swinging watch, the modulated to and fro sending listeners into a trance.

As the priest spoke, Eamonn sat upright, looking straight at him, while all the time reciting in his head the fare stages of the Inner Circle route. He glanced at Mrs O'Dwyer and could see she was doing something similar, embellishing her performance with the occasional vigorous nod and smile. A few others in the class had a comparable mastery of their own outward appearance. For many, though, the deceit was entirely beyond them. Patrick Wall was rocking on his chair, his neck stretched backwards, head resting on the desk behind him, staring up at the ceiling, mouth open, features slack. Mark Houlihan was assiduously mining his nose, his face a picture of profound loss. Marie Murphy was absent-mindedly jabbing a compass into her own arm over and over again and Bernadette Keenan was lightly napping on the desk beside him.

Eamonn detected a change in classroom pressure, a falling-away or dip. He switched his attention back to Father Maguire in time to hear him say: 'Well, we'll try again, shall we? How did God show his love to us? Hmmm? Anybody? How did God prove that he loved us?'

Marie Murphy tentatively raised her hand: 'He invented rainbows, Father.'

Father Maguire smiled with his mouth. 'Yes, well, that's right enough. We say "created", not "invented": God created rainbows. That's true, dear, but he showed his love for each and every one of us in a much more powerful and meaningful way.'

Silence.

'Come on, now. I've been talking about it for the last twenty minutes.' He gave a mirthless laugh. 'I just said it! Come on.'

With perfect timing the bell rang for home time and the sound of thirty chairs scraping on lino filled the air before stopping abruptly as a suddenly red-faced Father Maguire bellowed: 'No one is going anywhere until I have a satisfactory answer to my question! Do you think I just come here to talk to myself? Do you think I can't tell the ones among you who choose not to listen to God's word? I tell you now there are some of you here who are a very long way from God's grace and a very long way from being ready for communion, so you can forget any ideas you might have about pretty dresses and fancy bow ties, and presents no doubt from all the family. I want an answer.'

Mrs O'Dwyer looked panicked, as taken aback by Father Maguire's turn as everyone else.

'Come on now, children. Don't let me down. Who can answer Father's question?' It was clear that she herself had no idea what the question had even been. She smiled nervously at the priest. 'I think they're tired at the end of a long day, Father.'

'I'm sure they are. I know I'm tired, very tired indeed, but I have plenty of work still to do today and I hope I won't be delayed any longer waiting for this answer.'

Mrs O'Dwyer put her head to one side. 'Father, please . . .'

Father Maguire turned away from her and pointed directly at Eamonn.

'You, boy. You were paying attention. Not fidgeting and thinking about Scooby Doo. Tell the rest of them. Tell the rest of them, or we shall go through it all again.'

Eamonn looked back at the priest with a blank expression. He felt the eyes of his classmates burning through his head. He saw Mrs O'Dwyer with her head down, her hand over her eyes. He licked his lips and spoke in a quiet voice. 'How did God show his love to us?'

'Yes. Yes. That's the question. No points for just repeating it back to me.'

There was silence. Eamonn felt a strange buoyancy. He thought of his Bronze swimming test. Treading water while he inflated his pyjamas. He watched the second hand of the clock climb step by shuddering step. He noticed the smell of plasticine lingering in the air. He watched as something seemed to drain from Father Maguire's face and then said, 'God showed his love for us by sacrificing his only son Jesus to wash away our sins.'

They didn't say much to each other. Eamonn stood up next to the driver's cab. He liked to help his dad by telling him the number of people at each approaching stop. His dad had never asked him to do this, but Eamonn was sure it was useful information:

'Three coming up, Dad.'

'Oh, three is it? Well, I think we can manage that.'

Eamonn liked listening to the way his dad spoke to the passengers, the kinds of things he said. He thought he was very good at this. Friendly but in charge. Sometimes at home, when he was sure no one could hear him, Eamonn would stand in front of the bathroom mirror and pretend to be his dad:

'A filthy day, isn't it now?'

'I'd say we'd have rain before the afternoon's over.'

'Move along the bus, please.'

'I'm afraid that pass is out of date, son.'

Lots of the passengers were regulars well known to his dad, shift workers knocking on and off, men and women with whom he'd exchange complicated banter that Eamonn couldn't follow. His dad had told him that the number 8 was known as the Workers' Special as it serviced so many big factories. He said the city would grind to a halt without the Inner Circle. Many of the passengers were Afro-Caribbean and Asian. Eamonn leaned into the cab at one point and said in a low voice: 'Are there many other drivers like you, Dad?'

'What do you mean?'

'Like you. Not coloured or Indian.'

'What? Do you mean Irish?'

'Yeah. Irish. Or . . . just white.'

Dermot moved his eyes from the road for a moment to glance at him. 'That's a funny question. There are a fair few Irish fellas. You know that yourself, you've met the people I work with.'

'So it's not a job only for coloured people?'

'Has someone been saying something to you?'

'It was just something I heard.'

'It's a job for anyone who's willing to do it. As long as they have the patience of a saint. Some of the lads are West Indian, some from Pakistan, Bangladesh, Poland, Ireland, a few Brummies. The lot. It's a real mishmash.'

Eamonn liked that. He'd be sure to say it if Mark Houlihan ever said anything again. He'd look at him and say: 'For your information, it's a real mishmash.'

When he'd finished his shift, Dermot and Eamonn walked home together. They walked in silence, until they passed the church and Eamonn asked: 'Dad, why didn't he die himself?'

'Who's that?'

'God. Why did he let Jesus die instead of him?'

'I think you'd be better off asking your mother that.'

'But the priest was going on about it today. Why do you think?'

Dermot sighed. 'Well. I suppose they'd say it was a sacrifice. That he loved his son most in the world, so he was making a big sacrifice to let him die.'

'That is what they say, Dad. I don't think it was nice for Jesus though. It wasn't really fair on him.'

'No. I don't suppose it was.'

'It'd be like you letting me cross the road in front of a car, just because it would make you sad.'

'I'd never do that, son.'

Eamonn shook his head. The priest hadn't explained it at all.

14

It was a secret between them, something tender and private. Eamonn had shown Laura some of the scraps of writing he had done over the years, a drawerful of stories and characters, fragments of novels. He had loved writing since boyhood. He confided that his dream was to complete a novel and in the same breath he disowned it. It was a fantasy, an embarrassment, the whole idea of having a dream so trite, so deluded. His life was ruled by the kind of self-imposed restrictions that Laura found impossible to understand. Much of her time was taken up trying to persuade him to declare a ceasefire with himself. And alone with her sometimes he did, speaking about the future and the past without qualification or irony – telling her stories of his childhood and stories he wanted to write, stories about him and stories about her. It was an unspoken pact between them – these glimpses of the real Eamonn to counterbalance the daylight hours of his refracted self-contempt.

The writing was the hidden element of their new life, the part they told no one. 'But you're out in the sticks,' said friends, 'the arse-end of nowhere. What will you do?' And they smiled and said, 'We'll be OK.' Because the isolation was fine, the distance was good, they would earn money in the daytime and Eamonn would write in the evenings.

There were initial difficulties. In the first few weeks he found himself distracted by the environment, the faultless blue skies, the irresistible allure of the pool, the overwhelming heat. He allowed himself a holiday. Then, within three months of arriving, Red Dot Publishing, their sole source of income, collapsed. In the days that followed the announcement, panicked by their mortgage, they bombarded every contact they had in search of any paid employment. Laura picked up some lower-paid freelance work as a proofreader for a rival publisher, but Eamonn could find nothing until a friend of a friend mentioned an online language school called LenguaNet. On the basis of a TEFL course he had done more than ten years previously he got a job as one of their tutors.

With new sources of income secured, Eamonn was free to write, but he worried about Laura. What, he wondered, was there for her to do in the evenings while he wrote? He'd settle in front of his laptop, but find his attention wandering to what she was doing in the other room.

'Do you need some company?' he'd ask, and she'd say, 'No, I'm fine, I'm reading.' And he'd take the book from her hands and lean over and kiss her, pushing her gently back on the bed.

It was around then that Laura decided that she too would try to write, if only, she said, to encourage him and stop unwittingly distracting him. She didn't consider herself a writer, felt she had no particular flair or anything important to say, but she had an idea for a story, she liked the notion of research and loved the image of them spending their evenings at different desks, each working on their separate projects.

'So . . . Goya?' he said.

'Well – the focus isn't really on him, just one of his assistants. It was an interesting time.'

'I guess there are quite a lot of books about it already, then?'

'Possibly, but it's not like I'm ever going to get it published, or even finish it, it's just something to work on, keep my brain active.'

'It's hard work, you know, writing a novel.'

'Yeah, I've gathered.'

'Historical fiction.'

'That makes it sound a bit grand.'

'That stuff isn't really my cup of tea.'

There was a pause. '"That stuff",' she repeated.

'I'm not being funny. I just mean, I don't ever read books like that, so I don't have any knowledge about them. I might not be much good at feedback.'

'Look, Eamonn. You have a gift. You're the writer. You're going to write an exceptional novel. You know that, don't you?'

'No.'

'Well, I do. You're going to write an exceptional novel. I'm not. I'm just going to read some books and try to write a story. It's not going to be ground-breaking or important and I don't expect you to read it or like it, so don't be worried about that. It's just something to do.'

He smiled. 'We'll be a tiny artistic colony.'

She nodded. 'We'll need absinthe.'

15

'Have you seen that fella over there?'

'Which one?'

'The big tom, there on the left in the shade.'

'What about him?'

'Well, look at him.'

'I'm looking.'

They sat on the terrace watching the cats taking their evening *paseo* round the empty pool.

'Does he not remind you of someone?'

Silence.

'Tell me now if he isn't the dead spit of Mr Socks.'

'He isn't the dead spit of Mr Socks. Mr Socks was a little thing, nimble.'

'Never mind the size, I mean the markings, the white paws, and his face – don't you think he has a look of him?'

'Maybe. A little.'

'I'd say he's a long-lost relative. The Iberian branch of the Socks family.'

'You used to tell me we were descended from Spaniards, do you remember?'

'Well, maybe we were.'

'No, not maybe, you relayed this information as fact. I distinctly remember you telling me that we had Spanish blood.'

'The Armada was washed up on the west coast of Ireland. There was all kinds of intermingling. There's a very good chance.'

'Laura never stopped laughing when I told her. She seems to

think it unlikely that I've any Mediterranean blood in my veins. She's always amused by how easily I burn. There's no compassion there at all.'

'I don't think poor Mr Socks would have lasted long with these boys.'

'No, they'd have soon sniffed him out for the Little Lord Fauntleroy he was.'

'I used to get into terrible trouble with your mother. She couldn't stand the creature, didn't want him anywhere in the house.'

'I didn't know that.'

'Well, she didn't like to hurt your feelings, so she'd put up with him when you were around, but when you were gone the poor cat got an awful shock. She'd be raging at him, shooing him out the back door with the brush.'

Eamonn was indignant. 'But he didn't like it outside. It made him sneeze.'

'I know, you don't have to tell me that. I made sure he was all right though. I made a nice little bed for him in the shed and I'd take him out treats of tinned salmon or whatever I could find.'

'Didn't Mom notice?'

'Of course she did. She was always giving out about food going missing. I'd say I'd taken it to work for my lunch and she'd say, "Who takes double cream for their packed lunch?"'

'I can't believe she didn't like Mr Socks.'

'No, they didn't get on at all.'

Later they took a footpath through the woods around the western edge of the development. They emerged from the pines towards the bottom of Lomaverde. They made their way slowly back up the middle of the road. Dermot was transfixed by the sky. He had never seen anything like it. Billowing trails of cloud in golds, pinks and purples were sliced through with shafts of the dying sun. A Hollywood Technicolor extravaganza above their heads. It was entirely fantastical to him, the sight of Charlton Heston's face peeping from the clouds could not have astounded him more.

'Will you look at that,' he said, but when he dragged his eyes from the sky Eamonn was no longer beside him. He looked back down the road and saw him standing still, staring off to the side. He followed his gaze and noticed for the first time a children's play area, set down in a hollow off to the right. It was a forlorn-looking place, untouched as far as he could see by any child, the primary colours of the swings and roundabout vivid in the setting sun. It reminded him of an advert for something, he wasn't sure what. At first he saw only the motionless apparatus – the red swings, the yellow see-saw, the pirate-ship climbing frame – and then he looked again. Beneath the slide was a pool of dark liquid, slowly spreading.

They walked over together. He bent to dip his finger in the liquid and felt a drip upon his neck. It was only then they saw the chicken, strung up beneath the apex of the slide, blood draining slowly from the gash across its throat. They stood side by side taking in the scene. The only sound the buzzing of flies.

'It's OK.' They both jumped at the voice. Dermot recognized the Swedish woman from the residents' meeting. She was struggling down the hill, wearing rubber gloves, carrying a bin bag, brush and large bottle of soapy water. He went over to help her.

'Thank you.' She handed him the brush to carry. 'It's OK,' she called to Eamonn, 'I will clear it up.'

Eamonn looked at her. 'Have you seen it?'

She sighed and pushed some hair from her face. 'Yes, I've seen it. It's Ottoline.'

'Ottoline?'

'My hen.'

Eamonn looked horrified. 'Did you do this?'

'No. Of course not. I had two hens. Ottoline and Sonja. They went missing earlier today. I assumed an animal had got them.'

While they spoke, Dermot cut the bird down and laid it carefully on the ground.

'I was coming down the road, looking for any trace of them, and I heard a commotion – sounds of flapping and squawking. I knew her at once. She had a distinctive noise that she makes. I called her name and then I heard footsteps running. By the time I came round the corner it was too late to save her.'

'What do you think it means?' asked Eamonn.

Dermot looked at him. 'I'd say it means someone fancied chicken for their dinner.'

'But just leaving it here, like a macabre calling card.'

Inga spoke. 'I suppose I disturbed them, I don't suppose they intended to leave it.'

'But still . . .' Eamonn seemed intent on finding darker significance.

Dermot caught the eye of the woman. 'Can we help you at all? Clean it up for you?'

'That's very kind, but I'll be OK.'

'Right.' They carried on standing, awkwardly, not knowing what to do as she put the chicken in a plastic bag. She turned her head to look at them. 'Please, it's OK, you go.'

As they walked away she called after them. 'Excuse me!'

They turned around. 'Sorry,' she was looking at Dermot, 'I've forgotten your name.'

'Dermot.'

'Dermot, yes. I'm so sorry about this. What a holiday you are having!' And she laughed.

They walked back up the road. Eamonn was unsettled. 'Odd sense of humour.'

'Did you think so?'

'Well, she was all very jolly at the end, wasn't she? As she wiped up the innards.'

'Scandinavian did they say she was?'

'Swedish.'

'There you are, then.'

'What?'

'Viking blood. It'd take more than a few giblets to upset one of them, I'd bet.'

Eamonn said nothing.

'Nice bit of halal chicken she has there now anyway. I hope she doesn't let it go to waste.'

'You're joking, right?'

'What? Why not? Slaughtered very cleanly.'

Eamonn pulled a face. 'Did you kill chickens back in Ireland?'

Dermot turned to him and nodded solemnly. 'Indeed I did. Chickens. Rabbits. Sheep. Cows.'

'Cows? Jesus Christ.'

'That's how it was in the country. Up at dawn and out you were with a big knife cutting the throat of anything you could find.'

'Oh, I see. This is humour.'

'Leaving a trail of macabre calling cards behind us. Slaughtering and singing while we did it.' He began to sing:

'Last night as I lay dreaming of pleasant days gone by
My mind being bent on rambling to Ireland I did fly.'

He carried on walking, leaving Eamonn standing in the road. 'It was a reasonable question.'

16

He knew that he would never turn into his dad, never be one of those sons mistaken for their fathers on the telephone. His parents were Irish, that was what he said. Never that he was Irish. He had grown up in England, he had a Birmingham accent, he was so palpably different to them that it seemed preposterous to him to describe himself as Irish. But to call himself English seemed no better. His name and indeed his physical appearance declared his otherness.

As a boy, cocooned in the small world of his primary school and parish, where nearly everyone he met was first- or second-generation Irish, his Irishness was largely invisible to him. He sometimes saw comedians on television telling jokes. There was an Englishman, an Irishman and a Scotsman. The jokes were the same – the Irishman was always called Paddy and he was always stupid. He found them baffling. He'd hear the audience laugh and he didn't get it. He thought it was something grown-up, something secret.

When he passed the exam for King James he found himself in the minority for the first time, but it was not simply the nationality of his parents that made him different, it was their religion, what they did for a living, the area in which they lived, the names they called meals, the places they hadn't been on holiday and a hundred other tiny details that seemed to place them and him on the outside. Staff would correct him, would reprimand or sometimes belittle him. From Mr Johnson, his geography teacher, he learned about something less tangible than glaciated u-shaped valleys and limestone paving. The taint was there in the way the teacher looked at him, the way he said his name, the way he handed him his work – a faint, but unmistakable odour, a smirk, a tightening.

In his first year at university he lived in halls with a boy called Kev Callaghan from Bolton. In their second term, while others were discovering their sexuality, Kev came out as an Irishman. Overnight he sprouted Sean O'Casey badges and Brendan Behan quotes, he started playing the Dubliners and Planxty loudly each evening in his room, and calling himself Caoimhín. It was as if, Eamonn thought, Kev had been bitten by a radio-active Celt. Eamonn didn't know what to make of it. He imagined his own father's bemusement if he went home wear-ing an Aran jumper and playing the *bodhrán*. One night Caoimhín drank too much Guinness and told Eamonn that he was in denial, that he was a self-hating Irishman. Eamonn was happy to concede the self-hatred and the Irishness, but he didn't see them as connected. They both accused each other of pre-tending to be something they weren't and in their drunken state thought that must mean they were in agreement.

What began as Caoimhín's own personal identity crisis seemed to become more generalized in the years that fol-lowed. Eamonn returned from university to a Birmingham filled with pretend-Irish pubs. Being Irish had somehow become a mainstream leisure pursuit, like eating Thai food and taking salsa classes. To be Irish you just had to like the Corrs and U2, drink Guinness, wear a big hat on St Patrick's Day and be ceaseless in your quest for 'the craic'. Eamonn didn't do any of those things – he was fairly sure his father didn't either – and so wasn't sure where that left him. He went along once to a branch of O'Neill's with some friends. It was like no other Irish pub he'd ever been to either in England or Ireland. The big-eared old boys had been replaced by young men with red cheeks and striped shirts and girls in short skirts.

The relaxed atmosphere replaced by a supercharged frenzy. People everywhere were punching the air to 'The Whole of the Moon' and on every wall was mention of the fabled craic. At eleven o'clock, when Eamonn thought it could get no stranger, some inaudible signal sent the entire staff clambering on to the bar like weary automatons to perform a lengthy tribute to the Blues Brothers. He drank as much as he could to get through the evening and the next morning found he was unable to separate reality from his dreams.

17

They could hear the radio on in the kitchen, Aggie's high-pitched voice singing along, missing every note. There was a lingering smell of bacon in the hallway, though there'd been none at breakfast. She'd set down a plate of eggs, announcing 'Ash Wednesday' as she did, and Dermot's stomach had rumbled a blasphemous response.

The lino was loose on the lodging-house stairs and he cursed as he slipped a step. He turned back to Matty, coming down behind him: 'How is it you never fall?'

'I know which one to miss.'

'Would it hurt them to put in a light bulb?'

'It's the third from the top.'

'Or, God forbid, nail down the lino?'

'I just step over it.'

'I don't know what use he is at all. She may as well run the place by herself.'

'There's no point getting aerated.' Matty opened the front door. 'You'll be gone soon enough.'

After mass they walked up to the Vaults with the black smudges still on their foreheads.

'So, not long now, is it?'

'No. Three weeks. A gay bachelor no more I'll be.'

'You're the lucky one.'

'I don't know,' replied Dermot, but he smiled as he said it. 'The honeymoon itinerary keeps expanding. I tell her we're only there for a week, but her family seem to have made it a point to scatter as widely as they can across the country. She has an aunt in Donegal and a sister in Cork. I'm to meet them all, apparently.'

'You'll be kept busy.'

'I will.'

'I still say you're the lucky one.'

'I am. I know. I am.'

'She has looks and brains too, so she has.'

Dermot smiled.

'What?'

'You make her sound like a racehorse.'

'I didn't mean to.'

Matty looked embarrassed and Dermot felt bad for him. 'No, you're right. She's a great girl. I don't know what she's doing with me at all.'

Matty grinned. 'Neither do I.'

'That's enough of that. Some of those younger lads chasing her, Brylcreem boys. Flash Harries. They weren't her style at all.'

'Showering her with diamonds, were they? Now why would she want that?'

'I don't think there were many diamonds. All talk those boys. The patter, you know? She'd have you screaming, the way she sends them up.'

'Well,' Matty drained his glass, 'you're moving up in the world. Away from the old stamping ground. Soon there'll be no one left at all.'

He got the bus into town and waited for her in the Kardomah by Snow Hill. He was always five minutes early and she was always five minutes late. He'd say: 'You're not a truly late person. There's a consistency there. Always five minutes. Why don't you leave five minutes early?'

And she'd say: 'Why don't you leave ten minutes late?'

The truth was he liked the wait, the anticipation of her arrival. He'd look out the window and what he saw was a kind of chaos, an abstract pattern of faces and wheels and legs and bags and hats and umbrellas until the moment when it all came together, the split second when she emerged from the crowd and everything snapped into place. The world complete.

There was something dramatic about her entrances. Her hair blown from being on the bike, her face glowing, a slight breathlessness as she swept through the café. He always stood to greet a lady, but with Kathleen it was never courtesy or manners, it was an involuntary response. His legs straightening of their own accord, propelling him up to hold her, to catch her somehow. She kissed him on the cheek and he held her close for a moment, before she pushed him gently away.

'People are looking.'

'They should. Good God, we're a handsome pair.' He whispered, 'Can you imagine the children we'll have? People will weep when they see them.'

She laughed and they sat down.

'Did you get the train tickets organized?'

'I did, yes. And the boat. And the hotel for the first night. You've nothing to worry about.'

'I was having these funny thoughts cycling in.'

'Were they about the hotel? The honeymoon suite? A night of romance and passion?'

'They were not!'

'I don't know that I'm interested, then.'

'Do you remember Audrey Hepburn in *Roman Holiday*?'

'Was that the one with Bogie?'

'No. That was *Sabrina*. *Roman Holiday* had Gregory Peck. They were in Rome. On holiday.'

'Oh, I remember!'

'I was just thinking: imagine if we were going on honeymoon to Rome. Could you imagine that? Wouldn't it be magical?'

'We're going on honeymoon to Ireland, Kathleen. It's all booked.'

'I know. I know. And that will be grand. It'll be great to see everyone. I was just daydreaming. Just the idea of it. Can you imagine being in a place like that?'

Dermot smiled. 'Well . . . it would be something, wouldn't it? The history of the place.'

'That's what I was thinking. And the glamour. My God. The people there are so good-looking.'

'So, day one, what would we do? I'd say we'd go to the Colosseum, what do you reckon?'

'Oh, Dermot! *Ben Hur*! Do you remember that? *Spartacus*! Tony Curtis!'

'I don't know that we'd see him.'

'I can picture you in a toga.'

'I'm not sure about that.'

'I think you'd look regal. Imperious. Like Larry Olivier.'

'More like a Mint Imperial. Anyway, day two, what do you fancy? The Trevi Fountain or the Spanish Steps?'

'Well, maybe day two we should go and pay our respects to His Holiness.'

'Oh yes. His Holiness. I was forgetting him. He'd be most put out if we didn't pay him a visit.'

'So there'd be the Sistine Chapel and the Basilica.'

'St Peter's.'

'Then we could do the fountain and the Spanish Steps the day after that.'

'We'd be eating a lot of spaghetti.'

'And driving around on mopeds.'

The waitress brought their coffees. Kathleen smiled.

'Ah, well. If we squint, maybe we'll be able to imagine Thurles as the Villa Borghese Gardens.'

'You might be better off shutting your eyes altogether.'

'It'll be lovely anyway.'

'It will. We can go to Italy another time.'

She laughed and he looked at her.

'What? What's so funny? Maybe we will.'

'Maybe,' she said.

'You sound like you've gone off the idea.'

'We were just joking about, Dermot.' She reached across and squeezed his hand.

After weeks of rain, it was bright and blustery on the wedding day. Dermot's older brother Joe came down from Liverpool to be the best man; the bridesmaid's headdress blew off into a tree during the photos and the priest got Kathleen's name wrong. Matty wished them well and bought them a gift even though Dermot had told him not to. It was a figurine. A shoeless child sat at a well. A funny thing really. The child's expression somewhat sad, her eyes large. A faithful puppy nuzzling into her side. It sat on the dresser throughout their marriage, part of the sitting-room scenery, its provenance half-remembered, its strangeness gone.

18

His footsteps slowed to a stop. He closed his eyes and saw his mother in the kitchen. The blue dress she wore on Sundays to play the church organ. She would sing as she prepared the dinner. Dermot found the words were still there:

> 'Hail, Queen of heaven, the ocean star,
> Guide of the wanderer here below,
> Thrown on life's surge, we claim thy care,
> Save us from peril and from woe.'

'That's nice.' He opened his eyes. A woman was standing at her front door. It took him a moment to place her as the Swedish woman.

'I'm sorry.' He remained standing in the same spot. 'I think it was the smell.'

'Sorry?'

'Roast lamb. It reminds me of my mother.'

'Oh. Yes. One minute we are walking along a street, the next we are in another time and place, like we have fallen down a hole.' She blew smoke from a cigarette. 'It was lovely to hear someone singing though.'

He shook his head. 'There's something wrong with my brain. The things it decides to keep and the things it decides to lose. Like a maniac housekeeper in there.'

She smiled.

'We've not really met in the best circumstances. I'm Inga, hello.'

He held out his hand. 'Dermot.'

'So, come in, please, help me eat this lamb.'

He was mortified at the suggestion. 'Oh. No, no. Thank you, that's very kind, but no.' Did she imagine he just lingered around people's doorways, sniffing the air and waiting for an invitation?

'Why not? Have you already had lunch?' Her tone was almost abrupt.

'Well, no, not yet, I was just heading back for . . . something.'

'Is it roast lamb?'

'I don't know exactly what . . . I doubt it.'

'Well, then, you would be helping me. I have too much. I'll end up giving half to the cats.'

He found her directness quite unsettling. He had no desire to make conversation with a stranger, he had been looking forward to a little nap, but he saw no way now of refusing without appearing ungracious.

'Well, in that case, thank you. I wouldn't want the cats to be getting too fat now.'

The house was sparsely furnished. A wooden-framed sofa, an easy chair, a coffee table covered in books. She brought him a glass of water with a slice of lime floating about in it.

'Take a seat, please, I won't be long.'

He did as he was told and tried to look relaxed. Leaning against every wall were paintings in various states of completion. His heart sank. Eamonn had once tried to convince him that a cow cut in half was art. He'd told his son then that if that was art then he was welcome to it. He'd said if that was art, then so was his sock, to which Eamonn had said 'Exactly' and Dermot had wondered if his son was half-witted. Cautiously, he cocked his head to one side to look at one of the large canvasses. Some weeds sprouting up from the pavement. Why would anyone want to paint such a thing? He thanked God he could at least see what it was; that was a start.

She walked in and saw him looking.

'Do you like it?'

He said the only thing he could. 'You do them well . . . the weeds. They look like them all right.'

'Thank you. I suppose I don't really see them as weeds.'

'Oh, right.'

He waited to see if she would say what she really did see them as, but instead she said, 'Come. We'll eat outside.'

He'd grown used to the sun-drenched terraces of Lomaverde with their unvarying views of the horizon, but Inga's garden was small and enclosed. Around the perimeter was a high fence, covered in an array of vegetation.

He smiled at the improbability of the place – lush and shaded. It seemed at odds with the woman herself. 'You have a lovely garden.' He walked over to some geraniums. 'You've had more luck with these than I have this year.'

'You enjoy gardening?'

'I do. When we get the sun, which isn't so often.'

'Here it's the water that's the problem. I have to remember that it's a luxury and try to be as sparing as I can.'

Dermot wondered if she was going to start on about re-cycling and global warming and all the rest of it, she looked like the type who might, but instead she disappeared back into the kitchen and re-emerged with the food. She carried out a large bowl of salad as colourful as her garden, followed by some bread, wine and, last of all, the leg of lamb.

'Would you like me to carve it?' It was the wrong thing to say, he knew as soon as he'd said it. The kind of thing Eamonn would jump on him for. Why would a woman need a man to cut the meat? Didn't they have arms and hands just like him?

She considered the offer, then shrugged and handed him the

knife. 'Why not? It's nice sometimes to be served by someone else. When you live by yourself there are good things and bad things.'

He nodded. 'My wife, she always felt the cold. Some years we had the heating on even in summer. I got used to the heat, I suppose, but not the lack of fresh air. That stuffiness – sometimes I couldn't stand it. God help you if you opened a window though, she hated the draughts, so I'd go outside in the garden for five or ten minutes to fill my lungs. Now I sleep with my windows open and I feel the night air in the room around me and, well . . . it's a fine feeling . . .' He trailed off. It was the first time he had spoken of Kathleen to this stranger and it sounded like a criticism. 'I miss her very much though,' he added too loudly, and wished to God he'd gone straight back to Eamonn's.

Inga pulled off a chunk of bread. 'Is she dead or did she leave you?'

It was certainly a contrast to the small talk at Jean and David's. 'She's dead.'

She nodded. 'Was that recent?'

'About seven months ago, but she'd not been well for years.'

'I'm sorry. That must have been very hard.' She paused. 'My husband, he didn't die, so I don't have that grief. We divorced eighteen months ago now. Each day without him has been . . .' she paused, searching for the right word '. . . a joy.' He looked up at her sharply and she held his gaze for a moment before breaking into a wide grin. 'I'm sorry, you look so shocked.'

'No, no, not at all . . .'

'You are, I'm sorry. Forgive me, I get out of the habit of talking to people and then I get it all wrong.'

He shrugged. 'I get it wrong often enough, my son would tell you that.'

'Sons and daughters like nothing better than telling their

parents off.' She laughed. 'And the incredible thing is that they know absolutely nothing.'

Dermot smiled. 'So, you're from Sweden?'

'My accent gives me away.'

He shook his head. 'No. I heard an accent, but I didn't know where it was from.' He hesitated. 'If I don't recognize an accent I tend to assume the person's from Luxembourg. I don't know why.' He was silent for a moment. 'I've never been to Luxembourg.' He had no idea why he was making such admissions. He sounded like the village idiot.

'I don't think I've ever met anyone from Luxembourg.'

Dermot nodded. 'I don't suppose I have either.'

She laughed. 'And you, your accent is Irish?'

'Ah, now you're showing off.'

'OK, I confess, I'm cheating. I wouldn't really be able to tell the accent. I can hear it's not English, but it could be Scottish or – what's the other one?'

'Welsh?'

'Scouse. But I know your name is Irish, so I took an educated guess.'

'Like Sherlock Holmes.'

'Oh, please, I hope I'm not like him. I never thought he was a nice man. Always so unpleasant to Dr Watson.'

Dermot was surprised. 'Was that not because Dr Watson was an idiot?'

She laughed. 'Poor Dr Watson. I always wanted him to solve the case, just to show Sherlock Holmes that you didn't have to be rude and grumpy to be clever, but he always let me down.'

'You were backing the wrong horse there.'

'That's the story of my life.' She lit a cigarette. 'Do you mind?'

He shook his head and she looked at him. 'So, from Ireland and you live in England. We're both immigrants, then.'

Dermot frowned. 'I suppose so. I don't tend to think of myself as that.'

'Oh? You no longer consider yourself Irish?'

'No, I do, I do, of course, but I don't really think of myself as an immigrant any more. It seems a long time ago.'

'You don't miss Ireland?'

He thought for a moment. 'I miss all kinds of things, but I'm not sure I'd ever find them by moving back. I know people who've made a big to-do about going back home, the prodigal returning, and the next thing you know you bump into them round the corner.'

'It doesn't work?'

He shook his head. 'It's like . . . they've held this idea of Ireland in their head for forty years, you know, the place they sing about in all the songs. They get there and it's not the place they left, of course it's not, it never was, and they're not the people they were.'

She nodded. 'I don't miss Sweden.'

'Did you not like it there?'

'There are things about it I love, but also a lot of not so happy memories. It felt good to begin again somewhere new.'

'A fresh start.'

She smiled. 'When I first came here, my paintings were very simple, very clean. A sunset. The distant horizon. A white house against a blue sky. That's all I wanted to paint.'

'But not now?'

'No. Not now.'

'Now you like painting . . . wild plants.'

She laughed. 'Weeds. It's OK. We can call them that.'

'You like painting weeds.'

'Not just weeds. All kinds of things. The bits of Lomaverde that were not in the brochures. The weeds. The cats. The puddles by cracked pipes. The things that living places have. The things that cannot be designed.'

'I'm afraid I'm not very artistic. I see those things and I want to fix them, to tidy them up.'

'Of course. That's normal. Most times I do too.'

'That's a relief. I was beginning to feel bad about pulling up the dandelions.'

She smiled at him. 'Why feel bad? We pull them up, we concrete over them, but soon they are there again. They always break through.'

He took a sip of the wine she had poured for him. He had never been one for wine, but the taste was softer than he remembered.

'They do,' he said. 'There's something to be said for resilience.'

19

He asked Eamonn about an old house he'd seen on the first day. Walking along the brow of the hill, he'd glimpsed it in the distance.

'It's just an old farmhouse, I think,' said Eamonn. 'A *cortijo*.'

'I thought I might wander over there. Have a look.'

'Right.'

'Will you come?'

'Well, I should really ... you know ... I've got things I should ...'

'Sure, I know, I know, you're busy with work and all, but just an hour or two. Get a bit of air.'

Eamonn scratched his ear and then slowly closed the lid on his computer. It seemed to cause him pain to do so.

Outside the air already buzzed with heat and flies and the fizz of the electricity substation at the end of the road. Dermot looked out to sea and tried to breathe in the scent of it, but got only the faintly cabbaged tinge of drains and cats.

They followed the road downhill, zigzagging past the shuttered apartments and houses. The sun caught on the metallic lid of one of the empty recycling bins and Dermot was momentarily blinded by the light. When his vision cleared someone had appeared on the road ahead of them. He was dressed in a uniform like a policeman's.

'Hello, Eamonn. Hello, father of Eamonn.'

'Hey, Esteban,' said Eamonn, walking towards him.

'I saw you on the cameras. I decide to run down and give

you a surprise. Boo!' He pointed to the side of one of the houses. 'I came the quick way, down the steps.'

'Did you meet my dad already?'

'No, but Roger told me that your father visit.' He turned to Dermot. 'I'm very happy to meet you.'

Dermot held out his hand. 'Likewise.'

Esteban laughed. 'Ah! Now I hear the accent! I wanted to shake the hand of an Irishman. I wanted to tell you that I love your country.'

Dermot looked bemused. 'Is that right?'

Esteban beamed. 'Ask Eamonn. The first day I hear his name I said, "This is an Irish name." And I came and said, "Hello, I have a big surprise for you, I know your country very well."'

Eamonn looked at his father. 'I had to tell him it wasn't my country.'

Esteban laughed. 'When he told me, I said, "So your mother is Irish and your father is Irish? I think Ireland *is* your country."'

Eamonn muttered to his father, 'He wouldn't have it.'

'Mr Lynch . . .'

'Please, call me Dermot.'

'Dermot. I spent six weeks in your country. In Dingle. Learning English.'

Dermot was delighted. 'Did you now? Well, fancy that.'

'Yes. I love Dingle. It's a beautiful place.'

'Don't mention the dolphin,' Eamonn said under his breath.

Dermot ignored him. 'Did you travel about much? Did you visit County Clare at all?'

'Yes, one day we went to the Burren and the Cliffs of Moher. Eamonn said this is where you are from.'

'I lived there most of my boyhood, yes.'

'It is a beautiful place.'

'I suppose it is.'

Esteban laughed again. 'That is modesty.'

'We better get going,' said Eamonn. 'We were going to walk over to that old *cortijo*, towards Las Cruces.'

Esteban frowned. 'The *cortijo*? There's nothing there.'

'I know.' Eamonn looked miserable. 'We're taking the air.'

'Very good.'

'My dad likes looking at empty, old places.'

Esteban turned to Dermot. 'Then you have come to a good place. Enjoy your walk. Maybe we will talk again. I have lots of questions to ask you.'

'It'd be my pleasure.'

When they were out of earshot Dermot said, 'So that's the security, then.'

'Yeah. He was one of the original team. We took him back on again when the burglaries started. Laura and I were lucky never to have been hit.'

Dermot wondered if it was luck or the marked absence of anything worth stealing that had saved them.

The walk took longer than he'd expected. From the top of the hill the farmhouse had not looked far away, but the distance had been deceptive. Eamonn had taken them down the hill first, towards the sea, before turning east and cutting across the slope to where he thought the house was. After an hour though they still hadn't reached it. They ended up climbing back up the hill to get their bearings. They saw the *cortijo* some distance above the path they had chosen and realized that they had descended too far and missed it.

By the time they arrived it was almost midday and they were grateful for the shade. A crumbling wall traced a part of the boundary, and a few trees stood within it. The house itself was stone – large and plain. The roof and windows were long gone, but the iron railings around the small upper balconies remained.

Eamonn peered into the gloom beyond the windows.

'Did you want to go in?'

'Let's have a sit-down first.'

They rested under a tree. Dermot unzipped his holdall and handed Eamonn a bottle of water. When he'd finished drinking, Dermot put a pile of foil packages in front of him.

'I made some sandwiches. Help me eat them.'

They ate looking towards the house, their backs against the tree. When he'd finished, Eamonn screwed up the empty tinfoil into a ball and threw it into his father's bag.

'Dad?'

'Yes?'

Dermot turned to him. 'What is it?'

'I wanted to say, about Laura.'

'What?'

'You know she's gone.'

Dermot kept quiet.

'She said she needed time to think.'

'Not for ever, then?'

'I don't know.'

'How long since she went?'

'Ten days.'

'Do you know where she's gone?'

'Back to England. She said she was going to stay with her parents. No one answers the phone.'

Dermot hesitated. 'Did you do something to upset her?'

Eamonn shook his head, unable to speak for a moment. 'Yes. Lots of things, I suppose.'

'I don't know what to say, son.'

'There's nothing to say. I just thought I should tell you.'

'Maybe she'll see things differently after a few weeks back home.' He knew if Kathleen were there she'd have plenty to say. She'd blame the girl, say she was a fool, but Dermot had always liked Laura. His sympathies should be with Eamonn, but God knows it couldn't be easy putting up with him all day, every day.

Eamonn got up and and walked towards the house. He stood looking at it for a few moments and then turned back to Dermot. 'Do you remember taking me somewhere like this in Ireland?'

'Like what? An old ruin?'

'Yeah – well, not a ruin exactly – just an old house, derelict.'

'I don't know. Sure we went to lots of old places. Where was it?'

'Don't know. I suppose it must have been the summer holidays, but it was just you and me. I don't know where Mom was. I just remember wandering around an empty house, holding your hand. You showed me a room that had toy soldiers all over the wallpaper, and in the corner there was –'

'Something scratched into the wall.'

Eamonn looked at him. 'Yeah! The letter "D". D'you remember?'

Dermot saw his brother's small hand carefully carving the letter.

Eamonn shook his head. 'I'm an idiot. You must have lived there. I think I thought the "D" was some magical coincidence, I never thought you'd done it.' He paused. 'But that wasn't your house in Liscannor.'

'No, it wasn't in Liscannor and it wasn't me.'

'Oh.'

'There were two "D"s. A small one inside a big one. My brother Dominic did it. Dominic and Dermot.'

'Dominic. He was the younger one?'

'Yes.'

'So, where was that?'

'It was in Longford. Drumlish. Where I was born.'

'How come we only went once?'

117

Dermot shrugged. 'There was nothing to see. The family scattered after Mammy died. I went to live with my granny in Liscannor when I was fourteen. I went back to see the house that time with you and I didn't go back again.'

'Did the others move to your granny's as well?'

It seemed odd to Dermot that Eamonn wouldn't know these things.

'No. We all went our separate ways. Patricia had already entered the convent, and Peggy followed her. Joe went over to Liverpool. Gerard to the Christian Brothers in Dublin.'

'Is that when Dominic went to America?'

'How could he? He was a boy of twelve. He couldn't emigrate to the States for years.' Dermot looked over at the house. 'He and I used to have some adventures exploring places like this. There were enough of them about. Old ruins, not all big houses. Often just little ramshackle cottages, abandoned in the Famine. It was our idea of fun. We'd set up dens in them. Sometimes we were brave volunteers under siege by the constabulary. Other times we were gold prospectors, surrounded by Apache Indians. I was always the boss, of course, barking out orders to Dominic. "Barricade the windows!" "Take cover!"'

Eamonn smiled. 'So where did he go?'

'When?'

'When you went to Liscannor.'

Dermot saw the lines of toy soldiers on the walls, faded, as they were when he'd returned with Eamonn. 'Nowhere. He stayed where he was.'

He stood brushing crumbs from his lap. 'Come on, then. Let's go in and see what treasure we find.'

20

With the pain of separation came the relentless mental churning – the grinding business of processing, interpreting and conjecturing. Their final conversation played somewhere in Eamonn's head all day, every day. Each line, paused, analysed, redrafted, erased. It was like an illness, his brain infected, his thoughts overheated and circular. He tried, without success, to drown out the playback. He did not want to recall the things she had said. Remembering the words led to the same awful conclusion: he had driven her away; he had broken everything.

'You're leaving me?'

'I have to think. I have things to work out and I need to be away from you to do it.'

'I don't understand.'

'Eamonn, things haven't been good between us. I need some clear space to think.'

'Things have been fine.'

'You're self-deceiving. You can see exactly what I see, but you won't admit it.'

'What can you see?'

'You're not yourself. You're lost. You're so unhappy here.'

'So you're leaving? That's going to make me happier?'

'I'm not leaving you. I'm going to . . .'

'. . . Think. Yes I know. You said. About what? About leaving me?'

'About everything. There are things I need to work out.'

'What? Sums? Crossword clues?'

'No.'

They were both crying now.

'So you're going? Leaving me behind? Laura . . .'

'I just need time to think.'

'You don't love me any more.'

'You know I do.'

'I don't know anything.'

He exercised some restraint in his texts, though this in truth had more to do with his contempt for SMS as a means of communication than any real self-control. Texting seemed a retrograde step to him, like trying to have a conversation using Dymo Tape. Since she'd left, he'd texted her just once, every day.

His emails were more expressive and expansive, often disastrously so. He had not been able to resist occasional late-night outpourings. Regrettable lapses into florid self-pity, woundedness, the odd, empty accusation to try to even the score. The next day he would send an even longer apology, retracting certain points, reiterating others. Laura, wherever she was, whatever she was doing, was being bombarded with upwards of a thousand words a day, one half of them at least apologizing for the other half. Among that latter half were his first, tentative steps into poetry. Not verse, he was horrified to see in the cold light of day, so much as broken prose and half-remembered Joy Division lyrics, probably no better and possibly considerably worse than the solipsistic ramblings of American Web developers that Laura had once had to edit.

If she waded through the almost fifteen thousand words he had rained down on her in just over a week and a half, she would by now be aware of the general gist. He loved her, he was sorry if it hadn't always shown. He was sorry he had been so miserable. He would change. He would make a go of their life there. He vowed to make her feel loved again. He had over the course of the one-sided correspondence listed every single episode in the last fifteen months where he considered he had behaved shabbily. He wanted her to know that he understood. He insisted that he didn't want to pressure her. He said he wanted her to take as long as she needed to think. This was the only thing he wrote that lacked any sincerity at all.

He'd discovered that deep uncertainty opened the door to all kinds of forgotten playground voodoo. A childhood superstition had resurfaced: if you stopped expecting something to happen, then it would. The fact that a mail or a message had yet to arrive only indicated that he had not been thorough enough in exorcizing expectation. Each morning he sat before his closed laptop attempting to empty his mind of all hope, his eyes squeezed shut in a state of non-prayer. She would not have emailed, he told himself over and over. She was not yet ready. He could not hurry her.

21

He opened the wardrobe. The combined scents of dust, wood and perfume settled upon him. Here were the clothes Kathleen hadn't needed in her final years. The best coats, the going-out dresses, the wedding hats and silk scarves. They were folded neatly on shelves or hung from good wooden hangers, some still in the polythene sheaths of dry-cleaners; after years of such delicate handling he couldn't bring himself to let them drop into the bin bag he had ready beside him. He went over to the other wardrobe and reached for the suitcase on top. He laid it on the bed and started to fold the dresses and coats gently into it before stopping short. He would need the suitcase back and that would cause a problem at the charity shop. He pictured them tipping the dresses out into a heap on the counter and handing him the case. He wondered, should he have waited for Anne's help before he started with all of this? He took the dresses out again and laid them on the bed. He dismissed once more the idea of the bin bag and went in search of an alternative. He settled in the end for some of the good-quality carrier bags that Kathleen used to keep in the understairs cupboard. Large House of Fraser, Marks & Spencer and Debenhams carriers she had accumulated and preserved over the years. 'Is this what you were keeping them for?' he asked aloud.

Back upstairs, he sat down at her dressing table. It was unsettling to see his reflection in the mirror. He was used to seeing her face framed there, engaged in various arcane ministrations. He unzipped the large padded bag in front of him and the weighted compacts and pots slid out on to the surface. Here were the tiny tools she had used to perform her adjustments: miniature paintbrushes for her eyes and lips, compounds of colour and powder, a hundred different mysteries encased in shellac. He suspected they could all go in the bin, but he would let Anne make that decision. He started opening the drawers on either side of the dresser, mechanically reaching in and pulling out the various different subspecies of underwear and letting them fall into the bag. If it had been he who had gone first, she would have had to contend with only one drawer of pants and one of socks. He did not try to fathom the purpose or classification of the different items, he knew only that some were slippery, some springy and some tendrilled and knotted.

At the back of the bottom drawer he felt something solid. He reached in and pulled out an old shoebox, the lid held on with elastic bands. He placed it carefully on the bed and studied it for a moment before removing the bands and lifting the lid. Inside were bundles of letters in faded blue Airmail envelopes. He lifted a bundle; they felt light and insubstantial. He sat on the bed, the letters on his lap. In all the years he'd seen only a handful arrive. He had thought them sporadic updates, occasional good wishes, but they were the ones that had slipped through the net. The rest had been hidden from him. Their arrival, their reading, their storage – all concealed.

Later he gathered together the eight bags he had filled, put on his jacket and cap and set off for the parade of shops around the corner. He was buffeted by a stiff breeze, the bags bumping against each other and against him, but he kept up a good pace. When they were courting Kathleen would pull back on his arm and say: 'Can't we stroll? Do we have to march?' and he'd slow down for a few yards, but the brisk pace always returned.

The woman in the charity shop didn't seem thrilled at the

sight of him and his bags. She looked to Dermot like the type not thrilled by very much at all. She asked him to drop them on the floor at the rear of the shop and showed no inclination to examine their contents. When he returned past the counter he felt the need to say: 'It's good stuff in there, well looked after too.'

She nodded and smiled as if he were simple. As he was leaving he noticed a mannequin in the window. He imagined passing by in a few days' time to see it dressed in Kathleen's clothes. His wife rendered in white, polished plastic, surrounded by piles of jigsaws and DVDs, watching his comings and goings.

'God Almighty,' he said aloud, and hurried out.

He went home and sat, still in his jacket and hat, looking at the envelopes scattered across the bed. When it grew dark he gathered them together and put them back in the box. He felt its weight in his hands. So many words and only half the conversation.

22

The afternoons had always been difficult. Even with Laura there he had often found them long. Any promise the morning held seemed to burn off in the sun, and the night with its surrender to alcohol, or whatever other distraction could be found, remained a distant spot on the horizon. Since she'd gone the afternoons were deep, dark holes that he had to carefully edge his way around.

Still studiedly avoiding his mounting pile of work, he wrote an email to her, a follow-up to the one he had sent in the morning. He sent her his daily text. He refreshed his in-box in case she had been moved to reply straight away, but found only some submitted assignments from students and a couple of mails from friends in England. He left them unopened. There were already a dozen messages from friends awaiting replies he could not write. When he and Laura had first arrived in Spain, he'd send entertaining little summaries of their new life to pals back home: amusing misunderstandings, baffling encounters, culinary discoveries. Now he found it impossible to transform his daily life into anecdote. Moments of despair did not alchemize into nuggets of wry self-knowledge. Moments of despair only turned into hours and then days.

He regretted now not joining his father on his afternoon stroll. He felt the silence build steadily like snow falling around him until it seemed a palpable presence in the apartment, pushing him out. He closed the laptop, put on his hat and stepped out into the heat. He would call on someone. He would talk to another human being.

It was punishingly hot and the summer had yet to take hold. It had taken him only a few months of living in Spain to realize that there was nothing wholesome or cheering about the sun. The sun was straightforwardly malevolent, its hostility relentless. He lived his life coated in creams and charms to ward off its evil.

He walked with no particular destination in mind down the middle of the road, the silence as heavy as the heat. Increasingly he felt something curdled in the atmosphere of Lomaverde, though he did not know what. Whatever it was, it was there in the glare of the midday sun as much as the nighttime shadows of his room: a presence, a watchfulness. It was a generalized sense of unease not helped by slaughtered chickens and tales of the Civil War dead. It was ridiculous to think of ghosts and yet he felt himself sometimes irrationally fearful. He wondered if it was possible to be haunted by phantoms of an unrealized future. The lives that never came to Lomaverde. He imagined disembodied Dutch retirees, floating French Web editors, semi-transparent Danish designers, but these conjured-up presences remained banal rather than spectral in his mind.

The real ghosts of Lomaverde were the cats, legions of them now, snaking up and down stairwells, darting for cover at every footstep, yowling by the bins at night. Eamonn was fond of cats. Having grown up with Mr Socks for a pet, it was impossible for him to understand why the animals were seen as superior or haughty. Mr Socks was as affectionate as he was dim-witted. Sometimes, when Eamonn was little, feeling the loneliness of an only child, he liked to imagine that Mr Socks was his brother, but then the cat would get his head stuck in a crisp bag, or run around with a pair of Eamonn's pants stuck to his paw, and Eamonn would feel the need to dissolve the familial link. As a schoolboy he had read that come nuclear Armageddon, cockroaches would inherit the Earth, but in the smaller, less radioactive collapse of Lomaverde it was feral cats who were making hay. And these survivors were nothing like Mr Socks. They had not been spoon-fed rabbit-flavour Whiskas or given Dairylea triangles as a regular treat. They were skinny and twitchy. Eamonn had no idea where they had all come from. He had seen one once in Nieves the sales manager's office and somewhere in his mind lurked the theory that the tubby tabby reclined on the photocopier was the unlikely progenitor of the sprawling street gangs that now roamed the development. Whoever the original settlers were, they had been deceived, just as their human neighbours had, by the promise of good times and, more specifically, plentiful food to come. They had bred prodigiously and now there were too many of them for the leftovers and scraps of such a sparsely settled community.

He thought of Roger ranting about the cats and felt an unexpected surge of fondness for him. There was no polite conversation with Roger, no space for silence or thoughts or doubts. Eamonn realized that what he wanted to do more than anything at that moment was drink cold beer and listen to someone loud and inattentive.

His only qualm was Cheryl. She would join them and she would not allow Eamonn to be a passive observer. She would demand responses, interaction, capitulation of one sort or another. She communicated by shaking her big hair, alternating arbitrarily between disdain and flirtatiousness. He and Laura found her frequently hilarious. The pouting and the flouncing, the dialogue straight out of a bad soap opera; her entire conversational repertoire a ragbag of tired, old lines she'd been hoiking around since her heyday. She was not like any woman he had known. She was older of course, but it wasn't just generational. She seemed a different species, an exotic creature, a cartoon – both funny and fascinating. He found her face remarkable. High cheekbones, fiercely shaped brows, grey eyes. She looked like an evil queen from a children's book. A superbitch from an 80s TV movie. She had glamour, he supposed, a kind of harshness about her clothes and make-up. There was something both anachronistic and ridiculous about her, but behind Eamonn's laughter was confusion, because a part of him still fell for it.

This small, unwanted attraction was fed by a sense he had that she was there for him, available. That Roger and Cheryl wanted both Laura and him. There had been times when the flirting had turned into something else. A queasy, usually drunken blundering into sexual territory in conversation. It was always the older couple who initiated it – hypothetical questions, stories they'd heard, a kind of probing. Once Cheryl had cornered Laura and interrogated her about her sexual history. Laura had attempted to laugh it off, but Cheryl had seemed irritated at her unwillingness to tell all. On another wine-soaked evening, Roger had appeared to suggest that they swap partners but then insisted it was just a joke.

'Christ, Laura,' Eamonn said, 'did you see their eyes? They're like wolves. It's like they want to consume us.'

'You'd get off lightly. At least Cheryl is an attractive woman. I'd get Lovejoy!'

He shuddered. 'My God. Wife-swapping in El Dorado. We're trapped in retro-porn.'

After that they seriously started to extricate themselves from Roger and Cheryl's company. Laura was less extreme. She found them creepy but ultimately harmless. She would sometimes keep up appearances to avoid looking rude. Eamonn however was assiduous in his efforts to elude them. He had a terror that the older couple would somehow detect the hairline crack in his armour; that, like animals, they would pick up the scent of the tiny, unwilled grain of desire he had for Cheryl.

Lost in his thoughts he had walked too far, missing the turning for Roger and Cheryl's house, and now found himself walking down an uninhabited street at the bottom edge of the development. He swore aloud at the prospect of traipsing back uphill in the heat. His head pounded violently and he wished he had thought to have a drink before he left the apartment. He stood for a moment with his hands on his knees in front of one of the unfinished houses but had a curious feeling that he was not alone. Scaffolding surrounded the structure and loose plastic sheeting hung down over the partially built walls. He raised his head to look through the door frame into the empty shell of the building. In the shadowy interior he thought he saw something move across the opening.

'Hello?'

The afternoon silence hung heavily. He tilted his head, squinting into the dark. He shielded his eyes and took a step forward. There was a different quality to the darkness in one spot, something denser, more solid. He stepped closer and there, for a split second, he saw a pair of eyes looking back at him. He jerked backwards and as he did felt a shifting in his head, like sand sliding from one side to another, suddenly black flies seemed to be everywhere at the edge of his vision and as he batted them away his ears filled with a high-pitched screeching.

The first thing he became aware of was the heat of the tarmac pressing through his T-shirt. He moved his hand and discovered he was flat on his back. He was aware of a presence beside him. He opened his eyes and saw the outline of what appeared to be a boy's head looking down at him, silhouetted against the deep blue of the sky. He couldn't make sense of the image and closed his eyes again. Some time later there was a voice.

'Eamonn. Eamonn. Can you hear me?'

He opened his eyes once more to see Roger's face leaning over him.

'Jesus, thank God, I thought you'd carked it. Are you all right? Can you move?'

He sat up slowly. 'I think I fainted.'

'I thought you'd had a heart attack.'

'Sorry.'

Roger sat down heavily next to Eamonn. 'Fainted? What am I supposed to do? Loosen your stays?' He reached into a side pocket on his shorts and produced a small metal flask. 'Have some of this.'

Eamonn took a swig of brandy. 'You're like a St Bernard's. How did you find me here?'

'I was returning from the hunt.'

Eamonn focused on Roger's appearance, some kind of over-fed Bavarian assassin. 'You're carrying a gun.'

'Beretta. Very nice.'

Eamonn shook his head, trying to bring the world back into alignment.

Roger took a slug of the brandy. 'Been out since dawn. Going for the "Grand Slam".'

'You've been playing tennis?'

'Not tennis, you dick. The Ibex Grand Slam.'

'Are Ibex the sponsors?'

'Are you concussed?'

Eamonn felt helpless. 'I don't understand anything that's happening. Me. You. The pain in my head. The words coming out of your mouth.'

'An ibex, Eamonn. It's not that hard to understand. It's an animal. A goat . . . I think. Big horns anyway. You've got four types in Spain – your Gredos, Ronda, Sierra Nevada and . . . the other one.'

'Right.'

'So. You kill all four and that's your Grand Slam.'

Eamonn put his head in his hands. 'Oh God.'

'Here we go. Here comes the hand-wringing. I'm embracing the culture. You should try it sometime.'

'A day killing goats. All kinds of goats.'

'It was just something to do. Ian and I thought we'd give it a go.' He was silent for a moment. 'Another bloody con. No fucking goats in this country as far as I can see.' He pointed the gun at the empty house. 'The hunting element was getting all the gear really – choosing the guns and the clothes. After that it was a drag. I don't know what the fuck we'd have done with a dead goat anyway.' He wiped his face with his sleeve and spat. 'We don't see you any more.'

'I know. I'm sorry. Just been busy, work, you know.'

'We should stick together. All in the same boat. Sod all else to do.'

'Yes.'

Roger stood and reached out a hand to help Eamonn up.

'Thanks.'

Eamonn straightened up, rubbing the back of his head, which was throbbing steadily.

'Haven't seen lovely Laura for ages either. I thought we had a nice little scene going on. The four of us. We had some laughs.'

Eamonn said nothing.

'You need to unwind. Relax. You're too uptight. Both of you. Let yourselves go a bit. Let Uncle Roger and Aunty Cheryl sort you out.'

Eamonn forced a half-smile and started to walk away, but Roger called him back. 'Hey! Don't forget this.' He picked up a bottle of water from the road.

'It's yours, isn't it?' said Eamonn.

Roger shook his head. 'I stick with Señor Torres.'

Eamonn took the bottle. It was cold, wet with condensation on the outside. He looked over at the house. 'You didn't see anyone about, did you? Before you found me.'

Roger looked at him. 'No. Why?'

Eamonn hesitated. 'I thought someone else was here.'

Roger looked around. 'You see?'

'What?'

'Another reason for this.' He patted the gun. 'Something rotten in the state of Lomaverde.'

'What are you talking about?'

'We're not wanted here, Eamonn. Vultures are circling the stricken ship. Do you think Esteban's going to stand in the way of the mob?'

'What mob?'

'Whoever they might be. The country's in collapse. Civil unrest. It's just a matter of time. We need to be ready.'

'To shoot people?'

'Hopefully it won't come to that.'

'Is that part of the Grand Slam too?'

'I hope you find it funny when it happens.'

'Do you think it's possible that you're losing your mind?'

'Hey, I'm not the one who imagined I saw someone. I'm not the one who passed out.'

'It was probably just a local kid.'

'Yeah, casing the joint.'

They started walking back up the road.

'I can't believe someone gave you a gun licence.'

'You might be grateful someday.'

'Yeah, when the goats come for us.'

Eamonn glanced back over his shoulder. He felt them still, the eyes, watching his every step.

23

He walked down her road, but when he reached her door he hesitated and turned back. At their lunch together she'd spoken about her painting, how it helped clear her mind, focusing just on colour and texture, forgetting all the other things in her life. He'd asked her then: 'I'd imagine it would put you off, would it? Having someone there watching you paint. Seeing how you do it.' She thought about it and he saw that he had put her in an awkward position, so he answered for her: 'Oh it would, it would, I'm sure. Very distracting, having someone in the way.'

She shook her head. 'No. I don't think so. With some people, yes, but I don't think you would disturb me.'

'I just . . . I know nothing about it, really. I've never seen anyone paint. I'd be interested to see how it's done, like.'

She had smiled. 'It would be my pleasure.'

But now he wasn't sure what he had been thinking of when he made the suggestion. He had been easy in her company, had drunk a little too much of her wine and let himself be carried away. What did he know about painting? Why would she want some ignoramus sitting there, watching her and making idiot comments? Better to be suspected a fool, he thought, than open your mouth and prove them right.

He was walking back up the hill when he heard a voice calling his name.

'Hello there.' Esteban was sitting on a plastic chair in the shade of his security cabin. 'Are you exploring again? Another empty house?'

Dermot shook his head. 'No. No particular destination in mind. Just fancied a wander.'

Esteban smiled. '"Just fancied a wander."'

'I felt like a walk.'

'Yes. I understand. If there is no hurry, join me, please.' He disappeared into his cabin and returned with a stool, which he sat on. 'Here,' he gestured at the chair, 'please, sit.'

Dermot did as he was told.

Esteban was silent for a moment and then said, 'I worry that maybe I sound stupid the last time we meet.'

Dermot looked at him in surprise. 'Not at all.'

'"Your country is so wonderful. I love Ireland." All these things. I sound like a child.'

'It was nice to hear it.'

'It's a long time since I was there and I have happy memories. It's so different to here, so green of course, so . . . different. Perhaps I think everywhere is better than here.'

Dermot looked around at the deserted estate. 'I'd say it must be awful dull for you.' He saw from Esteban's face that he had not understood and he tried again. 'The days must be very long. There's nothing to do.'

'I check cameras. I read books.' He smiled. 'I speak to everyone to practise English.' He hesitated. 'Yes, the days are long.' He was silent for a while. 'But it is a job and not everyone has a job. Most of my friends?' He blew air from his mouth. '*Nada*.'

Dermot shook his head. 'It's a terrible thing.' He thought for a moment. 'It was the same when I was growing up back in Ireland. Nothing to do. No work. No opportunities.'

Esteban lit a cigarette. 'My mother did not want me to take

134

this job. She never trust the people who own it, the developers. They have a very bad reputation here. When they were building it, they did not do things in a good way. Everything cheap. One man, a worker, died. An injury to his head, bricks fell, he had no protection.'

'I didn't know that.'

'No. It's not what they tell people when they come to buy their houses. The man's family, they never got the money, the compensation. It was all bad. Some people have superstition about this place, said it was bad luck to work here, bad luck to build here.'

'Is that what your mother thought?'

'No, my mother, she's not like that. But she did not trust the developers. She said they would not pay me. She was right in the end.' He flicked a plastic bottle top into the road. 'Mothers are always right, aren't they?'

Dermot smiled. 'Always.'

'So when you were in my situation, you left your country, you moved to England?'

'I did.'

'To London, "where the nightlife is unequalled".' Dermot looked at him and Esteban laughed. 'I always remember that sentence from my schoolbook.'

'Ah, right, no, not London. Birmingham. The nightlife in Birmingham, well I'd say it was equalled, but it was good enough for me.'

'And for me too, I'm sure.' Esteban blew out smoke. 'I think about it often.'

'London?'

'Leaving.'

'Do you think you will?'

'I don't know. We always think it's better somewhere else.

The green grass – that thing. Maybe it's an illusion. I work here. Lomaverde. Even the name is a lie. I see the people who live here. Are they happy?'

Dermot shrugged. 'I don't know. I'm not sure what they were looking for. They didn't come here out of desperation. They weren't looking for jobs. Not like those poor souls in the boats the other day.'

Esteban sighed. 'People struggle to survive. It can make them do wrong things. Things people know are not . . . good idea.'

'Risk their lives.'

'Yes, that, but other things too.'

'I suppose so.'

'Things that are not in the law, you know? The black money – there is a lot of that.'

'Black money?'

'Hidden. The government doesn't know. Illegal.'

'Oh, right. Of course. It happens when times are hard.'

Esteban blew out smoke and Dermot looked at him.

'Can you drive?'

'Yes.'

'Well, there's an option.'

'What's that?'

'In England. They always need bus drivers.'

Esteban laughed. 'Maybe one day.'

'Why not now? It's easy these days, step off a plane, no need for visas or permits. Your English is good enough.'

'Getting there is easy, but leaving here, I don't know. My cousin, he is a few years younger than me. We grow up together, he doesn't speak English. I'd feel bad leaving him here. And my mother, we're good friends. If I go she has only my dad. He is nice man, but he doesn't talk much.' He threw his cigarette on the ground. 'Maybe I'm a coward.'

Dermot was silent for a while. 'I never thought much about all that.'

'About what?'

'I never stopped to think what I was leaving behind. I thought if I did that I'd never get away.'

Esteban shrugged. 'Perhaps you were right.'

24

In the first few months he'd spent his afternoons making notes about his novel. Some days he thought he had too many ideas and other days not enough. Some days the scale was too ambitious, other days too narrow. One week he was convinced it would be first person, present tense, the next week it was multiple viewpoint, past historical. In the densely packed document entitled 'Scope' there were twenty-eight different themes he thought the novel would touch upon. The main character was a hospital porter called Wayne, or possibly a banker called Justin, or a child detective called Pip, or maybe all of them and more in a literary maelstrom of fragments and traces that would be far greater than the sum of its parts. And throughout all these vital, preliminary considerations and crucial decision-making stages came the steady tap-tap-tap of Laura's keyboard.

'How's it going?' he asked.

'OK, I guess.'

'You seem to be writing a lot. You're like Ernie Wise bashing out a play a night.'

'Ha ha.'

'I thought you'd be doing research first.'

'Well, I do a bit of both each day. I think if I spend too long thinking about it, I won't ever actually write it.'

He said nothing.

As the weeks passed, his notes folder expanded.

She asked him eagerly: 'Is there anything you can read to me?'

'No, not yet.'

'But it's going OK?'

'It's OK.'

'I mean, you have actually started and everything?'

'It depends what you mean by "started". I mean, how do we define "the start"? I'm not sure that we can.'

After a while he stopped adding to his notes and shortly after that he stopped opening the folder. He found the contents unsettling. A tangled knot of half-ideas and desires with no discernible beginning or end. A list of resolutions and ambitions. He sat and stared at the folder icon on his desktop and listened to Laura's tap-tap-tap day after day until he finally realized his mistake.

'Laura!'

'What?'

'I've had a breakthrough.'

'Amazing.'

'I haven't been writing a novel.'

'No?'

'No. I've been writing about a novel.'

'Isn't that a start?'

'No. It turns out that was the work I was engaged upon. I've written thirty thousand words about a novel. Now I've finished.'

'Aren't you going to write the novel itself?'

'What? And spoil it?'

'Eamonn. Come on. Don't do this.'

'Do what?'

'You're attacking yourself. Giving yourself a hard time. What you're trying to do is insanely hard. It'd be crazy if you didn't get stuck sometimes.'

'You didn't.'

'I'm not doing the same thing. You're doing something more ambitious.'

'No. That's not it. I'm not cut out for this.'

'What does that mean?'

'I'm not the literary type, am I? I mean, look at us. Your father has written books, your mother has papers published in journals. You grew up with this kind of stuff. What the fuck do I know? I'm not from that background.'

She stared at him for a long time. 'Please tell me you're not turning this into a class issue.'

'I'm not turning this into a class issue. I'm just saying you have a confidence and I suppose a sense of entitlement. Why shouldn't you write a book? You know you can do it. I know I can't.'

'Why does this feel as if you're attacking me?'

'I'm not attacking you.'

'All I've ever done is encourage you.'

'I know, just as your parents encouraged you all through your life.'

'Will you stop talking about my fucking parents! It's not their fault that you're not writing your book.'

'No, I know, it's mine. I'm useless.'

'Jesus. Do you know how tiring this is?'

'I'm sorry if I make you tired.'

'It's fine that you show no interest in what I'm writing. I never expected you to.'

'I do show an interest, I'm always asking you how it's going.'

'Only so you can gnash your teeth and beat yourself up. You're not actually interested. After all, historical fiction isn't your "cup of tea", remember? But that's fine, I'm OK with that. And it's even fine that you can't be happy for me that I'm getting on OK, that I'm finding it interesting and rewarding. But yes I find it tiring, wearing, deadening that I have to constantly reassure you, to prevent you mentally self-harming. And I find it more than tiring, I find it pathetic, predictable and ultimately repellent that everything always comes back to the ridiculous, enormous chip on your shoulder.'

'"Repellent",' he repeated.

She looked into his eyes. 'Why are you fucking everything up?'

25

She entered his bedroom without knocking.

'Come on, Eamonn. Daddy's waiting to take you, he wants to get back and watch his programme.'

Eamonn was staring at the bed. 'Why are those there?'

'They're your clothes, Eamonn, for goodness' sake! I've laid them out for you.'

Item one: brown wool blazer, generous lapels; item two: white polycotton shirt with stiff, similarly generous collar; item three: brown corduroy trousers, slightly flared; item four: blue tie.

'They're the clothes I wore for Gerald's wedding.'

'That's right.'

'But I'm going to a party tonight. Not a wedding.'

'Well, you need to look smart.'

He had an indistinct image in his mind of how the other boys might be dressed. He saw ripped 501s. Hooded tops. Baseball jackets.

'No one will be dressed like this.'

'Like what? Smartly, you mean? Of course they will. You're going to a girl's house. Her parents will expect you to have made an effort, you can't just go out in your old jeans. Anyway, I've seen young boys your age out in ties and smart trousers –'

'Not like these!' It came out too loudly. He saw his mother's face change.

'Oh, I see. Are these not good enough? Are you embarrassed

by the clothes we buy you? Not expensive enough for your friends?'

He sat heavily on the bed and started to take off his shoes.

His father peered at the house from the driver's seat.

'How did you say you know this girl?'

'She's a friend of someone at the girls' school.'

His father nodded slowly. 'I'd say her father has a good job, living on a road like this. What does he do?'

He shrugged. There were many, many things Eamonn wanted to know about girls, what their fathers did was not one of them.

'Well, you'd better go now. It's five to seven, you don't want to be late.'

Eamonn got out of the car, but remained standing by the passenger window. His father mouthed at him: 'What are you doing?'

'I'll wait for you to go.'

His dad leaned over and wound the window down. 'I thought I'd wait here till you were in, check it's the right place, the right night. You don't want to be turning up in your finery on the wrong night. That would be a terrible faux pas.'

He put on his posh English accent. Eamonn used to find it funny.

He sighed. 'It's the right house, it's the right night. Dad, please . . .'

'All right, all right. I get the message. You want me gone. Not getting in your way with the young ladies, is that right?'

'Dad!'

'OK, son. Just be ready at ten.'

He stood waving, unconvincingly, until his father was gone and then took cover from the house in front of the high hedge.

He pulled off his tie, took off the jacket, undid his top shirt button and looked down at himself. Still the flared cords. Still brown. He looked agricultural. A lost young farmer cast adrift from the 1970s. He tucked his trousers in his socks.

He emerged from behind the hedge and walked up the drive. He had taken no notice of the house when his father pulled up, but now it loomed large ahead of him, looking like something out of a horror film. It was old and pointy with bits of plant growing all over it. A couple of balloons hung from an enormous brass handle, smack in the centre of the front door. They didn't appear to have a doorbell so he snapped the heavy letter box instead. He had to do it a few times before he saw a shadow appear on the other side of the stained glass.

The door opened to reveal a short man with a beard, a glass of wine in his hand and a puzzled look on his face.

'Oh. Hello. Are you here for Laura's little soirée?'

'Yes.'

'I almost didn't hear you there. Why on earth didn't you ring the bell?' He reached out and pulled a circular brass knob, setting a series of bells jangling somewhere further in the house. 'Come in, come in.' He glanced down at Eamonn's ankles. 'Did you come on your bike?'

'No.'

'Oh. Right. Well, I'll let Laura know you're here. I think she's in the beauty parlour at the moment with one of her coterie.'

Eamonn waited in the hallway. It reminded him of church. Tiled floor, heavy wooden furniture, framed pictures everywhere, though none, as far as he could see, of Jesus or the Virgin Mary. Footsteps came hammering down the stairs and then stopped abruptly.

'Oh. Hello.'

Eamonn looked up to see the girl whose house it was. He had never spoken to her directly before.

'Hello.' He pushed a box of Roses at her.

She took them and looked at his trousers. 'Did you come on your bike?'

'Yes.'

'Where are the others?'

'Who?'

'Jonathan Parker and the rest of your gang?'

'Aren't they here?'

'Not yet.'

'But they all live round here, don't they?'

'I suppose so. Don't you?'

'I live in Erdington.'

'I don't know where that is.'

Her mother appeared from a door. 'Laura, what are you doing? Don't keep your guest standing in the hallway. Take him into the party room.' She turned to smile at Eamonn. 'Hello, there. Nice to meet you . . .?'

'Eamonn.'

'Eamonn. Isn't that a lovely name, Laura?'

Laura was non-committal. 'He's come on his bike. From Erdington.'

'Goodness! You must be absolutely exhausted.'

He followed Laura into a dark room with loud music playing. He smelled the girls before his could see them. A sweet combination of hairspray, teen perfume and some-thing spiced. He made out their shape in the corner, four or five of them, their perms stiff with Shockwaves gel, like a pride of lionesses, swaying slightly to the sounds of Bros. One separated from the group, Harriet, their leader, the one who spoke to Jonathan. She had a plastic cup in her hand.

'Do you want some punch? It's got Martini in. Kate's already completely drunk.'

Trying to find the bathroom later he opened the wrong door and found her parents instead. He was shocked to see them eating their tea so late. They sat at a large pine table, with a bottle of wine open between them. There was music playing, a man with a terrible voice singing over guitar. Eamonn thought the scene looked like something from the telly. A programme on after the nine o'clock news, where men and women shouted at each other and then took their clothes off and got into bed together and his mom would get up and turn the TV off, saying, 'That's enough of that.'

Laura's mother stood up. 'Hey, Eamonn. Are you OK?'

'Sorry. I was looking for the toilet.'

'There's one by the back door.'

He noticed there were bookshelves even in the kitchen. There was no way they could have read all the books they had. Her father caught him looking at a shelf.

'Are you interested in psychiatry, Eamonn?'

'Erm . . . yes.'

'We took Laura to the Freud Museum last summer and she seemed most unimpressed.' He pushed a chair back with his foot. 'Come in, why don't you? Join us. Emily's made this wonderful tagine and we can't finish it.' Eamonn was about to say that he'd already had his tea, but then the father added: 'And I know for a fact Laura won't touch it. She'd much rather fill her face with the rubbish that McDonald's churns out.' Eamonn liked the idea of appearing more sophisticated than that. He made his way over to the table.

'I don't really like McDonald's.'

'No, we're not huge fans either. Don't really see eye to eye with their way of doing things.'

Eamonn shook his head. 'They put gherkins on everything.'

The mom served him up a bowl of something that looked really bad and he started to worry that he had made a mistake.

'So, Eamonn,' Laura's father said, 'tell us all about your interest in psychiatry? Are your parents in the field?'

He didn't see how the questions were connected. Then he remembered the clothes he was wearing – the agricultural look – there was some terrible misunderstanding.

'They're not farmers. They live in Erdington. My dad's a bus driver.'

There was a moment's silence and then both parents burst out laughing. Eamonn's face flushed and the food in his mouth felt slimy and alive. He pushed his chair back to stand.

'Oh, Eamonn,' said the mom, 'you are a real character.'

He manoeuvred the foul, mangled slugs to the side of his mouth. 'Thank you for the food.' He started walking quickly to the door. 'I'll go to the toilet now.' And he fled.

When he got back to the party the impasse between the boys and girls seemed to have been broken. Everyone now sat in a circle, with an empty bottle of cider in the middle. He was told where to sit and listened while Jonathan and Harriet bickered about the rules.

'If it points at a girl and it needs to be a boy, then it's the boy sat to her left.'

'No! If it does that, we spin again.'

'Well, we're going to spend all the time just spinning the bottle.'

'The main thing is that you have to kiss whoever it points at. You can't chicken out or say you don't fancy them.' At this there was much terrified laughter.

'Can we just get on with it?' said Matthew Goldsmith.

'Come on, girls. Matthew's bursting. He can't wait for a big snog.'

On the fourth spin the bottle pointed at Eamonn. After a couple of subsequent misfires, a girl called Emma was picked out. He avoided looking at her face to see any sign of disappointment.

He used to be around girls all the time. Playing British Bulldog, searching for worms, swapping dirty jokes about Batman. In two years at boys' school they had become distant and exotic. When he saw them they were changed – bigger and burdened with mysterious freight – magazines and bangles and electric-blue eyelashes. He glimpsed them only occasionally. He missed them.

No words passed on their way to the armchair. They banged teeth several times before the angle was right and an airtight lock was formed between their mouths. With his eyes tightly shut Eamonn felt weightless, flying through the darkness, travelling through her mouth and out into the universe. They clung to each other, deaf to everything and everyone, the world forgotten.

It was she who broke away first. Someone was calling his name and finally she had looked to see who it was. Eamonn found himself beached back in the physical world, Wet Wet Wet playing, his lips stinging, his head woozy, an urgent voice saying: 'Your dad's here. You have to go.'

He looked down at Emma, her face was closed and unreadable, but he could still taste her in his mouth.

'See you around,' she said, like someone delivering a line.

'See you around,' he repeated.

He found his jacket where he'd stuffed it in a corner and went out to the hallway. His dad was standing in the spot where he had stood and waited earlier.

'Where in God's name have you been? I've been knocking the door for fifteen minutes. Are her parents not in?'

Eamonn hurried his father out before he was seen or could say anything to anyone. The sound of the front door slamming brought Laura's mother to an upstairs window. She opened it and leaned out, calling: 'Bye, Eamonn. Nice to meet you. Put the bike in the boot, have you?'

'Bye. Thank you,' Eamonn said as he pushed his father towards the car.

'What bike is she talking about? Have they given you a bike?'

'No.'

'Seems like a madhouse to me,' Dermot said as he got in the car. 'You'd think they could spend some of their money on a doorbell.'

26

It reminded Dermot of bars in Ireland. A TV flickering in the corner. Stools up to the counter. Bags of crisps served on a plate. It was called El Rincón. He asked Inga what it meant and she told him: The Corner. Nothing fancy about it at all.

He had been restless that evening in the flat, unable to settle. He was standing on the terrace, watching the sky darken, when the buzzer sounded. Her invitation as welcome as it was unexpected.

It was a forty-five-minute brisk walk along the dirt road into San Pedro – a good preparation for a cold beer. When they got there, Inga introduced him to Luis, the barman, and ordered a couple of Cruzcampos.

'Just in time,' she said, as Luis turned up the volume on the TV.

Dermot looked up to see two teams lining up on a pitch. 'Is there a match on?'

Inga laughed.

He took a sip of his beer and noticed that the scarf she was wearing had something written on it.

'Helsingborg,' he said slowly.

She turned and smiled. 'My team.'

'Oh, right. A football scarf.'

'Of course. What did you think?'

'I just thought it was a scarf – you know, women often wear scarves.'

'Not like this! You must have thought I looked mad.'

'Not mad, no. Hot, I thought. Even allowing for the sun going down, I thought a woolly scarf could be hot.'

She looked back at the TV. 'Luis always has the big matches on here. It's the only place I can see them.'

Dermot saw the flags at the bottom of the screen and realized that the match was between Sweden and Spain.

Inga carried on talking. 'Perhaps you could become a temporary supporter of Sweden, given that your own side failed to even qualify.' She glanced at him, waiting for him to take the bait.

'Did they?'

She laughed again. 'Oh, very good. I'm sure it didn't hurt at all.' She turned back to the screen. 'No one in Lomaverde is interested in football. That's why I asked you – it'll be nice to have some intelligent conversation about it.'

Dermot was quiet for a while, drinking his beer. It wasn't long before Inga turned from the screen and peered at him. 'You weren't making a joke, were you?'

He looked down at his hands.

'You don't know anything about football?'

He shrugged. 'The truth is, I don't know where that Aston Villa bag came from. It's got me into all kinds of bother over the years.'

'Oh no, Dermot! Why didn't you say?'

'I didn't know we were coming to watch football. Anyway, I don't mind. It's a nice change.'

'But I said we'd be able to see the TV in the bar.'

'I just thought you liked TV.'

'And wearing woolly scarves?'

He shrugged. 'I take the invitations I get.'

She kept apologizing. He didn't know what for. In the end he told her to please just watch the match and let him drink his beer, and she did.

He was content enough to look about the place. He studied the pictures hanging behind the bar: a signed photograph of a basketball team, a poster of a red sports car, and a small picture of the Virgin Mary with a black face. She seemed to be watching him, her expressionless eyes following his each time he took a drink.

There was an odd selection of food on offer. A glass display case on the bar was filled with bags of crisps and two boxes of doughnuts. Next to the till was a large jar of olives. He eyed the murky contents with suspicion. He'd eaten one once. He'd thought it was about the worst thing he'd ever had in his mouth. He'd thought if people would eat them they'd eat anything.

Away from the bar and the buzz of the television two women of around Kathleen's age sat at a table playing cards, drinking something red and fizzy that came in small bottles. On another table a little girl, presumably belonging to someone, sat drinking a chocolate milkshake and colouring in a large picture of a palace. Dermot thought of Nagle's place in Ennistymon, people slipping in and out without much thought, using it like an extra room of their house. He wondered if Eamonn had ever been to El Rincón. It might be nice for him, getting out of the flat, a change of scenery. He could always bring his laptop for company.

Inga seemed unbothered at being the only Sweden supporter in the place. She shouted at the TV a couple of times and laughed occasionally with Luis and some of the other Spanish fans. When the game finished she apologized to Dermot for her team's defeat. 'It wasn't a game to convert you, I fear.'

'Is that what you were hoping to do?'

'I thought you might see the light.'

'I've never been much good at that.'

She took off her scarf and blew her fringe from her forehead.

'Are you a regular here, then?' Dermot asked.

'It depends what football's on. I don't come that often, but I know Luis now and one or two others.'

'I got the impression that there was some bad blood between local people and you all up there.'

She smiled at that. '"Bad blood" – I like that, very melo-dramatic, very Gypsy's curse.'

'Is it not the case?'

'I don't think so. I think maybe it's a fine line sometimes for people between isolation and paranoia. Some people down here are unhappy with the development, or unhappy with the developers, but I don't think they hold us personally respon-sible. If anything, I think we puzzle them. Why did we come? What were we hoping for? In our big homes and our funny woolly scarves.'

He smiled. 'Have you always been a fan?'

'Not always. I was never that interested in it as a young girl. I followed the local team in Norrtälje, but half-heartedly. When I met Anders though – my ex-husband – he was very keen, used to go to matches most weekends. I had an idea that I should try to share his interests. I'd pretend to be very enthu-siastic about upcoming games. Memorize facts about certain players.' She lit a cigarette. 'It's no wonder he thought me a fool.'

Dermot said nothing.

'It's OK. He was right.' She took a sip of her drink. 'It's hard to look back. My stupidity, you know?' There was a long pause. She shook her head. 'I have to be kind to myself now. That woman was punished enough.'

They sat in silence for a few minutes.

'Dermot, I'm sorry. I don't know why I'm saying this. I won-der, am I trying to give you the worst evening of your life?'

'I don't mind at all.'

'It's ridiculous. You have what my mother called a "listening face". It must be a curse.'

'It's not.' He looked around the bar. 'You seem quite at home here. Are you glad you came to Lomaverde?'

'I am. Is that surprising?'

'I get the impression not many people are.'

'I suppose you're right.' She hesitated. 'Can I tell you a secret?'

'Yes.'

'I'm glad Lomaverde has failed.'

He looked at her.

'Please don't misunderstand, I'm not glad about the unhappiness it has caused others, of course not. The people who can't sell their houses, the people who lost money, the workers who never got paid properly, all the disappointments. I'm sorry for all those things.'

'Of course.'

'I came here expecting the same as everyone else. A new community, a fresh start in this beautiful place.' She lit another cigarette. 'My marriage was over. Thirty years of trying to turn a blind eye, of thinking my husband would change. That felt like a big mistake, a terrible waste of time. I thought I could come here and lose myself in a new place.

'But imagine somewhere in which everyone is like that. So intent on happiness, on living a fairy tale. They have not emigrated from places with no work or money to a place with jobs and opportunities. No, they have left comfortable lives in search of somewhere even better. It's a kind of greed, don't you think? And if you'd have said that to me two years ago, I'd have said, "So what? Why not be greedy for happiness? What's wrong with that?"

'Shall I tell you what's wrong?'

Dermot nodded.

154

'Disappointment. That's what's wrong. If you're greedy for happiness then you will always be hungry. You can't just say happiness is in a certain place and move there, it doesn't work like that.' She put her hand over her mouth. 'My God. "If you're greedy for happiness then you will always be hungry." I sound like a fortune cookie. This is all obvious, old as the hills. You know all this already.'

He gave a little shrug. 'Maybe.'

'The point is, no one would want to admit to their disappointment, it would be something shameful, something hidden. Imagine living in such a place? Where failure or regret or despair are inappropriate, where such feelings are not allowed, don't fit with the blue skies and the sunshine. I would have lasted six weeks.' She exhaled a long plume of smoke. 'But that isn't how it worked out. Instead Lomaverde is a failed dream. Do you know the word for it in Spanish?'

He shook his head.

'"*Ciudad fantasma*" – a "ghost town". It sounds beautiful, don't you think? It is a melancholy place, crumbling at the edges, and I find that I love it. It's a place where you can admit to mistakes, you have no choice but to. I think the lack of people makes it more human.' She paused. 'Is that mad?'

He took a drink of his beer and thought back to his childhood. Exploring empty cottages with Dominic, a certain exhilaration buried in the sadness, a sense of familiarity in the unknown. He saw she was waiting for an answer. 'It's not mad. I like it there too.'

She stubbed out her cigarette. 'Shall we head back?'

'If you like. I'm sorry your boys didn't win.'

'It's OK. It was good to see the game anyway. For all that he took away, my husband gave me three wonderful things: my son, Magnus, my daughter, Pia, and my love of football.'

'You still love it, even when you lose?'

'A good defeat can be better than a bad victory.'

'Can it?'

She laughed for a long time at that. 'You really know nothing about football, do you?'

27

Dermot sat on the futon apparently engrossed in one of his library books. Like many autodidacts the spread of Dermot's knowledge was eccentric. Eamonn had long since stopped being surprised by the things that his father knew or took an interest in: Serbian heraldry, sheep husbandry, the films of Barbra Streisand. His knowledge, though broad, was shallow, usually just one documentary or book deep. He held his sources in great reverence, taking as gospel almost everything he read, assuming the author's word to be the last word. Eamonn found his habit of quoting as fact the crackpot opinions of long-forgotten commentators often exasperating.

He bent down to read the title: *Home Computing for You and Your Family.* The cover showed a sinister-looking middle-aged man in tinted glasses, beckoning two children towards his enormous desktop computer.

Eamonn sat down next to his father. 'Good read is that?'

Dermot looked up. 'It is. Very interesting.'

'Has the Internet been invented yet?'

Dermot thought for a moment. 'They haven't mentioned it, no.'

'Right.' He carried on staring at the cover for a moment before remembering what he'd come to say. 'So, I asked around, and apparently the nearest church is in Poliver.'

'I see.'

'I don't know the times of the services, but there'll be one on at some point this morning.'

'Oh yes, it's Sunday, isn't it? I'd lost track of the days.'

'I'll charge the car battery up and drive you over there. I could come in with you if you like. Obviously it'll be in Spanish, so I could help you with the words – otherwise you'll be standing up and sitting down at the wrong bits and you'll get sent to hell.'

Dermot smiled. 'Ah, no, honestly. Don't go to any bother. There's no need for that.'

'Maybe you're right. Maybe I'll find a bar and get a beer instead.'

Dermot turned a page. 'No, I mean, there's no need to go at all.' He examined a flow chart. 'I don't really do that any more.'

'Don't do what?'

'The whole churchgoing business.'

Eamonn laughed, as if he'd heard a joke. 'What do you mean?'

'Well, I just don't.'

'Since when?'

'I suppose since your mother died.'

'You don't go to church?'

'It's not such a big thing.'

'Oh. I see.' Eamonn considered this for a while. 'So, you lost your faith?'

'You make it sound more dramatic than it is. I didn't lose my faith.' He scratched his head. 'I just stopped going to mass.'

'But you still believe in God.'

Dermot was silent.

'You don't believe in God?'

'Now, Eamonn, you sound like a priest.'

'But you were always religious.'

'I used to go to church each week with your mother, I'm not sure that's the same thing.'

Eamonn was quiet for a while. 'I knew she went on about it more than you, but I still thought you believed in it all.'

'Everyone I knew growing up went to church, believing had nothing to do with it, it was just what you did. Your mother, though, she got more into that side of things as she got older. It just wasn't worth upsetting the apple cart and making a big song and dance about it.'

'Didn't you feel a bit of a hypocrite, standing there every week?'

'I wasn't forcing anyone else to believe. I didn't care when you threw it all in. Did you really think that everyone there attending church was thinking about Jesus's blood?'

'I suppose not.' He was silent for a while, considering the implications. 'I think I'll make a drink. Do you want something?'

'A cup of tea would be great.'

He stood with the box of tea bags in his hand and called through the hatch: 'Do you remember old Father Maguire?'

'How could I forget him? The hours I suffered listening to that voice. Honest to God, put a horse to sleep he could. That man was a terrible bore.'

'I was wondering, when did he start at St John's?'

Dermot thought for a minute. 'I don't know. In the 70s sometime. Your mother would have known. Why?'

'Do you remember when I came home for Mom's funeral and you asked me to go through the photos?'

'I do.'

'There was a pack of photos I couldn't work out. A couple had Mom in, maybe on a parish trip somewhere. There was a group shot on a ferry, probably early 70s. Then there was a whole load of the same bloke. They weren't all from one roll of film, lots of different shapes and sizes of photo, but all the same guy.' He paused. 'He was wearing a dog collar.'

Dermot said nothing.

'I suppose he'd be the priest before Maguire, would he?'

Dermot had got up and was looking out of the window. 'I don't know.'

'A youngish guy. Fair hair, big, wide grin? Would that be right?'

'That sounds like him.'

'Do you remember his name?'

Dermot took a while to answer. 'Walsh. His name was Father Walsh.'

'Oh, right. Well that solves it, then.' Eamonn frowned and then laughed. 'So why did Mom have so many photos of him?'

He came out of the kitchen with the tea, but Dermot had gone.

28

He waited with the others until the Sister came and let them in. Visiting time started at 6.30. She opened the door at 6.31. Third night in a row she'd kept them waiting. Still making her point.

Kathleen was at the far end of the ward. He went to the cot first.

'Is he going to wake up soon?'

'He's only just gone off.'

'Oh.' He leaned over and kissed her.

'He had his bottle and he was asleep within minutes.'

'I thought I'd be able to give him his bottle tonight.'

'Sister said it was better to get it out of the way before visiting time.'

'She looks at us as if we're litter blown in off the street. She'd be happier if there were no fathers to deal with at all.'

'She's an old boot.'

'Have they said when you can go?'

'Maybe tomorrow, or the day after that.'

'You should both be at home. Not this place.'

'I wish I was in the General. At least I'd have some pals there.'

He looked at the baby again. 'How's he been?'

'Miserable most of the time. You'd think I was beating him. He pulls a face that would break your heart.'

Dermot smiled, stroking the baby's face lightly. 'What about you?'

'Just a bit tired. Did you bring me anything?'

'Some magazines.'

She looked at them.

'What? Did I bring the wrong ones?'

'No. They're fine. I'm just sick of magazines. The same rubbish in every one.'

'Also a box of Maltesers and a bottle of Super Jaffa.'

'Thanks.'

'Well, I thought they'd get a better response from you. Are you sure you're OK? You seem down compared to yesterday.'

'I'm fine. I just want to go home.'

'I know, love.' He looked at the cards on the bedside table. 'Did you have any visitors this afternoon?'

'Just Rita Barry.'

'She talks enough for four people.'

She was quiet for a while.

'She said something I can't stop thinking about.'

'What was it?'

'She looked at him and said, "Well, God bless him. He's a little miracle. Just what you were praying for all that time."'

Dermot looked at her. 'That sounds like Rita Barry all right.'

'Is that what she thinks I was doing when she saw me down at church?'

'What?'

'Praying for a baby? Asking God for something? Like he's a shopkeeper?'

'This is playing on your mind? Something the Barry woman said? God's sake, Kathleen.'

'Maybe she's right.'

He saw now she was worked up.

'We had all that time. We both worked all the shifts we could and still there was time. I used to pray: if I wasn't to be a mother, what was I to be? What was his plan? I helped out in the parish. I visited the sick. I typed the newsletter. I arranged flowers and spent hours listening to the twitterings of Rita Barry, Pat Quinlon and Margie Maher, which believe me would try any saint.' Her voice was louder now. He worried others would hear them.

'I don't understand why you're upset.'

'But maybe it was all with an ulterior motive in mind. Do you see? Maybe it was all saying: "Look at me, God, I'm a good person, why can't I be a mother?"'

He rubbed his face. 'Well, what's wrong with that? I thought you were supposed to ask God for things you wanted.'

'Is that all prayer is? Begging letters. I thought it was meant to be a conversation.'

'I don't know what you want me to say. You seem to be arguing with yourself.'

'I don't want you to say anything.'

She was quiet for a moment before saying: 'I hold their hand when they go.'

'Who?'

'If there's no family. One of us will sit with them when they're slipping away. I hold their hand so they're not alone at the end. I sometimes wonder – is someone waiting to take their hand on the other side? When they pass I search their faces for any sign of knowledge, for a clue. What is it they see, Dermot?'

Nothing, he thought. Nothing at all. He pushed the thought away and took her hand, speaking quietly. 'Should I talk to the doctor?'

She shook her head. 'It's not like that. I'm fine. I'm not blue. I'm happy, you know that, never been happier since he was born . . .'

'But what?'

'It just makes you think, doesn't it? Birth, death. That's when you think about these things. When I do anyway. About God. About what it means.'

He wanted then to tell her how much he loved her. He wanted to tell her to forget about God. He tried to think of something to comfort her.

'Maybe you could try speaking to Father Phelan when you get home? Isn't that what he's there for? He must be there for something.'

She smiled at that. 'I've tried to talk to him sometimes in the past, but he never seems to listen.'

Dermot was unsurprised. They didn't listen. They had no answers.

'Well, he's not there for much longer. Maybe the new priest will be better.'

'Probably another old relic who thinks women are there to make cakes and sing sweetly.'

'You'll soon disabuse him of that belief.'

She laughed and he felt a surge of hope. Maybe this was the push she needed. If the lack of a baby had led her to the Church, maybe now she would pull away. End her search for whatever it was she thought she was looking for.

He took his hand from hers and laid it on the baby's back, feeling the rabbit pulse of his heartbeat. 'What are we going to call this one?'

She leaned over and stroked the baby's head. 'I don't know. We had so many prepared, but then you see him and none of them seem right at all.'

'I had Peggy on the phone from the convent last night. She rang to offer her congratulations and tell us that he'd been born on the day of St Polycarp.'

'Polycarp? What was he, patron saint of fish?'

'Burned at the stake apparently. When the flames couldn't touch him, they stabbed him to death.'

'Good God.' They both started laughing, becoming momentarily hysterical before getting control of themselves.

She looked at him. 'I was thinking. If you want to name him Dominic, I'd understand. I'd be happy with that.'

Dermot thought. 'No. He's his own man. He deserves his own name.' He hesitated. 'But maybe as his second name. I'd like that.'

'There we are, then. Halfway there.'

29

'Your mother would have appreciated an incline like this.'

They walked along the shaded side of the street, the sun finally weakening its grip and sliding down the sky.

As with so much his father said, Eamonn could think of no particular response.

'Was a time she was a devil for the slopes.'

'Right.'

'A real terror.'

'Because she liked hills?'

'On her bike! She was a devil.'

'Mom? On a bike?'

'"Handlebars Hegarty", that's what we used to call her.'

'"Handlebars Hegarty"?'

'Back when I first knew her, she was awful windswept-looking, like she'd just stepped in from the storm. She'd be out on it any hour of the night or day, cycle back on her own from a late shift at the hospital, she would, no lights, like a bat on wheels.

'First time she agreed to go out with me, I was stood waiting for her down at the bottom of Corporation Street. It was hellish busy. Rush hour. I was getting knocked and nudged by everyone hurrying to get home for their tea and I was cursing myself for picking such an idiot place to meet. I was looking for her face in the crowd and then suddenly I spotted it, way off in the distance. There she was, on the bike, coming down the hill towards me, and there were cars and buses and people everywhere, but to look at her you'd think she was on some quiet country lane. Floating along, she was, without a care in the world, the wind blowing her hair back, the afternoon sun on her face. Handlebars Hegarty.'

Eamonn tried and failed to conjure up a picture of it. They walked on in silence. He found stories of his parents before he was born quite fantastical, impossible to relate to the people he'd grown up with.

Laura's parents were an open book. Their life together a never-ending panel discussion. He considered unnatural the amount they had to say to each other. Nothing escaped the searchlight of their opinion. They would talk with passion and at length about the local shops, Philip Roth, mushrooms, wheel-clamping, Neil Young, dim sum, their next-door neighbour's recycling boxes and the mental illnesses of their friends.

His parents, in contrast, were borderline mute. Sometimes they bickered, sometimes they remarked on the obituaries, but generally they coexisted with few words.

'Your tea is on the table.'

'Did you get the peas?'

'I'd say you'd need a coat.'

They chose often to communicate by proxy, with Eamonn acting as a shuttle between them.

'If your mother wants to get to Brendan's for lunch she'll need to get a move on.'

'If your father doesn't mow the grass soon, we'll never find the cat.'

He found it hard to imagine how they talked to each other when he wasn't around. He wasn't sure that they did.

As they turned the corner now, Cheryl was standing, apparently waiting for them, on the pavement. Eamonn had never seen her beyond the confines of a house or terrace before. The sight of her on the street was incongruous.

'Hello, you two. I spotted you from afar.'

'Is that right?' said Dermot.

'I was up in the bedroom, gazing out of the window, and there you suddenly were, like two handsome princes come to rescue a damsel in distress from the terrible ogre.'

'And where is this terrible ogre?' asked Dermot. Eamonn looked at him. It occurred to him that maybe his father had had a lifetime of this on the buses. An endless line of Cheryls charmed by his twinkling Irish eyes. He thought of skimpy polyester negligees, of Reg Varney . . . he made himself stop.

Cheryl waved an arm. 'Oh, on the couch of course, empty bottles scattered around him, watching the tennis with Ian. Keep me company, won't you, before I die of boredom.'

Dermot smiled. 'Well, we couldn't allow that.'

'Come and join me on the terrace, we can ignore the tedious people inside.'

Eamonn intervened. 'Thanks, but we've got dinner waiting for us back at the flat. I've left it in the oven cooking while we went out for a walk.' It sounded unconvincing even to him.

'Oh, Eamonn! Don't be so bloody boring. Isn't he painful, Dermot? Just one drink. An aperitif, for God's sake. That's only civilized. We won't let your precious dinner burn, you old woman.'

She marched Dermot into the house. Eamonn stood on the street for a few moments before following on reluctantly.

On the roof terrace she settled Dermot in a chair and then commanded Eamonn to assist her getting drinks from the little bar they had set up there in the corner. Once out of Dermot's earshot, she spoke sharply. 'Well, I've heard about Laura. Jean let something slip to Becca. Frankly I'm a little hurt, Eamonn, that you didn't come to Roger and me when this happened. We're your oldest friends here.'

'I didn't really want to talk about it.'

'You should have come straight over here. We wouldn't have

had to talk about it, we could have just had a drink like old times. We used to have some good nights. I don't know what happened.'

'No.'

'Well. Now she's gone, maybe we'll see a bit more of you. You need your friends at a time like this.'

She touched his arm. 'All I'm saying is: I'm here if you ever want to talk about it. You're not on your own.'

He looked at her hand. Golden-brown skin, diamond rings, red fingernails. He wanted to brush it away like a mosquito. He wanted to cry.

Dermot's voice drifted over to them. 'Can I give you a hand?'

Eamonn pulled his arm away and walked over to join his father. Cheryl followed on with Dermot's drink.

'So, Dermot, you have us all in a stir.'

'How's that?'

'Well, it's been a while since we had a visitor, and with it being your first time abroad, there seems to be a sense that it's a bit of an occasion.'

'Oh?' Dermot laughed. 'Like a papal visit?'

'Something like that. Becca in particular is very animated about it. I assume you've heard about the barbecue?'

Dermot and Eamonn spoke together. 'What barbecue?'

'Oh, my goodness, listen to you two. You sound as if I'd suggested a funeral.'

'I don't want anyone going to any bother for me.'

'Becca wants to do it; you're just an excuse. She needs something to lift her spirits. Well, don't we all? Something to break the monotony. We haven't had a big get-together for ages. They used to happen almost weekly. Everyone invited, a chance to catch up; but then it all started to go sour. Suddenly it was just a roomful of people moaning and drinking too much. Everyone sick of the sight of each other.'

Dermot looked unsure.

'Oh, don't worry, she has it all under control. Listen, I'm sorry if I spoiled the secret, maybe it was meant to be a surprise party. Don't look so miserable, Eamonn, it'll be a chance to put on our glad rags and forget our troubles.'

Eamonn gave a mirthless smile.

'We'll see if we can put some colour back in those cheeks, eh?' She turned to Dermot. 'After that Laura upped sticks and deserted our lovely Eamonn. How could she do that?'

Dermot glanced at his watch. 'Oh, Eamonn, the dinner.'

Eamonn stirred. 'Yes, the dinner. It'll be burned.'

Cheryl stood to see them out. 'What culinary delight is it tonight?'

'Chicken,' said Dermot at the same time as Eamonn said, 'Chilli.'

Eamonn nodded. '*Chilli con pollo*. An experiment.'

Cheryl looked at Dermot. 'Fingers crossed it'll be burned.'

They walked back up the hill towards Eamonn's block in silence. As they climbed the stairs Dermot asked: 'What did Laura reckon to that one?'

'Cheryl? OK in small doses, I suppose. Why?'

Dermot said nothing for a while and then: 'Do any of them have any jobs?'

'Well, Ian and Becca have their business, but I think it's pretty much dead in the water. Laura and I did our stuff, everyone else is retired.'

Dermot headed for the kitchen. 'I worked with a fella named Moran. He retired eighteen months before me. You wouldn't know it though. He was always around the garage, having a chat with the lads on their break, checking out the buses when they came back in. He shouldn't have really been there, you know, wasn't insured to be on the premises any more, but the gaffer turned a blind eye.' He paused. 'Turned out he was slashing the tyres with a penknife. Never done anything like that in his life. The company didn't press charges. His wife came down and spoke to them. That was the last we saw of him.' He poured some baked beans in a pan. 'It does funny things to people. Time on their hands.'

30

Dermot called from the front door: 'I'll be off now, leave you to it.'

Eamonn looked up from his laptop. 'Are you going for a walk? Did you want me to come with you?' Not *Do you want me to come with you?* A linguistic feint. A hypothetical offer. Dermot responded as Eamonn knew he would.

'No, not at all. You have work to do. I don't want to get in the way.'

'I should get on with it really. I've let it mount up since Laura went.'

'You can't do that – you have to earn your living.'

Eamonn felt a flicker of irritation. It passed as quickly as it had come. The point was inarguable.

'So . . . another walk?'

'I'm not walking today. I'm getting a lift with your one down the way.'

His father had some strange reluctance to use people's names. 'Your man', 'the fella with the hat', 'your one with the limp'.

'Which one?'

'The Swedish lady.'

'Inga?'

'That's right. Apparently there's a big DIY place out off the motorway. She's off to buy some stuff for her painting and I thought I'd maybe go along and pick up one or two things.'

Eamonn nodded vaguely, having already opened up his work email and become distracted.

'OK. Well . . . have fun. I'll see you later.'

He didn't notice the door close. He stared at the screen: fifty-three assignments to mark plus the six phone tutorials he had booked in. He headed straight to the kitchen to find some kind of coffee substitute. Since Laura had gone, he'd started speaking his thoughts out aloud, issuing abrupt little snorts at his own internal commentary. He didn't want to be the kind of person who did such things. He thought consuming less caffeine might help. He settled for a bracing pot of laugh-free yoghurt and returned to his laptop. He thought he'd just write a quick email to her, letting her know what he was up to. He liked to keep her informed. When he'd finished that, gone to the loo, checked the kitchen cupboards one more time, there was really nothing for it but to open up the Beginner-level assignments. 'Lesson Twelve: At the Shopping Mall'. Robert was looking for a new jumper. The students had to fill in Julia the shop assistant's half of the exchange.

> R: Hello, I'd like to buy a sweater.
> J: . . . .
> R: That's nice. Can I try it on?
> J: . . . .
> R: Do you have it in blue?
> J: . . . .
> R: No, it must be blue, to match my blue trousers.
> J: . . . .
> R: Thank you. Goodbye.

Eamonn used to think Robert was a dick, with his weird need to match his jumper to his trousers. But now, post-Laura, he felt a tenderness towards Robert. He saw Julia for who she was. Robert was a man in need of help. He clearly had no idea what he was doing. He'd evidently lost his way in life. But Julia wouldn't throw him a line, not even to say: 'You know, a grey sweater would look fine.' She'd let Robert carry on searching high and low and when she saw him that night in the bar, on his own, in his matching blue sweater and trousers, she and her girlfriends would laugh remorselessly. Eamonn shook his head. Julia was a complete cow. He didn't know how he hadn't seen it before.

Lenguanet were based in Madrid and had contracts to provide online language tuition to civil servants across several autonomous communities. Students submitted their work online and tutors returned the work marked within an agreed time frame. In the face of massive cuts in government spending, however, many communities were cancelling their contracts and the company were laying off tutors. Having fallen badly behind, it was fortunate for Eamonn that his cohort of Asturian health workers were particularly slow in making their way through the course and that his manager was too preoccupied by the implosion of the company to check up on his activity.

The work was repetitive, enlivened only by the monthly phone tutorials that each student was obliged to complete. Eamonn had sent mails the previous night to his Advanced-level students to arrange slots for the day. He had enough self-knowledge to realize he was currently nowhere near robust enough to conduct Beginner-level phone tutorials. Although straightforward in theory, with the student simply following a script, the reality was different. The students, with effectively no English language at all, understandably found the idea of a telephone conversation with a faceless teacher terrifying. They rarely understood what was required of them, or which part of the script they should read, or even that there was a script.

Eamonn would answer the phone to the sound of a stranger hyperventilating. Random words – some English, some

Spanish – would start coming at him like stray bullets. He would tell them to look at the script, would try to reassure them, but his English outpourings only made them panic more. Sometimes, against the rules, he attempted to speak to them in Spanish, but his Spanish was so poor that it either went entirely unnoticed or caused even greater confusion when they spoke Spanish back to him. The calls generally descended into both student and teacher throwing out words they did not themselves fully understand and which could not be understood by the other. Latterly Eamonn had adopted the approach of grimly ploughing on through the script regardless of the students' utter incomprehension and mounting anxiety. It was a gruelling and baffling ordeal, a kind of anti-communication, and the perfect inoculation against any desire to learn a foreign language.

Within each call, though, there was a small epiphany. No matter how rocky the crossing, how fraught the previous nine minutes had been, there was always a brief moment of connection at the very end. Eamonn would say 'Goodbye' several times until the student heard and recognized it. The student seized upon the word like someone adrift at sea for weeks – both because they had finally understood something and that what they had understood was that their ordeal was almost at an end. There was always a second of stunned silence and then a flurry of reciprocal goodbyes. Despite himself, Eamonn found something moving in the moment, the pure thrill of communication against the odds; he felt much as he thought Alexander Graham Bell must have felt as he made his first ever phone call. In his current emotionally raw state, though, Eamonn wasn't sure he could withstand that instant of redemption and hope without bursting into tears.

As it was, the calls with the Advanced students were bad enough. It was the responsibility of the tutor to keep the

conversation going for twenty minutes. Often it wasn't a problem, the students loved practising the language and were happy
to chat about whatever came into their minds, but Eamonn
was aware that he was failing to return the conversational ball.

'So . . . José María . . . what have you been doing since we
last spoke?'

'Well, actually, it has been a very interesting time. My wife
and I went on a fascinating holiday.'

'Oh, good. Good. That sounds nice. I'm glad you did that.'

Long pause.

'Would you like to know where we went?'

'Oh. OK, yes – that would be great.'

He saved Encarna till last. He found something quite intimi-
dating about her. It wasn't just that her English appeared to be
the equal of, if not superior to, his own. It was more that she
seemed to be humouring him, as if she were the one being
paid to make small talk. He found this impression confusing
and unnerving.

'Hello, Eamonn, it is Encarna.'

'Hello, Encarna. How are you?'

The sound of smoke being exhaled.

'So-so.'

'OK. Good. So how did you find Unit 18?'

'You want my honest opinion?'

Eamonn could think of little he wanted less. 'Of course.'

'I thought it was ridiculous.'

'Oh. I'm sorry to hear that.'

'Why must we read such stupid articles? Always a silly thing
from the newspapers. A funny story. I don't even think this one
was true. This woman from Korea, who ends up in Torquay
rather than Turkey? Please – it's preposterous.'

There was a pause.

'Yes. You're right. It's bollocks.'

He heard Encarna laugh for the first time. 'Bollocks. That's the right word for it.'

'Encarna, why are you doing this course?'

'I thought it might be interesting.'

'And has it been?'

'Not really. Not until now.'

'Why now?'

'Because now we are really communicating. We are finding out things we want to know. We are not talking about the weather in Scotland, or Christmas shopping on Oxford Street, or . . . what was it? . . . morris dancers.'

'Those fucking morris dancers.'

She laughed again. 'Exactly.'

'You have a nice laugh.'

'Thank you.'

'I wish I heard it more often.' Eamonn felt slightly out of control, as if he were reading a script someone else had written.

'Really?'

'We should do this more often. A proper conversation. Maybe I could visit you?'

'I'm sorry?'

'Maybe we could meet up sometime? I could come up to Asturias. You could show me the grass and the cider.'

'Erm . . . we're a long way from each other.'

'You sound sultry. I don't think I've ever told you that. It's probably the fags.'

'I'm sorry?'

'You're right, too far. Anyway, what's so fucking special about grass and cider? Jesus, I could go to Hereford for that. Fucking morris men!'

'Eamonn, are you OK?'

'I'm just saying, it'd be nice to do this more often. To talk.

177

On the phone. Have you ever had phone sex?'

'Eamonn! I think this isn't a good day for you.'

'No, no it's not, you're right, but when is? Can't sit around waiting for a good day to come along, can we? Never get anything done.' There was silence at the other end of the line. 'I was joking about the phone sex. I don't even understand what it is.'

'Please stop talking about it!'

'I'm not talking about it. I'm just saying it was a joke.'

'I won't have phone sex with you!'

'Well, you keep mentioning it –'

The line went dead. He was still staring at the image of the red telephone receiver when a new call came through on his headphones. The screen showed the caller identity as Francesca, his manager at Lenguanet.

'Hello, Francesca, I've been meaning to call you.'

'Hello, Eamonn.'

'You might have seen I'd let a little backlog build up, but I'm getting back on top of things now . . .'

'Yes, I saw you had a few phone tutorials scheduled for today . . .'

'Yeah. Sorry about the last couple of weeks. I've had a few problems, but . . .'

'. . . And as you know we randomly monitor the quality of the service our tutors provide.'

'. . .'

'So I thought today would be a good day to do that.'

Eamonn was quiet for a while. 'I would describe today as atypical.'

Silence.

'I was joking about the phone sex.'

More silence.

'I'm fired.'

'Correct.'

He closed the laptop. Walked to his bedroom, climbed into his bed and curled into a tight ball. He awoke hours later to sounds of hammering and the smell of fish fingers.

31

After a thorough inventory Dermot was almost impressed to discover that not a single thing in the flat worked the way it should. Nothing. Not a tap, not a cupboard door, not even the toilet seat. It reminded him of his pal Jack Dempsey, who took up DIY in his retirement and just about destroyed his family home. Whenever Dermot saw Jack in the pub, he would ask him what he was up to and the answer was always the same: 'Making improvements' – followed by a short nod of the head and a sip of his pint. He managed to hang the front gate backwards on a slope, rendering it impossible to open. Dermot would see the post flung on the garden path whenever he passed by the house. According to Kathleen, Jack's wife resorted to crushing up her Temazepam in his tea to keep him in his chair.

For all that Eamonn's place had been badly put together, none of it, as far as Dermot could see, was really beyond hope. The walls were good enough for a dry climate, the ceiling and floor sound. It wasn't going to fall down, which he knew was more than could be said for some of those other foreign developments. He'd seen the programmes on the telly: dream homes with cracks right through them; condominiums built on shallow foundations; stucco bungalows sliding down hillsides.

He'd gone around with a pad and pencil, making a note of everything that needed doing, and it was clear that every one of the problems should have been tackled a long time ago. The initial snags had been allowed to bloom into more serious issues. He found himself underlining words and adding exclamation marks as his incredulity at Eamonn's inaction mounted. Screws that could have been tightened before cupboard doors started hanging off and hinges became misshapen. Sealant that could have been applied before water pooled on the bathroom floor and the skirting board rotted. Doorstops that could have been fixed before handles made holes in the plaster walls.

Eamonn had never been handy, Dermot knew that. Some of the pieces he had brought home from woodwork as a boy could almost make Dermot weep. The amount of effort and glue that went into them was heart-breaking. 'My son's no labourer,' Kathleen used to say with pride. But he did not go on to be the doctor or solicitor that she had always assumed he would. Neither she nor Dermot had ever fully understood the different jobs he had done, in part because he never took the time to explain them. They were never anything simple or straightforward that Kathleen could tell the women at church. It was always: 'Something with computers.' Or 'Something to do with books.'

After Eamonn graduated, Kathleen became increasingly indignant that many of his cousins who had left school with far fewer qualifications seemed to be better off than him. John drove around in a BMW while Eamonn went most places on his bike or in Laura's old Renault. Brendan had moved into a brand-new, four-bed semi out in New Oscott, while Eamonn and Laura lived in a little Victorian terrace on a tatty road in Moseley. She blamed his employers. 'Your bosses are taking you for a ride, son.' 'You're too soft, that's your problem.' But he would roll his eyes and say that he didn't want to drive a BMW and he didn't want to live in New Oscott.

It was true that he and Laura went away on holiday a lot, but never anywhere that anyone else Kathleen and Dermot knew went. Rainforests and teeming cities, obscure islands and frozen peninsulas. Never once to Florida.

For Kathleen and Dermot, Eamonn's adult life was like a film with a plot they couldn't quite follow. They tried, but nothing made complete sense, as if they had missed a key scene, or the sound was turned down too low. Dermot was less concerned than Kathleen. There had always been an idea that she and Eamonn were on the same wavelength, that they understood each other in a way that Dermot did not, and yet the opacity of her son's choices threatened this. Heartbroken though she was when he announced his emigration, Dermot knew that a part of Kathleen was glad that Eamonn was moving to Spain. A friend of a friend's son had done the same thing. There were programmes about it on telly. It made for a story that was easy to tell and made their son seem like everyone else.

Dermot didn't feel any disappointment in Eamonn. He was mildly baffled by his life, but felt, above all, that it was his to live. For Kathleen, the disappointment was not in Eamonn, but in herself. She reproached herself for always saying the wrong thing, for failing to understand him as she felt she should. He'd always been interested in books and films, but if ever she mentioned one she'd heard of, it was never one he was bothered about. He never wore the jumpers she bought him each Christmas. Dermot would hear her testing the water, sending out depth charges:

'Peggy said that Brendan has all the Sky channels – the whole caboodle.'

A shrug.

'I hear 3D is making a comeback in the cinemas. They're all doing it now.'

A grunt.

'I don't care for that Home Secretary. I think he's shifty.'

A roll of the eyes.

And yet their bond remained. It was to her, not Dermot, that Eamonn had spoken on the phone each week. He could be impatient with her, irritated by her, but there was a certain closeness there that Dermot knew he and his son did not share. In latter years Eamonn had refused to accept how ill his mother was and for her part Kathleen had not wanted him to know. Dermot had heard them discussing the idea of Kathleen visiting Eamonn out in Spain. He wasn't sure who was kidding themselves more. When he tried to speak to Eamonn about it all he got back was:

'Dad, you've been saying she's at death's door for years. She'll outlive us all.'

He had put his arm around him at the graveside. The first time he had held him since he was a boy. He was all bones.

He was painting the wall behind the front door, where he had filled a hole, when Eamonn emerged from the lounge.

'Is this ever going to end?'

'Sorry?'

'All this.' He gestured vaguely in Dermot's direction: 'Is that going to make the flat smell?'

'What?'

'The paint. It gives me a headache. I don't want the flat stinking of it.'

Dermot looked at him. 'It's matt, son, not gloss. It has no smell.'

'Good.' He walked off.

Dermot finished painting and then carefully laid the brush down and crossed into the lounge. Eamonn lay on the couch, staring at his laptop. Dermot picked up the machine and, without closing it, placed it gently on the other side of the room.

'Dad! What are you doing?'

Dermot sat in the chair across from Eamonn.

'Back on the buses, you'd get these characters. Young boys in particular. They liked to carve their names in the windows with their Stanley knives, or cut out pieces of the upholstery as if it were prized animal hide, or spray meaningless scribble all over the top deck. What would you call people like that?'

'I don't know what you're talking about.'

'Just answer me, if you can. What would you call people like that?'

Eamonn was exasperated. 'I don't know. Vandals.'

'Yes. I'd say that was right. They were vandals. Destructive and shameless vandals. But the thing is, son, they weren't idiots. They had no respect for property, but at least, you'd have to say, at least, it wasn't their own property.'

'Good, well that's –'

Dermot spoke over him. 'At least they hadn't spent all their money on a brand-new flat and been too idle to lift a finger to stop it falling apart. They didn't worry that a spot of paint might give them a headache and then stare at a computer screen all day and night. They didn't sit in their pyjamas in the middle of the afternoon feeling sorry for themselves.' He stood up and retrieved the laptop, placing it back in front of Eamonn. 'No. Someone like that, son, would be a vandal and an idiot.' He turned and left the room.

32

'Eamonn.' She spoke softly. 'Let's get out.'

He smiled. 'Out where?'

'Away from here. Let's leave. Let's not come back.'

He gave a little laugh. 'That'd be nice.'

'Well, let's just walk away.'

'What?'

'Give the keys back to the agents. People do that.'

'They do, and they lose their deposits, everything they invested.'

'We could start again.'

'Over a hundred and eighty thousand pounds.'

'It's just money.'

He laughed.

She didn't.

'But you're the one who's always saying everything's OK. "We have each other." "Give it time." You know, all that upbeat, positive stuff you do so well. You're the one rattling out the novel. I thought you were fine.'

She held his gaze. 'I am.'

His face changed and he rolled back on the pillow. 'It's me. I'm letting the side down.'

'It's nothing to do with letting the side down. You're really not happy here.'

'I'm just adjusting.'

She hesitated before speaking again. 'I think you had higher expectations than me.' She paused. 'Unrealistic expectations.'

'What, the writing?'

'Partly that.'

'Well, what else?'

'I don't want us to fight.'

'We're not fighting.'

'I'm worried we're about to.'

'Why don't you just say whatever you want to say?'

'You thought you'd be a different person here.'

He said nothing.

'And I don't know why you wanted that. I loved the person you were.'

'"Loved"?'

'I still love you, but I'm worried about you. I don't think this place is good for you.'

'Why?'

'Oh, Eamonn, come on. You're not yourself, you're lost.'

'I'm just getting used to it.'

'You need stuff around you to rub against. There's nothing here.'

'While you have such a rich interior life . . .'

'I'm not saying all this so that you can sneer at me.'

He closed his eyes. 'I'm sorry.'

She was quiet for a while. 'You have no one and nothing to pick apart here but yourself.'

He had his head turned away from her, his eyes screwed shut. He tried to control his breathing. When he looked back at her he forced a smile he did not feel, affected a lightness in his tone.

'I thought you were writing about Goya, not studying GCSE psychology.'

But she remained serious. 'If we've made a mistake, we can admit it and walk away. There's no virtue in punishing ourselves.'

'Laura, honestly, it's fine. I'm sorry if I'm grumpy sometimes. I'm finding my feet. The fact is we're living in a beautiful place, we have each other, we have total freedom. How could anyone be unhappy? Only an idiot would consider that a mistake.'

She looked at him for a long time, searching his face for something, and finally gave up. She flopped back on the pillow and sighed. He leaned over her.

'Why has that made you sad? I thought it would make you happy.'

She seemed resigned. 'I know you did. I know you did.'

33

The toll motorway was abandoned. Signage in every tunnel warned them to keep their distance from other vehicles. They had driven over ten kilometres and were yet to see another car. He had been up and out early that morning, managing to recharge the car's battery with David's help, and that had felt like an ambitious and successful start to the day. But now, as he sped along the empty road, he could think of few experiences that could engender such a sense of loneliness.

The trip was his way of an apology after the incident with the paint. His father had seemed surprised and pleased by the suggestion and Eamonn hoped their argument was forgotten. It was a rare and unsettling thing to see Dermot angry.

In the early days he and Laura had often taken daytrips and excursions to places near and far. But, contrary to expectation or logic, as he had grown disenchanted with Lomaverde he had also grown increasingly reluctant to leave it. Laura would suggest escapes to cities, the distraction of other human beings, of bars and museums, even of traffic, but Eamonn knew that they would have to return, and in that way seemed to drag Lomaverde and its attendant atmosphere of failure and despair with him wherever he went.

Sometimes, sitting on the terrace, he'd see a distant plane passing mutely overhead and he would be filled with the urge to spell out SOS in patio furniture. The sense that they were stranded – isolated but also captive – was at times overpowering. He would try to remind himself of all the people who would give a great deal to be where he was at that moment, to remember that he was free to come and go as he wished and could rejoin the wider population by just walking to the nearest town, but it rarely convinced. And now, the silent motorway seemed to confirm his worst fears, leaving the troubling impression that the wider population had fled. The passing landscape provided no comfort. Arid hills flattened out into vast agricultural planes encased in plastic, interrupted only by the occasional bright green, intensively irrigated golf course. Everywhere were sun-bleached advertising hoardings for new towns and developments just like Lomaverde, and the horizon was scattered with motionless cranes.

Dermot broke the silence. 'It's a lovely bit of road, eh? I wish there were more like this back in Brum.'

Eamonn smiled weakly in agreement.

'Did you hear they wanted to put cycle lanes along the Stratford Road?'

'No.'

Dermot nodded, his eyes wide with incredulity. 'Yes. The Stratford Road. Did you ever hear anything like it?'

Eamonn was unsure what response was required.

'I said to Sammy, "Sure there's not enough room for the cars let alone the bikes!"'

Eamonn turned his head briefly. 'I think that's the idea. Prioritize bikes . . . and buses.'

'Jesus, you wouldn't want more of those lunatics weaving in and out of the traffic.'

'But they wouldn't have to weave in and out because they'd have their own lane.'

'Everything has to be green now, doesn't it? That's the latest fad.'

'It's not really a fad, is it?'

'Like the last thing, what was it? "Nouvelle cuisine".'

Eamonn stared ahead. His father had read an article about

nouvelle cuisine at some point in the 1980s and had never really gotten over it.

They drove to the small town of San José and found some-where for lunch. When Eamonn had visited the restaurant before with Laura the place had been bustling, but now, on an early-season Tuesday lunchtime, the only other diners were a nervous-looking German family sat in the corner. He couldn't think of a single other occasion on which he and his father had eaten in a restaurant together.

'They've got all kinds of fish, or they do chicken if you'd prefer; it says with chips, but I'm sure they could do it with boiled potatoes if you want.'

Dermot pointed to the menu: 'Doesn't that say "*paella*"?'

'Yes it does.'

Dermot closed the menu. 'I'll have that.'

Eamonn looked at him. He had never seen his father ven-ture as far as a hamburger, much less anything more exotic.

'*Paella*? Do you know what it is?'

Dermot tutted. 'I'm not a complete ignoramus. Of course I know what it is.'

'But you don't eat seafood.'

'There's me thinking I grew up eating mussels and whelks and seaweed.'

Eamonn looked at him doubtfully. 'What about the rice, it'll have stuff in it. Mom was always careful to never give you spicy food.'

'That's because she couldn't stand the smell. I worked along-side men from Pakistan and the West Indies all my life, do you think I never ate anything spicy?'

Afterwards, they walked over towards Playa de los Genoveses. He had noticed that his father had developed a habit of launching into anecdotes halfway through, as if the story had been running in his head for some time before he started to speak.

'She kept saying she was getting fat. Her skirts didn't fit her any more. She'd give out about it, asking me why she was putting on weight when she wanted to lose it. As if I had any idea. To be honest I'd barely noticed. I thought anyway that just happened to women as they got older, got a bit thicker round the middle. I knew better though than to say a word. It would have been bad enough agreeing she was putting on a few pounds without telling her it was because of her age. I knew to keep my mouth shut.'

'You're talking about Mom, right?'

Dermot looked at him as if he were simple. 'Of course. Anyway, then she got ill. A tummy upset of some sort that wouldn't go away. She'd always been terrible for avoiding doctors, said she saw enough of them at work. She told me it would clear up by itself.'

'What was it?'

'I had no idea. One day I got home from my shift and there she was lying on the bathroom floor. Her face green. I'd had enough. I took her up to the surgery myself, her protesting all the way.

'I'd never set foot in the place before. I felt like her gaoler dragging her in to see the doctor. Left to her own devices though I knew she'd say nothing.

'Anyway, the doctor, Wiley he was called, he examined her stomach and I got a bit of a shock when I saw how swollen she was. After he'd prodded her about she sat back next to me and squeezed my hand and I knew then right enough that she was terrified. She said: "Doctor, is it some sort of growth?"

'He peered at her over the top of his glasses, just like they do on the telly. "Yes. Some sort of growth, Mrs Lynch," he said. "A baby."' Dermot shook his head as if hearing the news again. 'My first reaction was to hit him. Some stuck-up old bastard having a laugh at the Paddies. But he carried on talking, saying she'd have to have some tests, but assuring us she was pregnant, a good way along. I remember he said: "Given your past history and your age, I'd say it was something of a miracle." Then he smiled and said: "Congratulations." I'll never forget that smile. It was a good one.'

Eamonn gave a short laugh. 'What? That was me?'

'Who else would it be?'

'That's a great story. I can't believe I've never heard it before.'

'Your mother didn't really like to talk about it, to be honest. I think she was embarrassed not to have picked up on the signs. It was such a shock.'

'So was I not planned?'

'You were indeed. Good God, you were planned. You and all the others.'

'What others?'

'The ones that never came. There was never any question that we wanted kids. Jesus, we had you all named before we were married, but it just didn't happen.

'We were careful for the first year, we just wanted to wait until we'd moved from the flat to a house, that was all. But for years after your mother insisted that us being cautious for a few months had jinxed us for ever. "We sent a message that a baby wasn't wanted," she'd say, and I could never understand who she thought we'd sent this message to, who would so deliberately misunderstand our intentions. God, I suppose.

'Anyway, we were married fourteen years and everyone around us was on to their fifth or sixth kid. It was tough, especially on your mother, very tough. All the false alarms and disappointments.' He paused and lowered his voice. 'The cycles, you know, all that business, apparently hers had never been regular, so it was awful hard for her to know what was going on and avoid building her hopes up.' He paused again. 'It was hard for both of us.' He looked at Eamonn and grinned. 'And then you came along. We just couldn't believe it. It was like a miracle.'

Eamonn winced at the word. He connected it with uncles and aunts ruffling his hair and pinching his cheeks. He'd never considered the meaning as a child, just thought it was one of the many mystifying or irritating things that relatives came out with.

'I bet you'd got used to just being the two of you.'

Dermot shook his head. 'We had not. Not at all. That was never the idea.'

It was a rare, overcast day. The beach was largely deserted and the wind blustery. They walked along the sand. Dermot marched briskly with his head up, while Eamonn meandered and stopped often to examine the small towers and circles of stones he found on the sand. San José had a vaguely hippy vibe and he wasn't sure if the stones were some neo-Pagan trimmings or just pretty patterns on the sand. Either way he found them unsettling, reminiscent only of burial mounds. They reminded him of the bodies washed up on San Pedro beach. He tried to imagine what the migrants might have made of the Promised Land had they lived. An unfathomable fantasy world of golf courses, polytunnels and empty streets. He imagined their ghosts, restless spirits roaming the Costa, huddling in sandy bunkers and silent shopping malls.

His father was waiting for him at the water's edge. As Eamonn approached, Dermot dropped his Villa bag on the sand and crouched down to look through it. He pulled out a neatly rolled-up towel.

'So. I'd say it's been long enough since dinner.' Eamonn was aghast to see, inside the towel, a pair of swimming trunks at least as old as him.

'Are you thinking of going in?'

'Of course I am. Are you not?'

'I hadn't really planned to.'

'What? Look at it. You'd be mad not to.'

'The water will still be cold, it's only June.'

'Ah come on. It'll do you good. Nothing like a plunge in the sea to clear the head.'

'I've not brought my stuff.'

'Sure you could swim in your pants, no one's going to notice.'

Eamonn ran his hand over his face. 'Oh God. OK, OK.'

Dermot grinned and clapped him on the arm.

Eamonn shook his head. 'It's going to be horrible.'

Dermot got changed quickly and Eamonn watched him stride into the water up to his knees and then stand motionless. His arms and the back of his neck were a deep red, but the skin on his back and legs was a creamy white. It looked newborn set against the dark, weather-beaten extremities. He felt an unexpected tenderness towards his father's body. A sadness that there was no one but him to see its trueness and beauty. Dermot walked forward and plunged head first into a wave.

Eamonn's own entrance into the water was typically protracted and tortuous. He waded gingerly up to his knees and then launched into an ungainly, jumpy kind of run into deeper waters, the cold like a hard kick to his balls. He thrashed about furiously and when the pain finally receded he lay on his back and trod water.

Looking up at the sky, he wondered for the first time how his and Laura's childlessness might have seemed to his parents. Did they assume that they wanted children? Did they pity them?

The question had bobbed up to the surface between him and Laura occasionally over the years. In their twenties they had been baffled by the appeal of parenthood. They looked at every stage, from pregnancy, through childbirth, to the arrival of a baby and saw only pain, terror and hardship. When they thought of a baby they thought only of all the things they would lose.

After she'd hit thirty Laura became more ambivalent. She still didn't actively want a baby, but neither could she be certain that she would never want one. She found the finality of the decision unsettling. She shared her doubts with Eamonn:

'What if we change our minds and it's too late?'

'What if we can't have children anyway?'

'What if not having kids sends us funny and we start collecting figurines?'

What she wanted above all else was certainty. She read discussion forums on the Internet of the defiantly child-free and the fervent breeders, each group accusing the other of selfishness. The research, she said, had been inconclusive.

Eamonn's position had changed. He had grown to like the idea of children, or at least a child, but still found the prospect daunting.

'Maybe no one is ever certain,' he said.

'But it's a big decision.'

'Maybe you have to just jump.'

'Do you think we should?'

But he didn't want to persuade her; he wanted her to be completely sure.

He thought now of Dermot's words. His parents had not considered themselves complete without children. They seemed to see themselves on the periphery of their own relationship. He found the idea stranger the more he thought about it. It suggested that falling in love created rather than filled an emptiness. He imagined them living in their three-bedroom house for all the years before he came along, waiting. He wondered if he and Laura had been waiting for something all these years and not even known it.

When he raised his head he saw he had drifted further out than he had realized. He saw his dad, a distant figure on the beach, a towel round his waist, walking away back to the line of prickly pears beyond the sand. Eamonn tried to stand but found he had floated out of his depth.

His legs were beginning to ache and he decided he too would go back. He started to swim, but seemed to make no progress. He put his head down again and swam harder, thrashing his arms and legs until he was short of breath. He lifted his eyes from the water and felt a small pulse of panic as he saw the beach still just as far away and the orange buoy still bobbing out of reach in front of him. He tried once more but was unable to free himself of the current. He turned around to see if there was anything he could drift out to, but instead was hit full in the face by a swell and took in water through his mouth and nose. He tried to float on his back again but the waves rolled over his head. His arms and legs were heavy now and hard to lift out of the water. He felt himself being dragged down and only then considered that he might drown. For a split second he felt not fear but surprise and a kind of disappointment that this is how it would all end. Then another swell washed over him and straightforward terror gripped him. As he came up from the next submersion, he heard a voice calling for help and recognized it as his own.

It seemed only seconds before he felt his father's hand clutching him, his other arm encircling his neck and pulling him along. They struggled for a while, the two of them, and he heard Dermot's ragged breathing as he fought the current with one arm, saying over and over again: 'I've got you. I've got you.'

When they reached shallow water, Eamonn's legs were too weak to walk. Dermot dragged him up on to the beach and lay him on the sand. He disappeared from Eamonn's view for a moment and returned with the towel. He placed it over his son's body and tucked it in all around. Eamonn wanted to ask if Dermot was OK, but he found it hard to speak.

'I saw you were in trouble. I was on my way back out to you before you started calling.' He was rubbing Eamonn's chest, trying to warm him up. 'What a fecking idiot I am, forcing you in there when you didn't want to go and then walking off and leaving you. If your mother was alive, she'd murder me.' He kept on rubbing. 'I'm sorry, son, I'm sorry. You're all right now. You're all right.'

Eamonn was watching his father's face close up. A scar on his chin. His wild eyebrows. The blue of his eyes.

'You're all right, Eamonn. God, I'm sorry. You gave me such a fright.'

Eamonn pulled his arm out from under the towel and laid a hand on his father's cheek. Dermot stopped rubbing, kneeled back on his haunches and held his son's hand to his face.

34

He stepped from the warm evening air into the church. He dipped his fingers into the stone font, dabbing holy water on his head, chest and shoulders, and then stood for a moment, unsure where to go, unmoored without Kathleen and Eamonn at his side. They sat in the same pew every Sunday. Eamonn squeezing between his legs and the iron bars of the radiator, seemingly finding the clankings and clicks of the ancient heating system more mysterious and significant than the words of the priest. While Kathleen was deep in prayer, her eyes shut, her lips moving, Dermot would pass sweets to the toddler. A rainbow drop. A Flump. A foam shrimp. Tiny points of colour in the half-light.

He hadn't been to confession since he was a boy. Father Cahill had been his priest then, a giant crow of a man. He'd manifest himself in the schoolroom unexpectedly, shoulders hunched, knees cracking, stalking up and down the desks, rapping boys' heads with his knuckles if they gave a wrong answer to questions of faith.

Dermot's father made them attend confession every week.

'What will we say?' Dominic would whisper to Dermot in a panic on the waiting pew.

'You've to confess your sins.'

'But I don't know what sins I've done.' His brother's voice high, terrified by what he had failed to do. Dermot would invent sins for them both. Dominic had broken his mother's teapot and blamed the cat. Dermot had written bad words in the back of the family Bible. Dominic had been gluttonous at table. He invented sins to confirm to the priest that boys were essentially feral creatures and that penance was a blessed and necessary sacrament.

Most weeks the only bona fide sin he could think of was the previous week's fabrication of sins. He tried to imagine what the priest would do if he confessed to that. He was sure that lying to a priest was a very bad thing. The kind of thing for which he might go to hell. But hell seemed distant and unconvincing. Like God and Jesus. Cahill, on the other hand, and particularly his right fist, was close and ever present.

He moved away from the porch and took a pew on the far side of the church where he could watch unseen. Over by the two doors there were quite a few waiting their turn. Five thirty on a fine Saturday evening. He hadn't known what to expect.

Back home you'd just had to work out who was ahead of you in the queue and then go in when you saw them come out. Now there were lights above the confessional – one red, one green. They looked festive. Reminiscent of parties or doctors' waiting rooms.

He noticed a lag between people leaving the booth and the green light going on. He wondered what the priest was doing in those intervals. Recovering? Praying? Listening to the final score? He imagined Father Walsh, sitting in the dark, preparing his words carefully.

He had yet to see anyone looking distraught. Cahill had always managed to reduce at least a couple of sinners each week to tears. Dermot and Dominic used to speculate how he did it. Did he refuse them absolution? Rain down hellfire and damnation? Did he pull back the screen and give them a punch?

Whatever he'd done, Walsh was not doing it. The penitents emerged from the door looking relaxed, serene, often smiling. They made their way over to a pew in front of the altar, kneeled and bowed their heads for a few moments and then left. Two Hail Marys, Dermot estimated, at most.

But Dermot knew of course that Walsh was no Cahill. He was a modern priest. Kathleen was always telling him so. A friend to all. Feared by none. Guitars in church. Jokes in the sermon. The once-annual parish trip now augmented with prayer retreats, youth weekends and summer camps. Walsh would tell Kathleen of his plans to make the parish more vibrant, to re-energize the whole community in Jesus's love. 'Renewal' was the word Dermot heard her use a lot.

When Tommy Nolan suffered a heart attack the previous month, it was Pat Quinlon, not Kathleen, who pestered Dermot to step in as driver for the parish trip. Kathleen would know how little relish the prospect held for him. The worst kind of busman's holiday. He'd planned a day with Eamonn at Dudley Zoo, showing him the sleepy lions and the old castle, but found himself making a pilgrimage to the shrine at Walsingham instead.

It was a hot day. Four hours there and four hours back. Kathleen sat directly behind Dermot with Eamonn asleep on her lap and Walsh beside her. The priest was in high spirits, very talkative. He told Kathleen all about his time at the seminary, his travels in Africa, the year he spent in France, the books he had read, a quiz he liked on Radio 4. The only time he stopped speaking was to stand up and lead the congregation in a sing-song. Not all hymns. 'Leaving on a Jet Plane', 'Fernando'. Dermot recognized them from the radio. He was a modern priest.

Once they got to Walsingham, Dermot learned that there was to be a pilgrim mass. He tried to speak to Kathleen alone.

'It's not really suitable for Eamonn.'

'Why not? It's only like going to church on a Sunday.'

'On a Sunday he hasn't spent four hours on a coach.'

'He was asleep for most of it. Anyway, he enjoyed the songs.'

'There are no other kids on the trip at all. It's not really been planned with children in mind.'

'He's fine.'

'We're not that far from the coast. Why don't we slip off for a bit? We can be back in a couple of hours. You can still visit the shrine.'

'I can't do that.'

'Why not?'

'I want to go to the mass, that's the point of this, Dermot. And anyway, Father needs me to help.'

'Right.'

She hesitated. 'Why don't you take Eamonn off? I don't suppose you'll really be too sad to miss the service yourself, will you?'

She and Walsh were late getting back to the coach. Everyone was waiting. Eamonn tired and teary. They'd been walking the 'Holy Mile', they said, Walsh explaining the medieval symbolism of the statue of the Virgin.

'You know how I am when I get going,' he said by way of apology, and the other pilgrims laughed.

Dermot was alone in the church, the last penitents having made their reparations to God and left. The green light remained on over the confessional door. The style of the priest might change but the church remained the same – a menacing Victorian pile, the stained-glass windows clogged with dirt, the interior impermeable to sunlight. Dermot looked up at the murky oil paintings on the wall depicting the Stations of the Cross. He read the title under each image, something dogged and awful in their detailing of every humiliation: Jesus falls the first time, Jesus falls the second time, Jesus falls the third time, Jesus is stripped of his garments. Images from a horror film. Muddy renderings of cruelty and pain hovering above Eamonn's head every Sunday. The nails going on. The spear in the side. The boy was three years old.

He went in then. Closing the door firmly behind him.

The priest began automatically, like a coin-operated side-show: 'In the name of the Father, and of the Son, and of the Holy Spirit, Amen.'

Dermot didn't join in. He felt too big for the space, as though he were in a Wendy house.

'I'm ready to hear your confession now.'

He didn't want to kneel down.

'In your own time.'

He could smell Imperial Leather soap. He stood against the back wall, looking down at the grille. The silence was longer this time.

'I'm here to listen.'

He could hear him breathing.

Walsh cleared his throat. 'Will you not say what you've come here to say?'

Neither man spoke for minutes. There was a shuffling, the priest moving closer, trying to see, then quietly, as if not wanting to be overheard, he said, 'Dermot. I know it's you.'

Dermot nodded slowly, waiting.

Walsh tried again: 'What is it you want to say to me?' He sounded wary. A long pause and then, almost a whisper: 'Does Kathleen know you're here?'

Dermot scratched his nose.

'Keep speaking, Father. You have a talent for it.'

35

Eamonn left Rosemary and Gill's air-conditioned lobby and stepped out into the clammy night. He was a little woozy with whiskey. He had felt an aching kind of emptiness in his chest since being dragged from the sea, as if something had come out of him. Scotch had seemed a good remedy, the heat somehow masking the hollowness.

They'd been pulling into the development when the two women had flagged them down. They had insisted he and Dermot join them for the evening. His dad hit it off with the two of them instantly and they in turn seemed to find him a scream.

Eamonn was aware that he policed his father's attitudes. There was really no evidence that Dermot was racist or sexist or homophobic, but that hadn't stopped Eamonn charging both his parents with these crimes over the years. He picked them up on the things that they said. They might not hold hatred in their hearts for a gay couple, but that wouldn't stop his parents referring to them as 'that funny pair'. They might love Fats Domino but still refer to him as 'coloured'. It was what you said, not just what you felt, Eamonn tried to explain. Maybe it was a generational thing, but he had always thought it should be monitored, addressed, fixed.

'It's strange that none of my mates have ever corrected me,' Dermot once said in a rare moment of frustration. 'And they come from Trinidad and Jamaica and Pakistan and Bangladesh. You're always telling me what I should call them, but I never see you with a friend that isn't white.'

And Eamonn had tried to brush that away, insisting it was an exaggeration and moreover an irrelevance. But it lingered between them, an inconvenient truth.

Dermot had of course said nothing remotely questionable all evening. He had been in high spirits. Possibly, Eamonn reflected, a reaction to the earlier drama and shock. They had not been at Rosemary and Gill's long when his father spotted the pack of cards.

'Do you like to play a hand or two?'

'We do,' said Gill. 'How about you? Could we persuade you to a few rounds of Whist? And Eamonn? Could you bear it? Would you humour us?'

'What do you say, son? Shall we have a go?' Dermot said. 'Now, Whist?' He turned to Eamonn and winked. 'Which one is that?'

They had played for hours and Eamonn had grown tired. He decided to leave as his father was setting about teaching the two women the many idiosyncrasies of the game of Twenty-Five. It wasn't until Eamonn walked away from their building that he realized how dark it was. The sky was cloudy and the streets black without the benefit of moonlight. He held out his mobile phone as a torch.

He remembered nights on holiday in Ireland. Walking back to the caravan site, after similarly interminable evenings of cards with relatives, the air thick with cigarette smoke, the atmosphere serious, the games impenetrable. His father holding his hand as they walked between towering black hedgerows. The air smelling sweet and strange. One time they walked straight into a donkey wandering the empty road in the moonless night. Eamonn screamed, the donkey brayed and his parents giggled. The memory felt like a dream.

He stopped and looked around him. He didn't know where he was. It was possible that lost in thought and muddled by alcohol he had strayed off course, or maybe it was simply that the familiar looked strange in the darkness. He stood still to try to get his bearings. The light from the phone was faint and he could see little more than a few feet in front of him. He had no idea how long he had been walking. It felt a long time, long enough certainly to have reached his own door. He peered into the blackness and had no inkling which way to go.

He continued a few steps in the same direction, hoping that his subconscious had been successfully navigating all along. But after just a few yards he stopped. There it was again: the sense he had had outside the half-built house. He was not alone.

He attempted cat speak. 'Psss wsss wssss wssss.' But no cat emerged. Squinting into the darkness he saw nothing. He started to walk again before remembering that he was lost. He was tired and uneasy and wanted very much to be home in his bed. He could think of no other option but to phone for help. Calling his father to rescue him for the second time in a day. As he dialled the number for Gill and Rosemary, he heard movement nearby.

'Dad? Is that you?' he called out.

Then, up close, a voice on the phone: 'Hello?'

'Gill.' His own voice too loud.

'Hello? Who's this?'

'Gill. It's me. I've got a bit lost. I can't see a thing out here.' He spoke more quietly, tried to sound light-hearted; it came out wrong.

'Eamonn, is that you?' There was laughter.

'Gill, listen, can you put my dad on . . .' The phone slipped from his hand and clattered on to the road, leaving him in total darkness.

'Fuck. Fuck.'

He dropped to his hands and knees, patting the ground around him. He had his arm outstretched. One moment the phone was nowhere, the next he felt the corner of the plastic casing pushing against his fingertips. He reached to grab it and as he did he felt something else touch his hand. Warm, light, gone in an instant. He yelped.

'Who's there?'

He stood up and turned in a circle, his arms out straight.

'What do you want?' There was nothing. Silence. Blackness. Suddenly he felt a disturbance of air behind him and he fled, no longer wanting to know who or what it was. He ran blindly, his breath ragged, until he saw a light bobbing in the distance and heard his father's voice.

'Eamonn? Eamonn? What are you up to?'

Eamonn ran right up to him.

'What's going on? Are you drunk?'

'There's someone out there. I dropped my phone and I felt someone touch my hand.'

'Who?'

'I don't know.'

Dermot shone his torch around and then back at Eamonn.

'Are you drunk?' he asked again.

'It happened the other day. Someone hiding. Watching me.'

Dermot looked around again. The street was empty and silent.

'Where did it happen the other time?'

'Over by the building site.'

'All right, then. You stay here and keep a lookout. I'll head down there, find out if someone's messing around.'

'No . . . let's just go home.'

'What? Why would we do that?' He shone the light in Eamonn's face. 'Are you scared?'

'Yes! A bit. Of course. It's scary.'

'There's no need to be scared. I'll leave you with the torch.'

'Dad.'

206

'What is it?'

Eamonn tried to laugh. 'You don't watch horror films, you don't understand. You don't split up.'

'For the love of God. It's not a horror film, son.' Dermot handed over the torch and started to go but Eamonn's hand shot out and held his father's arm tight. He turned and looked at Eamonn's face.

'OK, son. We'll head home.'

Back in the apartment he made him some sugary tea, which Eamonn found undrinkable.

'Some people pick up on these things,' said Dermot.

'What things?'

'Oh, ghosts and atmospheres and all that. I never did.'

'I don't believe in ghosts.'

'I don't reckon believing's anything to do with it. Just a sense. There are just some that have it and some that don't.'

He was quiet for a while and then said: 'Dominic and I were always out exploring old abandoned houses. Most of the time we were like wild animals running about the place, but every now and then something would scare him. He'd say he didn't want to go in a particular room, or didn't want to play in certain places. It drove me mad. I was forever trying to convince him there was nothing there, it was all in his imagination.'

'Not everyone shares your love of crumbling old ruins.'

'I remember one time, in the old Dempsey cottage, I asked him to look in one of the rooms for any old furniture or bits of wood we could try and burn. He just dithered about next to me until I shouted at him: "Will you go in the other room like I told you!" and he turned and said: "But, Dermot, I should wait till the man's finished fixing the door."'

He laughed. 'He wasn't even scared. Very matter-of-fact. He could see the funny side though. After that whenever we'd go anywhere I'd tease him. "Is that phantom carpenter doing any work here today?"'

He shook his head. 'I'm making him sound cracked. He wasn't. He was great company.'

Eamonn smiled.

Dermot looked at him. 'You're very like him sometimes.'

36

Dermot was awake again. Something about the heat had him waking and dozing, waking and dozing all night long. He drifted in and out of dreams. Each time he woke, the same breathless struggle to work out where he was. No sound or shape to give him a clue. He wondered at the time, his watch useless in the dark. He closed his eyes and saw a different shade of black.

He remembered another summer's evening, sitting in golden light watching shadows lengthen on the floor. His mother in the bed. Her black hair unfurled upon the pillow, as if she were underwater.

'Are you still there?'

'I am.'

'Come over and talk to me.'

'I thought you were sleeping.'

'I am and then I'm not. I don't know if I'm dreaming or awake. Let me hold your hand.'

He walked over to the bed and took her hand. Her fingers were dry twigs in his palm.

There was too much to be said, so they remained in silence. He sat on the bed and listened to the ticking of the clock, the rhythm of her breaths, the crows outside. After a while he laid his head on the pillow and she stroked him as if he were a little boy once more. He closed his eyes and felt that God was nowhere.

After her death they all sought to escape. An unseemly scramble to get away: first from their father, useless in grief, self-pitying and mean-tempered, and then from his new wife. There was nothing especially malign about Teresa and perhaps they should have been glad of someone to look after the old man, to cook and clean for all of them. But she was not their mother and her presence served only to deepen the fathomless hole left by the absence. Two of Dermot's older sisters became nuns. One brother left for Dublin, another for Liverpool. At fourteen, Dermot had finished school but was too young to leave home. He was sent to live with his grandmother over in Liscannor, who had room enough for one, leaving behind his baby sister, Eva, and his younger brother, Dominic.

Something buzzed past his head. He waved his hand and made brief contact, pushing the creature onwards through the darkness. A moment later it was back again.

When he thought of Liscannor now the memories were vivid but fragmentary: tearing down the road on Donal's motorbike; chasing Delia Byrne through the dunes; diving into giant waves under purple skies. He remembered exactly the hit of steam and vinegar from finger holes in chip wrappers, the lustre of Mary Fallon's lipstick, and the taste of his first Capstan.

The mosquito dived again and Dermot batted the air.

'If you had any sense you'd lay low.'

It wasn't so strange. Families dispersed, children scattered, homes were abandoned. It was the way things were. He kept in touch with Dominic. Postcards, visits at Christmas. But his own new life in Liscannor was full of incident. Eighteen months of tiptoeing about the house, of speaking in whispers, of feeling an unbearable heaviness pressing down on him were blasted away by the Atlantic. He had little interest in looking back, scant time or space for reflection on the way life had changed.

But when he contemplated those years now, it was not the

hijinks and antics in Liscannor that absorbed him, it was the thought of Dominic back at home with his father, Teresa and their new baby. He tried to imagine what his younger brother had done during gaunt winter afternoons and the long dusks of summer nights. Who had he gone gallivanting with? Who did he wake with frozen hands in the middle of the night when he was scared?

A sudden vibration by his ear and he sat up swinging his hand through the thick black air, missing over and over again.

If Dominic bore any bitterness or sadness at being left behind, he never let it show. It was, after all, the way things were. He got out himself soon enough. Leaving home at six-teen and heading to the States. Dermot had always thought that Dominic would follow him to England and he had often worried that America had been a kind of rebuke. A statement that Dominic was his own man, the little brother no more.

When he heard the whine again, he reached for the switch, flooding the room with light, revealing the insect on the wall. He got up and delivered a close blow, his open hand bursting the mosquito's swollen body on to the white plaster. He sat back on the bed, the room too bright, a trace of blood on his palm.

Young and careless. Stupid and preoccupied. He had let go of his brother's hand and he had lost him.

37

In the morning he wandered back down to the building site to investigate what he thought he'd seen the other day. His father now apparently thought he had a sixth sense. There were things Eamonn had to accept about his recent low state. Being single, being unemployed, being a poor swimmer – all these things he had no choice but to acknowledge as true, but possessing supernatural abilities was, he felt, overstretching his role.

Zigzagging down the winding roads, it was easy to lose track of where one was – each swathe of development looking the same as the one above it. Eamonn had learned to pick out small details of decay as landmarks on the many uninhabited stretches – a rust-coloured stain on a wall, a particular grouping of weeds, cables poking from the front of a lamp post.

The failure of Lomaverde was an excuse he could give for his own disillusionment with life there, but he feared the real reasons lay within himself. He had never been any good at fitting in. He was wary of people who didn't look like him, and contemptuous of those who did. He noticed things he did not want to notice, judged things he did not want to judge. A commentary always running somewhere in his head. He had really believed that away from England, away from the familiar, tedious triggers and his own tedious responses to them, he would be a better person. He would be his true self.

But on arriving in Spain he quickly discovered a terrible longing for all the things he'd thought he wanted to leave behind: lifestyle supplements, late-night bookies, teeming

Poundshops, television programmes about food, fluttering balloons outside flooring outlets, John Humphrys, Pudsey Bear, smug young men with beards, angry young boys with Rottweilers, the sounds that weathermen made. Without them all he flailed. What was there for him on the side of a hill in Spain? A view. An unwritten novel. His own shortcomings. Laura.

And Laura knew all this, she knew it long before he worked it out for himself. And she knew too that he thought it was something he could master. He would not be defined by what he was not. He would stay there on the side of a hill in Spain and try, by force of will, to evolve into a better, more complete human being. And he would fail.

He was down now at the building site and he made his way over to the half-built house. He lifted the plastic sheeting and stepped inside, unsure what he was expecting to find. What he did find was unspectacular – empty plastic tubs of sealant, broken breeze blocks, a plastic chair on its side. Nothing clandestine or eerie. He pulled back the blue polytarp across the doorway to leave and released a high-pitch scream as he came face to face with someone.

'Fuck. Jesus. Fuck. Esteban! What are you doing here? You almost killed me.'

'Eamonn. My God. Sorry. What's the matter?'

'You! That's what the matter is. Creeping about.'

'I was on patrol. I see someone is in here. I check.'

'Right. Well, it gave me a shock.'

'Why are you here?'

'I was just having a look.'

'For what?'

'I thought I saw someone. The other day.'

'I think no one comes here.'

'No. Probably not.'

'It's not safe here. Building places are dangerous. Your mother never tell you?'

'I'm sure she did.'

'Something could fall on your head.'

They were back on the road now and Eamonn noticed another, older man waiting there. He raised his hand and the man nodded in his direction.

'That's my uncle. He brought me some melon.'

'Right.'

'He grows them.'

'Oh. Nice.'

'Would you like some? I have it up in the cabin.'

'Maybe later.'

'OK.'

'Esteban?'

'Yes?'

'You haven't seen anything funny around the place recently, have you?'

'Like what?'

'Anyone who shouldn't be here.'

'Who?'

Eamonn felt foolish. 'I don't know. Just a couple of times recently I've thought someone was hiding from me.'

'Maybe it's Laura, hahahahahaha. "Surprise, Eamonn! I am here all along."'

Eamonn looked at Esteban until he stopped laughing and collected himself.

'My God, Eamonn. I'm sorry. This was bad taste. I heard you had problems and I'm sorry for them, really. What were you saying?'

'It doesn't matter.'

'No, Eamonn. Don't be that way. I'm sorry. Really.'

'I was just wondering if you'd seen anything strange. You know someone stole Inga's chickens?'

'Yes. Yes. This I know. She tell me.'

'Well, someone must have done that.'

'Yes. I have theory about that.'

'Which is?'

'I think Inga did it.'

'That's an interesting theory.'

'It sounds crazy, but some people . . . Women. Some women. They find killing animals difficult.'

'Some men too.'

'Maybe. I think she wanted to do it away from her house. Somewhere she could have a distance. You know' – he tapped his head – 'mentally.'

Eamonn stared at him for some time. 'That makes no sense. Why would she do that? Where's the other chicken?'

Esteban shrugged. 'Best not ask.'

'Christ, Esteban. Don't ever become a detective.'

'Look, you ask me if I see anyone. Anything suspicious. The answer is no. Are there any burglaries? No – OK, OK, this chicken – but that's not theft. Any car robberies? No. Any red paint all over buildings? No.'

'Right.'

'Promise me one thing, Eamonn.'

'What?'

'Keep away from this part. It's dangerous. A builder – he died at Lomaverde. These places are not for your exploring.'

Back in the flat Eamonn ate a sandwich and sat down in front of his computer. That morning, before setting off on a walk with Jean and David, Dermot had given him a little job-hunting pep talk.

'You've never been out of work. You're a bright lad. They'll be queuing up to offer you jobs.'

Even he hadn't looked terribly convinced by this, but Eamonn appreciated the effort. He spent a while staring at an empty Google search box before deciding to write a mail to Laura instead.

It had come as a surprise to him to learn that he was an optimist. He would have laid money against it. But hope, it seemed, clung on tenaciously, like the most insidious of weeds. He spent his waking hours hunting down its tendrils and subjecting them to ruthless dousings of cold facts, but still they returned – a fresh web of low-lying rhizomes each day.

She couldn't maintain the silence for ever. At some point she would surface. At some point her mysterious and secretive ruminations would be concluded and a verdict delivered. Even if she made up her mind to leave him there were still a thousand loose ends to be tied up – bank accounts, insurance policies, book collections. And knowing that he would speak to her again meant he found it hard to believe in the permanence of their separation. There was another conversation still to come, another chance. He had tried to prepare himself for the worst. To really believe that he had lost her and that the rest of his life would be spent without her but, in his more rational moments, he would admit to himself that it didn't feel entirely honest. He recognized the lure of pathos. After speaking to her every day for eight years, the idea that they would really part felt like a thought experiment. He found it hard to imagine that it wasn't the same for her. They still loved each other, he was sure of that.

He opened a bottle of Fanta Limón and performed the familiar ritual of checking his various in-boxes and portals. He found no voice or text messages on his phone that had somehow escaped his notice. No new mails of any description in his

Thunderbird account. Finally he signed into Facebook, though Laura had rarely used it when they were together and not at all since she had left. He looked only to see if any of her friends had posted messages, any clues about her whereabouts or state of mind. He was startled to see a new profile picture. Laura sitting outdoors somewhere. He felt a kind of obliterating grief creeping over him as he failed to recognize the setting, or the occasion. She had updated her status. 'Lovely to catch up with everyone at the weekend. Good to be home.'

He lost track of time as he stared at the words, breathing faintly, something unravelling slowly somewhere deep in his chest. He jumped when he heard his father's voice, apparently returned and standing beside him. Eamonn stood up too quickly, feeling light-headed and strange.

'What? What is it? What happened?'

'Nothing's happened. I was just saying we should be on our way to this barbecue thing.'

Eamonn nodded. 'Right. Yes. I'm ready.'

38

It wasn't much of a party when they arrived late afternoon. A bunch of people standing around muttering and looking awkward. Dermot had the idea that no one really wanted to be there. The hostess, Becca, had a kind of wild look in her eyes, talking nineteen to the dozen, laughing so loudly it set everyone on edge.

'Look!' she shouted to the assembled guests. 'Here he is, the man of the hour! I think you've all met Dermot – Eamonn's dad. He's come all the way from Ireland . . .'

'Birmingham,' Dermot said quietly.

'. . . And I want us all to show him that we know how to have the craic!'

People smiled politely, evidently puzzled by this, and then Simon shouted: 'Crack? Well, I didn't know it was that kind of party!'

Raimund laughed and said, 'Will you be handing out the pipes, Rebecca?'

'Hahahaha – "pipes"!' said Becca, then shook her head, laughing crazily and repeated just the word: 'Pipes!'

Dermot smiled and said to Eamonn under his breath: 'I've no idea what's going on here at all' – but Eamonn was heading away towards the drinks.

To Dermot's relief Jean and David came over and rescued him. While he chatted with them about their walk earlier in the day, his eyes wandered to the group around him. An inevitable consequence of working on the buses was a certain knowledge of human behaviour. Ninety per cent of the time he'd guess a passenger's destination before a word was spoken. As his bus approached a stop he'd already know who among the queue was the type to cause trouble, and who the type to stand and talk the ears off him for the next forty minutes. It wasn't a talent he particularly wanted. Most of the time he wished to God somebody would do something to surprise him, say something different just for once, but that wasn't the way it was. Most drivers were the same, reluctant possessors of a tired kind of sixth sense.

The affluent-looking French couple stood nearby, quite clearly discussing everyone else at the party. A few yards away, Roger was casting glances at the Frenchman and Dermot sensed some issue between them. Rosemary was keeping a close and furtive eye on what Gill drank and Becca was whispering furiously at Ian about something he had failed to do. Simon and Raimund were on the other side of the pool laughing with Cheryl. Dermot thought he'd detected a hint of Geordie in Simon's voice the other day. It was an accent he liked. He associated it with a driver he'd worked alongside in the 70s called Joey who was prone to quoting poetry at abusive passengers. It made them no less abusive apparently but it gave Joey a tremendous sense of satisfaction and Dermot thought it a shame more people didn't respond to provocation in a similarly inventive manner. He looked around for Eamonn and finally saw him leaning against the wall on the far side of the terrace, his face a mask, a full glass of wine in one hand, the rest of the bottle gripped tightly in the other.

As the afternoon wore on, others arrived and introduced themselves. He found it a little tiring, the faces and names hard to remember, the range of topics at times bewildering. The music was loud and people were shouting to be heard. Esteban had now joined the party and so had Inga. He saw her chatting to Rosemary by the pool. He caught her eye and raised a hand in salutation.

He was trapped in a corner with Henri, Danielle and Raimund all enthusing about a sausage, or possibly a beach, he couldn't quite understand the Frenchwoman's accent and hadn't liked to ask her for clarification. He looked across the terrace again and saw Eamonn. He seemed highly animated now, his facial expressions exaggerated, his laughter false. He stood talking to Simon. At a pause in the music, his voice rang out loud above the others: 'For example I never shaved my scrotum and maybe that might have made a difference. Would you recommend it?'

'Jesus, Mary and Joseph,' muttered Dermot, he started to head in Eamonn's direction, but his exit was blocked by Roger.

'Henry, could I have a quick word?'

Henri gave an unconvincing smile. 'Of course.'

'It's a polite request.'

'Please go ahead.'

'I was wondering if there was any chance of you giving up the nocturnal joy rides?'

'I'm sorry? What are "joy rides"?'

'The little drives you take in the middle of the night.'

'Drives?' He looked at his wife, who in turn shrugged. 'I'm sorry, I don't know . . .'

Roger smiled and shook his head. 'Look, we all know you have a big, manly BMW 4x4 and I'm sure we're all very impressed by it, but I for one would prefer it if you didn't drive it around in the wee small hours, because it's a noisy bugger and it wakes me up.'

'My car?'

'Yes. Your car.' He raised his hands in a mime of driving. 'Brum, brum, in the night.'

Henri laughed. 'What a strange accusation.' He looked at

Dermot and Raimund. 'Maybe it is a joke? I don't know what it is you think you hear in the night, but it is not me. Or my car.'

'Look, I'm sorry if this is getting you into trouble with your wife, but wherever you're going to or coming from, if you could just do it more quietly.'

'What has this got to do with my wife?'

'You tell me.'

'What? This is making no sense.'

'I'm just telling you to pack it in.'

Henri's face changed. 'I'm not sure if you are deaf or stupid, but I will say it again: I'm not doing anything. And, excuse me, you're "telling" me? You? Are you the mayor? I don't remember you being elected.'

Dermot had heard enough. He excused himself as the two men continued to squabble and went looking once more for Eamonn. Throughout the evening he had caught glimpses of him. At one point he seemed to have taken command of the music, which was a relief at first, but Dermot noticed later that it was just the same song he kept playing over and over. Later still he'd seen him talking to Jean, and Dermot had got the distinct impression that Jean had been trying to get away from him. Another time he'd heard him shouting in the distance. Each time Dermot had tried to get to him but Eamonn had either slipped away or Dermot had been pulled aside by someone else wanting to know how he was enjoying his stay in Lomaverde. Now that he was free there was no trace of Eamonn at all. Instead he found Inga sitting on her own by the pool. She pointed to the chair next to her:

'Hello.'

He sat and closed his eyes for a moment.

'Are you as drunk as everyone else seems to be?'

He opened his eyes. 'I don't think I am, no. I was just listening to an argument about engine noise which made me think I've not nearly had enough to drink.'

She laughed. 'Oh yes, Roger. He is a funny man. He is always very cross with me because I feed the cats.'

'I think I heard him mention that.'

'I'm sure you did. I told him this evening that he should be happy, as they seem to be leaving.'

'Is that right?'

'There's nothing for them here, the few scraps I give them aren't enough to stop them starving. I told him I'd noticed their numbers declining. I thought he'd be delighted but it just seemed to offend him. He said: "Bloody charming. Like rats leaving a sinking ship!" He was so hurt by their disloyalty.'

Dermot smiled. 'So, are you enjoying the do?'

She nodded. 'I didn't really expect to, but it's nice. I don't speak to my neighbours much. With some' – she looked over at Roger – 'that's maybe a little intentional, but with others, well, it's strange to say in such a small place, but our paths don't really cross so often and it's pleasant to speak to them properly and remember that there are good people here.' She looked at him. 'How are you finding being the centre of attention?'

'Is that what I am?'

'Of course. A new face. Fresh blood. A new audience for the old stories.'

'Oh, there was I, thinking I was charming company, but I just have novelty value.'

She smiled. 'Oh dear, I've said the wrong thing.'

'No. I think you have it right . . .' He stood up suddenly, his gaze directed at the far side of the terrace. Eamonn was slumped on the floor, his head buried in his hands. Dermot turned to Inga: 'I'm sorry, can you excuse me?'

He knew then that he should have taken him home hours

ago. He didn't know what had set him off. He'd been fine that morning when he left him and then seemed a changed man when he returned. He hadn't been right from the moment they'd arrived at the barbecue, and God knows how much he'd had to drink since then. Dermot walked over and crouched down, as best as he could, beside him.

'Eamonn?'

Nothing.

'Eamonn, get up, you can't stay here like this.'

A long sniff.

'Eamonn, come on, son, people are looking.'

A muffled response.

'What? I can't hear you.'

'Please go.'

'Come on, son, let's get you home.'

Suddenly Eamonn shouted: 'It's not my fucking home!'

The terrace fell silent. Dermot felt everyone's eyes upon them. He turned and tried to smile. 'I think he's had a bit too much to drink.' He turned back and spoke quietly. 'Come on. You're causing a scene now. Get up.' He braced his back and reached out to try to lift Eamonn off the ground, but Eamonn hunkered down.

'Dad, please, just leave me alone.'

Becca laid a gentle hand on Dermot's arm. 'Don't worry, Dermot, happens to everyone sometimes. Roger! Ian! Come and give Eamonn a hand.' Dermot was well able to lift his son by himself, but he deferred to the younger men, thinking Eamonn might be persuaded by them.

As they approached though he started shouting louder than before: 'Don't fucking touch me! I'm not going back there.'

They ignored him and tried to grab an arm each.

'Get off me!'

'Eamonn, don't be a prick.'

'Ow! He hit me!'

Ungainly tussling and slapping broke out with all three men at varying stages of drunkenness; a bottle was dropped and smashed on the stone tiles and then a voice rang out.

'Get your hands off him!' Cheryl appeared, the setting sun igniting the colours in her tropical-print maxi dress, her pearl-ized eye make-up shimmering. Ian and Roger stepped back obediently and she stood over Eamonn.

'Eamonn. What are they doing to you, sweetheart?'

He looked up at her with ceramic-puppy eyes. 'Cheryl. Help me.'

'It's OK, honey, I'm here.' She turned to Dermot. 'I'll take him back to ours for a bit, give him some coffee and a shoulder to cry on. He'll be fine.'

Dermot hesitated. 'If that's what he wants.'

'Come on, Eamonn, let's go next door.'

He struggled to his feet, resisting the assistance of Roger and Ian. As Cheryl linked her arm through his to steady him, she turned and whispered something to Roger.

Dermot watched her lead his son away. He wished he'd carried him home when he'd had the chance.

39

He was sitting on a bed in a dimly lit room. He was waiting for someone to return, he was pretty sure of that. He couldn't remember who they were or where they'd gone but he thought it was OK.

It was nice in the room, dark and soft. Everything was good in there. Apart from the music. Something awful was piping through from somewhere. A terrible noise. A constipated saxophone, trying over and over again to void its bowels. He was in danger of sobering up. Unpleasant shards of memory were starting to jab at him.

He needed another drink. He hoped that's what he was waiting for, that any minute now someone would enter the room with something tall, cool, refreshing and alcoholic. Not *calimocho* though, he felt quite strongly about that. There had been some indefinite period of time spent in a bathroom, cold tiles on his face, someone holding his head, comforting him as he vomited the filthy combination of red wine and coke. 'Fizzy sick' – he remembered thinking it important that he repeated those words over and over again, turning around, trying to speak between retches, as if the person gently holding his head needed to know, as if the words might help with some diagnosis.

Sparse, asynchronous glimpses of the evening now started to flash in his mind. Jean and Rosemary practising some dance steps. Someone trying to convince him of the benefits of Reiki. Lionel Richie's voice. Roger's hand on Becca's leg. 'Everyone you meet, they're dancing in the street.' Somebody sobbing.

His father's voice. Gill threatening to do a handstand. Endless Lionel. David dancing on his own. 'All Night Long'. Shovelling *gambas* into his mouth. His father's face in the crowd.

The saxophone had stopped. Now there were synthesized pan pipes playing the song, the inevitable song. He sang quietly: 'I'd rather be a hammer than a nail.' He lay and pondered. Would he? It was quite a conundrum. It was a song he had previously loathed, played on an instrument he detested, but now he reconsidered. The sound was soothing, the lyrics challenging, maybe even profound. Hammer or nail? Who could say? He'd wasted so much of his life sneering. Maybe this was the start of his re-education. Pan pipes. Synthesized pan pipes. What the hell was wrong with them? Why couldn't things be easy and nice? 'El Cóndor Pasa'. There was so much he could learn from the condor. What exactly were the virtues of difficulty and cynicism and just constantly . . .

The door opened and Cheryl walked in. He smiled.

'How are you, sweetheart?'

'I like your music.'

'Oh. Thank you.'

'Can I borrow it?'

'Ask Roger, he has it wired up to come into all the rooms; I think it's just random tracks from his computer.'

'Amazing.'

'You look better anyway. Here.' She handed him a drink.

His worst suspicions were confirmed with the first sip. Iced water. He put it down on the side table. 'Thanks.'

She looked at him. 'Oh, Eamonn, what are we going to do with you?'

He had an image in his mind of Cheryl doing something with him while Roger watched in the background. 'What do you mean?'

'I just mean, how can we help you?'

'Oh, right.'

She sat next to him on the bed. He could smell her perfume, something heavy and sweet. He looked at her legs stretched out beside him. Her feet looked soft and delicate, imprisoned in the cage of her high-heeled sandals.

'Is Roger home now?'

'No, he won't be back tonight. He'll crash out on their sofa. He normally does.'

Now he saw Roger and Ian taking turns with Becca. There was something wrong with his head. Everything was turning to pornography.

'Eamonn, you need to come to terms with Laura's departure.'

'I don't want to talk about it.'

'OK, but you're not handling it very well; look what happened tonight. Sobbing on Jean's shoulder. Shouting about circumcision. Constantly playing Lionel bloody Ritchie.'

He put his head in his hands.

'Look, I'm not trying to make you feel bad. Everyone gets drunk and makes a fool of themselves sometimes, and you've got more cause than most, but I just want you to know that if you ever feel you need to talk, you can talk to me. I'm actually a pretty good listener.' She squeezed his leg.

He kept his head buried. He felt the weight of her hand on his thigh. Normally he would move his leg, find an excuse to gently brush her hand away. Always polite. It had been hard work, constantly policing the borders of their relationship with Roger and Cheryl; this pressure he felt from them, low level, almost imperceptible, but constant. He pondered now the nature of that pressure, the intent within. It wasn't simply sexual, it was something wider, looser, impelling them to let go, a call for Eamonn and Laura to abandon themselves; to what, he wasn't sure, as he had always fiercely resisted. He thought of

227

the condor again. The wise bird. The old Eamonn was always resisting, always putting barriers between himself and simple, uncomplicated pleasure: pan pipes, trashy TV, wife-swapping.

'Have you fallen asleep?' she asked gently.

He lifted his head from his hands and looked at her. 'You're beautiful, Cheryl. I know you know that, but you are.'

She gave a half-smile. 'I was once.'

'You still are. You have an incredible glamour.'

'Not glamorous, please. Only grannies are glamorous.'

'Something powerful about you. Something different.'

She looked at him and he felt something change in the room.

'Does he appreciate it?'

'Who?'

'Roger, does he know what to do with you?'

She gave him a strange look.

He reached down and slid her hand up to his crotch. 'I do.'

'Eamonn.'

'It's OK.'

'I think I should get Roger.'

Eamonn was unsurprised. 'He likes to watch, doesn't he?' He moved his face closer to hers. 'The old Eamonn would have said no, but the new Eamonn . . .' He shrugged. 'It's all about letting go.'

Cheryl stood up. 'Eamonn. You're very drunk.'

'I know what I'm doing.'

'I'm calling Roger.'

He smiled. 'I'm going with the flow.'

She ignored him and started searching for her phone.

'I know I've resisted in the past, sent out the wrong signals.'

At this Cheryl turned and looked at him. 'Resisted what exactly?'

'You and Roger. I know how you must see us. Repressed.

Uptight. I don't know why I've fought against it so hard. Not tonight though, I'm past all that, tonight you can have me.'

Cheryl laughed. 'I can have you? Listen, sweetheart, there are only so many allowances I'll make for alcohol and a broken heart.'

He stood up and held her hands. 'I'm saying it all wrong, but you know what I mean. One night. Come on.' He tried to push her back towards the bed, but she freed a hand and delivered a powerful punch to his nose.

He fell back, holding his nose, a terrible sobriety lapping at his shores.

'Listen, Eamonn. You're drunk. I'm trying to keep that in mind, but you're making it difficult. I need you to hear what I'm saying. You have fantasies about me, fine, whatever, you're not the first, you won't be the last, but that's just what they are, fantasies, and they don't interest me at all. Maybe Roger and I like to flirt, we like to play our little games, but I thought we were all adults and we knew the rules. Jesus, it's not the fucking 1970s, Eamonn. I do not and never have thought of you as . . .' she trailed off, as if unable to even put the idea into words. 'I just don't think of you in that way. Now, you're upset, but you've done your crying now and you need to stop being a boy and start being a man. Laura's left you. Deal with it. Move on or get her back.'

Eamonn still had his head buried in the pillow when Roger came in.

'What's going on?'

She spoke quietly. 'Eamonn got a bit confused.'

Roger walked over to the bed and, with a small cry of effort, lifted Eamonn over his shoulder and left the room. Dawn was breaking as he carried him up the road.

'I thought better of you, Eamonn. I mean, I'm not going to hold it against you, don't worry about that, but I'm just surprised and I suppose disappointed. I mean, if you marry a woman like Cheryl, you know there are always going to be pricks who want a piece of her. That's how they think, like she's a fucking cake and they can just take a slice. No understanding, no respect, she's just a body to them. Those kind of men, they don't even like women, not really. I never thought you were that type, to be honest. I mean, we'll forget about this, we'll put it in the past, you can't carry these things around with you, especially not in a tiny place like this, seeing each other every day, but just now, while we're clearing the air, I'm just saying, well, I don't know, I suppose you're not the man I thought you were. I'm damn sure your father raised you better than this.'

There was the sound of the buzzer and a few minutes later his father's voice through the intercom. Roger dumped Eamonn on the ground in front of the door just as Dermot was opening it.

'Sorry to wake you, Dermot. 'Fraid it didn't work out at ours; thought he'd be better off back home.'

'Right.'

'Do you need a hand getting him in?'

'No, I'll be fine.'

Eamonn kept his eyes closed as his father dragged him into the lobby. He lay completely motionless while Dermot went upstairs and returned moments later. He offered no resistance as a pillow was pushed under his head and the blanket placed over him.

'Night night, son.'

He felt his father wipe away a tear that was making slow progress down his cheek and then everything went black.

40

He heard his footsteps moving quickly and lightly, like a wood-land creature scampering from bathroom to bedroom. He got up to catch him, but was too late, hearing the firm click of Eamonn's door as he shut himself in once more. He knocked lightly.

'Eamonn, are you awake in there?'

Silence.

'Eamonn, I just heard you. Why don't you come out and have some breakfast?'

'I don't want any, thanks.'

'You can't hide in your room for ever.'

'I'm not hiding. I have a migraine.'

'There's no point feeling bad about last night. You had a bit too much to drink. Sure everyone's done that.'

Long pause. 'I have a migraine.'

Dermot sighed. He seemed to have spent a lot of the last fortnight addressing Eamonn's door. It was reminiscent of the confessional box. 'Should I call a doctor?'

'No. I just need to lie in a dark room.'

'For the love of God. You can't spend your life lying in a dark room!'

Silence.

He left the apartment and went out for a walk. He'd intended to head down to the town, to get some supplies, make sure Eamonn's cupboards were full before he returned to England. It occurred to him that that was the kind of thing sons might do for their elderly parents, not the other way round. Not for the first time he considered that his presence wasn't helping at all. Without him around Eamonn would have to pull himself together. Maybe it was a case of sink or swim. The thought failed to reassure him. The memory of watching his son dipping beneath the waves was still lurid and nightmarish.

Despite his intention to walk into town, he found himself a few minutes later outside Inga's door. He was more surprised than she seemed to be at his arrival there. She was putting out food on the street for the cats. A bowl of leftovers and, next to it, a large bag of uncooked rice. He frowned at the rice.

'What are the cats to do with that?'

But she just smiled and said, 'Come in. I was just making some coffee.'

He glanced again at the bag of rice and then followed her in.

'How's Eamonn?'

He ran his hand through his hair. 'My wife was always worrying about him. Fussing. It used to drive me mad. He's a grown man, I'd say. He has a life of his own. Now it's my turn.'

'They never stop being a worry.'

'I don't know what goes on in that head of his. I don't pretend to.'

'Love can make us strange.'

'I'm not sure it took love to make Eamonn strange.'

She smiled. 'He frustrates you.'

'Why doesn't he go after her? The only fight in him seems with himself.'

'Perhaps he's giving her space and time.'

'Well, give someone enough space and you won't find them again.'

She looked at him. 'Is that an Irish saying?'

'I don't think so. Though I just said it and I'm Irish. Is that the same thing?'

'You're very good. You could do a line in tea towels.'

232

He seemed to consider this and said solemnly, '"The sayings of Dermot."'

'I'd buy one.' She smiled at him again. 'So. I was going to spend the day painting.'

'I should go.'

'No. I'd like you to stay.'

He sat in the same chair for hours. The room itself as absorbing as a picture. The sunlight coming through the window. Inga's small movements, transferring paint from a palette to the canvas. The painting at the centre of it all. He shifted focus from the abstract blur of colour where her brush met the canvas, to the resolved image of the broken chair that she was painting, to the wider room which framed her. He heard the brush sink into the paint, the creaking of the easel, her irregular breathing as she concentrated. The sun moved across the room, the pool of light shifting throughout the afternoon. He must have dozed off at some point. He woke up and saw the painting, imperceptibly augmented, richer, denser. Much later on, as it started to grow dark, he spoke, unprompted, and she didn't seem to mind:

'I wake up sometimes in the night and I can't work out where I am, or what year it is. I think I'm back in the house I was in as a boy. I think my brother's asleep in the room with me. It's like, without Kathleen there to anchor me, I'm just floating about in my own life.'

She stopped to listen when he spoke, but didn't turn around. When he finished she went back to painting. He wondered when she would think the painting was finished. He did not want her to finish.

'My brother Dominic died a long time ago. In America. A car crash. He and his wife, both killed. Her name was Della Schwarz. I never met her. Della Schwarz. It's a nice name to say. She was pregnant.' There was a long pause. 'Six months or so. A baby. We got a letter.'

She sat down on a stool in front of her painting and laid the brush on the palette. She didn't look at him.

'It was his name in the letter. And she was his wife. He'd sent a telegram when they married, just a year before. It was them all right. I didn't know him at all then. I hadn't seen him in years. There were letters, but it was as if they were from a stranger. I didn't know him as an adult, just this voice in the letters, talking about trains and jobs and roads and hamburgers and the people he had met.

'It was a lorry that hit them. I imagine one of those big ones you see in American films, all chrome and pipes and a blaring horn. Crossed the carriageway and hit them head on. I suppose the driver had fallen asleep, or was drunk. I don't know. They must have seen it coming. They must have known.

'I remember him as a boy, waking me in the night, scared of ghosts, scared but not scared. Scared but brave. He'd call out my name, then get into bed beside me, his body frozen, like he'd been sleeping in the fields, teeth chattering with the cold, telling me about the ghosts he'd seen. I'd squeeze his hand and the chattering would slow and then eventually stop and then he'd be asleep again.

'I think sometimes you lose people and you barely know it at the time. It starts as a small crack. That's all it is. It takes years, a lifetime, before you notice what went out through the crack. How much you lost.

'He sounded happy in the letters. He never mentioned ghosts. He was grown up, I suppose. He was in love. I'm sure she loved him too. He was going to be a father.' He paused. 'I can't imagine that at all, but then . . . it never happened anyway.' He coughed. 'I don't suppose he was ever scared any more, not as an adult. I hope not. Probably it was Della Schwarz he called for. Terrified for her and the baby, not himself. He was a grown man. Three lives about to end. I hope she held his hand. I hope they both held hands.'

They sat in the dark for a long time until a noise from outside broke the silence. Dermot stood up; Inga looked at him and put a finger to her lips. She indicated that he should follow her to the window. They stood in the shadows looking out at the street. The bag of rice was gone and the food bowl empty. Dermot craned his neck expecting to see the unlikely sight of a cat dragging the heavy bag. He saw nothing, but heard the distinct sound of light footsteps running away.

41

The electricity had been off for five hours. Each time there was a power cut Eamonn wondered if the lights would ever come on again. He thought that one day the electricity company would give up on them. Just a handful of people. More trouble than they were worth. He often imagined himself close to a survival situation. In the last power cut he'd asked Laura if she thought they should start burning the furniture or barricading the doors, but she hadn't seemed to share his sense of emergency.

It was late now and he wondered where his father was. He emerged from his room and found some of Laura's scented candles. He put them on the table and lit them. They gave off a peppery smell reminiscent of church incense.

He sat still but his body buzzed. A vibrating pulse, small but insistent. It felt very much as if a tiny creature were trapped inside him.

'There was an old woman who swallowed a fly.'

A song from infancy. He shut his eyes tight, trying to drive it away. It seemed designed, like so many childhood entertainments, only to perplex or infuriate. The thought of them now still maddening. London Bridge is falling down. There's a hole in my bucket. Ten green bottles. Small tortures, ceaseless, repetitive, neither funny nor clever, just stupid people saying stupid things.

'There was an old woman who swallowed a fly.'

She swallowed a cow to catch the dog. He remembered the version they used to play on the radio: a creepy-voiced man, giggling as he sang, as if there were anything remotely funny about the whole grotesque chain of events.

'There was an old woman who swallowed a fly.'

The song trapped like the fabled insect inside him. He resisted the temptation to smack himself hard in the face.

'I don't know why she swallowed a fly. Perhaps she'll die.'

He had made a list in his room. He smiled to think of it: his great novel had in the end amounted to little more than hundreds of lists. It was appropriate that he should be methodical even in this. A neat array of bullet points – for once the implicit violence seeming appropriate. He looked at it.

- Laura gone
- Sexually assaulted neighbour
- No money
- No job
- No prospect of job
- Unable to write
- Unable to escape Lomaverde
- Unable to remain in Lomaverde
- Source of worry to Dad

It was like striking a match. Each time he looked at it, the self-loathing flaring brightly once more.

As a teenager, unhappy at school, he had once or twice entertained the usual fantasies. Seduced by the grand operatic vision, drunk with self-pity, passing exquisitely miserable hours planning the staging, the note, the playlist, the eulogy. They had never been anything more than desperate bids for autonomy. Comforting fantasies of death, to make life temporarily more bearable. This was not like those at all. He had no vision of after. No note. No self-pity. No self-aggrandizing. No self. That was the point. He just wanted to end. To draw a line under it all.

But despite the list, despite the Internet research, despite even choosing the spot, he knew with a heavy, stone-like certainty that he would not do it. Suicide involved blinding himself to the pain he would cause his father and Laura. Covering his eyes and trying to believe it wouldn't happen because he wouldn't be around to see it. Even he was not capable of such self-deceit.

He heard a key in the door and his father came in carrying a torch.

'You're up, then?'

'Yes.'

'Migraine better?'

'A little.'

Dermot went into the kitchen and returned with some beers. He sat down on the futon beside him and said nothing for so long that Eamonn thought he had fallen asleep. Then he spoke:

'Losing someone is hard.'

Eamonn said nothing.

'I understand that.'

Eamonn nodded. 'I know.'

'Your mother too. She would have understood.'

'Yes.'

'She lost someone once, you know, someone close to her. She found it difficult.'

'Who was that?'

'Walsh. The priest you were asking about.'

'He died?'

'No, no. He just got moved on, you know the way they do. Your mother took it hard.'

'I never heard her mention him.'

Dermot was quiet again for a while. 'He was a breath of fresh air after Phelan. An educated fella, very energetic, full of the books he'd read and the ideas he had. He and she became pals. I suppose she'd have stood out from the other women that hung around the presbytery. I'd say he'd have been delighted to find someone he could have a conversation with.' He paused. 'And I suppose the same was true for your mother.'

'But Mom had you.'

Dermot rubbed his face. 'She did. But I'd never really shared her interest in religion. It wasn't such a big deal back when we married. But all those years we were waiting for you, the Church edged its way in. That's what it does, doesn't it? Find the chink. She was looking for something. I couldn't talk to her about those things.

'Anyway, Walsh came along. Stepped into the breach, you could say. He got her interested in all kinds of things. She started doing night courses – theology, that kind of thing – you know all those books she had. The truth was I wouldn't have minded doing a few classes myself, wouldn't have minded going along. I don't know why I didn't tell her that.' He reflected for a moment. 'I suppose I got the idea it wasn't really me she wanted to be discussing these things with.

'He came round the house one time for his tea. She was in a mania for days beforehand. All of a sudden we needed a book-case in the lounge. I had to build one double quick to show off all our books – only it wasn't our books that went on it, just hers.'

He was quiet again for some time.

'She told me once that I had nothing to worry about with Walsh.'

'What did that mean?'

'Oh, you know, there'd been talk. Gossip in the parish. I think it was just that the other hangers-on were put out about the time he and your mother spent together. I never thought there was anything like that between them.'

'Did you not ask her?'

Dermot ignored him. 'She said: "You've got nothing to worry about with Walsh, he and I are just kindred spirits." She said it to me as if that was OK' – he paused to take a drink – 'as if I'd never thought she and I might be kindred spirits.'

They sat in silence for a while before Dermot spoke again.

'I've known plenty of clever people – you get them on the buses – maybe that surprises you, but you do. Philosophers and thinkers of all types – some educated in universities, some educated by themselves. But the thing about clever people is they don't shout about it. Your mother, for example, she was one. She was brighter than he was, though she couldn't see it. A few more of those night classes and she'd have outgrown him. Realized how much of his talk was just noise. She and he weren't kindred spirits. I never believed that.'

'So he was never a real threat?'

'Not really. I don't think so. I don't think that's arrogance. I knew her better than anyone. But the problem was, I wasn't so clever. I didn't like the man and I let that get in the way of things. I should have let him be. Let things run their course.'

'What did you do?'

'I went to see him.'

'What did you say?'

'Not much. I didn't have to. He knew well enough. And he did what I knew he'd do.'

'What?'

'He skipped off. Moved on. Another parish. A word in the bishop's ear. His work with us was done. I think they saw him as a high-flyer.'

'Where'd he go?'

'Latin America somewhere – it was probably a short cut to being a cardinal.'

'That's far enough. Better than you must have hoped.'

'I don't know what I hoped. I don't know what I thought.'

He was quiet for a while.

'I found a box when I was clearing your mother's things. Stuffed with his letters. I counted them. A hundred and sixty-one.'

'What did they say?'

'I didn't read them.'

Eamonn looked at him.

'You don't even know that she replied. Maybe he was wasting his time.'

'You know, you can always tell the married couples on the bus. They're the ones not speaking to each other. Everyone else chats, but the husbands and wives sit in silence. It makes you wonder: are they silent because they know each other's minds and there's no need for words? Or are they silent because they're imagining conversations with other people? Or is one doing one and the other doing the other? Two different silences side by side?'

'But they were just letters. Nothing real. You and Mom were happy in your own way.'

Dermot smiled. 'We both thought the world of you, son.'

Eamonn shook his head, wanting more. 'But with each other. You weren't unhappy, were you?'

Dermot studied the backs of his hands. 'I always loved her.' He placed them flat on his knees. 'But I've been less lonely since she's gone.'

42

Eamonn made a big deal of it being his last full day. Dermot found him up and dressed before him in the morning, waiting to embark on a full itinerary. They drove out to a little town on the coast and had breakfast in something that looked like a chip shop but served a kind of extruded doughy thing. *Churros*, Eamonn called them. He had Dermot say it aloud, making sure he rolled the 'r's. They tasted like doughnuts. Dermot said they were nice, but in truth he would always favour a decent fry for his breakfast.

They walked along the front and Eamonn waited on the beach while Dermot took a final swim in the sea. He did breaststroke, slow and steady, watching his arms coming together and moving apart in the water in front of his face. Something eternal in the action. The same eyes seeing the same arms that swam as a boy. The sound of his own breathing. He thought he was never as alone as when swimming. Never so conscious of his own being. Seventy-six years old. He didn't know what to make of that. He saw Eamonn smiling and waving out at him now and then. He was trying awful hard.

Afterwards in the car Eamonn said that he was sorry.

'What for?'

'This past fortnight.'

'There's nothing to apologize for.'

'I've been pathetic. I know that. I'm sorry you've had to see me like this.'

Dermot shrugged.

'It was your first time abroad. I didn't even take you any-where.'

'You did so. Anyway, I've enjoyed it.'

'I don't want you to worry about me. I'm going to change. The other night, the party – that was a wake-up call. I'm going to pull myself together. Turn my life around.'

Dermot looked at him. They sounded like lines he'd heard in adverts. He patted Eamonn's arm.

In the afternoon they drove to a place in the middle of the desert called Mini Hollywood. It was a tourist attraction and as such exactly the kind of place Dermot imagined that Eamonn would hate. He'd always had a fearful objection to tourists. Kathleen would mention some place Brendan was going to on holiday and Eamonn would say: 'Full of tourists.' As if that was that. So it must have cost him something to go to such a place. Dermot knew he was doing it for his benefit.

It turned out it was the place they'd filmed all the old Clint Eastwood films he and Eamonn used to watch together on the telly on a Sunday afternoon. Hadn't been the Wild West at all, but a desert in southern Spain. Not even Italy. The whole Spa-ghetti Western name was misleading. Should have been Paella Westerns. *Pie-ay-a*. That's how you said it. He'd learned that.

It seemed an unfortunate choice at first. A day out from a real ghost town to a pretend one. He wasn't sure that tumble-weed was what Eamonn needed to see. They arrived just in time to see a staged bank robbery and a shoot-out. Dermot thought the fella playing the baddie had been miscast. He was more David Dickinson than desperado. It was a bit of fun though. Even Eamonn laughed when Dickinson fell down dead before the shot was fired. Dermot had always enjoyed Westerns, but never John Wayne. Couldn't stand the man. He used to have fierce lunchtime debates with his mate Ernest about the films of their boyhood. Ernest was loyal to Wayne, but Dermot maintained that Fonda outclassed him in every department. Ernest had gone back to Trinidad in retirement, but each year he sent Dermot a Christmas card with some quote from 'the Duke' and Dermot would reciprocate with 'ain't no cow country' – or some other Fonda obscurity.

They took a drink in the saloon and watched young women dressed as gaudy prostitutes perform a high-kicking dance. Eamonn looked across at him.

'Well, you've shown great restraint so far.'

'In what?'

'I thought you'd have done it the moment we got here.'

'What are you talking about?'

'The voice.'

'What voice?'

'Oh, Dad, come on – it's the only impression you ever did.'

'I don't remember any impression.'

'You do! You did it all the time when I was a kid.'

Dermot shook his head. 'I'm sorry, son, I don't remember.'

Eamonn was incredulous. 'But you must. That's half the reason I came here.'

'What? To hear me do some funny voice?'

'Yes! I can't believe you don't remember.'

'So, what you're saying is, you wanted me to do it?'

'Of course.'

'Which one was it again?'

'You know!'

'I don't, you'll have to remind me.'

Eamonn shook his head and then said quietly, 'Wallach.'

'What was that?'

'Eli Wallach. Dad. Can you just do it?'

Dermot frowned. 'Maybe if I rack my brains.' Then he leaned in close, pulling back his lips to expose his teeth: '"There are two kinds of people in the world, my friend. Those with a rope around the neck, and the people who have the job of doing the cutting."'

He was taken aback to hear Eamonn laugh. Unchanged since he was ten. A kind of explosive, spluttery chuckle. Dermot looked at him in amazement.

'My God, son, but you're an eejit.'

43

They stopped off for dinner in a small town. A strange kind of restaurant, set way off the tourist track and yet apparently Spanish-themed. It presented a fantasy of the country familiar to anyone who had grown up in Britain in the 1970s, all bull-fighting posters, flamenco dolls and sangria. It stopped short of portraits of Franco.

'I think it's the Spanish equivalent of a Toby Carvery,' he whispered to his dad.

'Very nice,' said Dermot.

The proprietor gave them English menus.

'I reckon we're the first to ever handle these.'

Eamonn frowned at the card. 'The translations are terrible. I need the menu in Spanish.'

'Don't call him back. Let him have his moment, son.'

Eamonn shrugged. 'OK. I'll have the "Landfill of pork". Why don't you try the "Vaporized fish"?'

'That sounds grand.'

It was late when they left, and a long drive home on empty roads. They had been silent for some time when Dermot asked: 'Are you tired?'

'No, I'm OK.'

'Easy to nod off on a drive like this.'

'I was thinking about my first night here with Laura. We came in on a late flight. Drove across the desert. Didn't pass another car for hours.'

'The roads are quiet here all right.'

'We'd been excited on the plane, talking a lot, but I just

remember silence in the car. Tired, I suppose. Suddenly there was something in the headlights. Huge and white it looked. Then a bang.'

'What was it?'

'A wolf. Two of them had run out in front of us.'

'Good God. Did you kill it?'

'I don't know. We stopped the car, but Laura said we shouldn't get out, in case the other one came back. We sat there in the middle of the road, shaken up. We didn't know what to do.'

'I'd say you did the right thing.'

'I'd forgotten all about it till tonight.'

'Maybe it's the full moon.'

Eamonn smiled. 'It was a clear enough omen really.'

When they got back to Lomaverde Dermot said he wanted to take a look around.

'But we'll have time in the morning.'

'I know, but I'd like to see it at night, one last time.'

They covered the length of the development, walking unhurriedly, saying little. They reached the end of the road, where the tarmac ceded control once more to scrubland, weeds, rocks, and the creatures that lived among them. They stood looking out towards the sea, tracking the movements of distant lights on the water.

'It's not all plain sailing,' Dermot said.

'What?'

'Making the crossing. Starting somewhere new.'

'No.'

'That sense that you don't belong. You're not wanted. It's hard to shake.'

'You never really had that, did you?'

'Didn't I? We thought about leaving Birmingham, you know.'

'And going back to Ireland?'

'No, not back there. Just away from Birmingham.'

'Why?'

Dermot turned to him. 'Nineteen seventy-four, son. It wasn't a good year.'

'Oh. Yes.'

'It started before then. It was all kicking off. Your mother was worried. She'd had a few comments at the hospital. Stupid things. Then there was a big hoo-ha about McDade's funeral.'

'Who was McDade?'

'Fella from Sparkhill, your Uncle Mike knew him, drank with him sometimes. Turned out he was a volunteer. Blew himself up trying to plant a bomb in Coventry.'

'A volunteer? For the IRA?'

Dermot looked at him. 'Well, it wasn't the Salvation Army planting the bombs.' He paused. 'Apparently some old cow at work had asked your mom why she wanted to be a nurse when all the Irish wanted to do was kill people. Your mother was upset. It wasn't long before you were due and she got herself in a state.

'She started worrying about how you might be treated, growing up with people like that about. People judging you just by your name.

'I told her it was nonsense. She couldn't be going and getting het up about one daft bat.

'But she wouldn't have it, said others were thinking the same thing. I remember saying people weren't going to start thinking all Irish were terrorists because some lad had blown himself up in Coventry.'

He was quiet for a moment. 'Sure, I didn't know what was coming.

'When we saw the news the next night the first thing I did was ring John Healey to make sure his girls hadn't been up there; I knew the youngest drank in the Tavern in the Town. I heard from some other drivers that it was pandemonium up there. They'd had to use taxis to ferry the injured to hospital. The coppers were all out at the airport with McDade's coffin.

'We heard later that the presbytery over at the Sacred Heart had been petrol-bombed; your mother looked at me and said, "You see? You see what's happening?" It didn't matter that there were Irish among those killed. The Irish were still to blame.'

'Did it get bad?'

Dermot shrugged. 'There were lots of calls for calm, for reason. Some people surprised you. Do you remember old Mrs Stokes next door?'

'Vaguely.'

'I'd always thought she was a bit snooty, but she was very nice to your mother afterwards. She told her to pay no notice to the idiots.

'I suppose it wasn't that people thought we were all terrorists, but they thought we probably knew who they were, that we were protecting them. There was a lot of insinuation.

'To be honest, it wasn't so bad for me on the buses. There were enough of us Irish, and the rest of them stood by us. There was a lot of solidarity in the garage – the lads had come out for Civil Rights in '69. But other places were pretty bad. There were walkouts and demos at Longbridge and some of the other big factories.'

'Against the Irish?'

'No, no, against the IRA, but some of them saw little difference.'

'But it all died down after a bit, didn't it?'

'I don't know if it died down, or we died down. We tried to make ourselves scarce – which is some trick when there's a hundred thousand or more of you. No more St Patrick's Day parades . . .'

'You were never into all that though.'

'All what?'

'All the St Patrick's Day nonsense – the big hats and the shamrocks.'

'I don't know about big hats, but certainly we celebrated St Patrick's Day. I remember the first parade just after I'd come over in '50 – there must have been a thousand of us from the buses – we had our own banner. It was a great day. There'd always be a big dance on the night. The first time I met your mother was at one of them. All that seemed to stop overnight.'

He sniffed. 'After those bombs in London last year . . .'

'IRA?'

'No, the other lot: 7/7 – the bus blown up. I said to Sunny who runs the shop round the corner, I said, "Do you know what's coming?"'

'What did he say to that?'

'He shrugged. He said, "It's already here."'

Eamonn followed the light of a fishing boat drawing closer.

'But you stayed in Birmingham.'

'We did. We got through it. We didn't want to leave. It felt like home.'

They'd been standing so long that Eamonn had grown cold.

'It's late, Dad.'

'You go on. I want to stay a while. I won't be long.'

Eamonn walked slowly, looking up at the moon, bigger than he had ever seen it. It was not the moon he knew. Its familiar, mournful face was lost in craters and shadows. He longed then to be home.

When he looked down there was a boy standing in the road in front of him. They stood immobile, neither breathing. The boy stopped in his tracks, frozen mid-run. Eamonn looked into the wide eyes he had seen before.

'You.'

His hand reached out slowly towards him. Fully outstretched, still he could not touch him. The boy glanced down at the hand, hanging there in the air between them, and then back at Eamonn. He gave the briefest smile and then he was gone, running silently towards the empty houses.

Eamonn was standing by a cement mixer when Dermot reached him.

'Were you waiting for me?'

Eamonn held his finger up to his lips and then pointed to the left of the building site, where the last completed house in Lomaverde stood. Dermot followed his gaze. The windows and front door were hidden behind metal shutters. Eamonn waited for a moment or two and then heard his father breathe in sharply. He had seen it. Tiny gaps in the shutters revealing dark shapes moving back and forth, some at a downstairs window, more upstairs – barely perceptible, shadows through keyholes.

'Ghosts,' said Eamonn.

44

Inga was still up painting. She welcomed them in and served them bitter coffee with spiced biscuits.

'You knew already,' said Dermot. 'I remember the bag of rice. For the cats.'

'I didn't want to worry you with it.'

'How did you find them?'

'That day down at the playground. When we found Ottoline. After you left I had a sense that someone was watching me. I had my suspicions about who it was.'

'So you knew before then?'

She shook her head. 'No. Not at all. My suspicion was wrong. It's shameful to admit it. I thought it had to be someone here and the only person I thought who might possibly ever do such a thing was Roger.'

Eamonn shrugged. 'That's not so crazy.'

'Oh, it is. Poor Roger. I just thought how angry he was with me for feeding the cats and how he liked hunting. I thought he might be trying to teach me a lesson. I sound quite stupid.'

Dermot smiled. 'Like Dr Watson.'

'Anyway, I thought I'd leave the carcass in the bag on the ground and then pretend to leave. I waited to see if anybody came back.' She got out a cigarette. 'I got a terrible shock when I saw him. Not Roger. Some poor young man. He looked so scared. He picked up the bag and I followed him.'

Eamonn asked, 'Do you know how many of them there are?'

'Twelve at least. The lucky few that made it across.'

'Does anybody else know? What about Esteban?'

'He knows, I think. His uncle has a farm, and the farmers, they need cheap labour, you know, and the migrants, they need work. It's been going on for months. A van collecting them at night.'

Dermot had an image of a rusty old transit. He remembered Matty Keegan. Frozen winter's mornings, the sound of him dressing in the room.

'Have you told the police?'

She shook her head. 'I found a charity that works with illegal immigrants. I spoke to them today. They are going to come and talk to the men. I wasn't sure what to do. I didn't know who to tell. I didn't want the authorities involved. The men have been through enough, I think. I hope they will get some help now.'

Dermot nodded. 'I don't know what else you could have done.'

She looked out of the window. 'We talk about strange noises, things that go bump in the night; I think we almost enjoy the idea of ghosts. But real people? Confined to darkness and silence, living among us? It's so sad. So awful.'

It was after one when Eamonn went, leaving Dermot and Inga talking. It was only when the sky started to lighten that Dermot stood and said, 'I should be going.'

'Oh yes, of course. It's very late. You must have packing to do.'

'I didn't bring much.'

'Well. Later today you'll be back in England, happy by your own fireside.'

Dermot imagined opening the front door. The familiar smells. The familiar things. Suffocating.

He gestured over at her painting. 'I would have liked to have seen that when it's finished.'

'Oh. Well. Maybe I can send a photo. It's not the same thing, but if you wanted to see it, I could email you an image.'

He nodded. 'Email. I'd need a computer for that.'

She smiled. 'Or I could just post a photograph.'

'No, you mustn't go to any bother.'

'It would be my pleasure. I could send it to you as a postcard and then maybe you could send me a postcard in return.'

'Of Birmingham?'

'Why not?'

'I'm not sure they make them.'

She smiled. 'Well. Maybe we will keep in touch anyway. I would like that.'

There was suddenly an awkwardness where there had been none. Without warning she leaned forward and kissed him on both cheeks.

'Goodbye, Dermot, it was really very good to meet you. I hope we will meet again.'

He remained standing in the same spot, feeling the brush of her lips against his skin, the light touch of her fingers on his arms. He looked at her for a long time and then he said, 'Did you say you had a computer?'

'Yes, a laptop.'

'Can you get the Internet on it?'

'Yes.'

'And you know how to work it?'

'Of course.'

'Do you think you could help me with something?'

45

They ate their breakfast on the terrace.

'You've hours yet. Did you want to do anything?'

'I'm happy enough here for now.'

Eamonn thought that he should say more to reassure Dermot before he left. Absolve him of any worry.

'I've been thinking – if this is how it ends with Laura, then this is how it ends. It'll be hard, but life will go on. I'll get over it in time.' He paused and then added in a voice that wasn't his own: 'Plenty more fish in the sea!' He made an expansive gesture at the barren landscape around them and gave a big smile. He was finding it hard to judge the tone correctly. Dermot ignored him and looked out at the horizon.

'I like it here.'

Eamonn nodded. 'Yeah. Oh yeah. I mean, me too. It's great really. A few teething problems, but I just need to give it more time.'

Dermot carried on studying the vista and then turned and looked directly at Eamonn. 'There's no future for you here, son.'

Eamonn froze. A distant memory from childhood. His father could read minds. Somehow he had forgotten this.

'You should speak to Laura.'

Eamonn breathed out. 'Well, that's difficult when she won't speak to me. I've emailed her, I've texted her, I ring her all the time.'

Dermot shook his head. 'But that's not speaking to her, is it? Face to face. That's a conversation.'

'She's not here. Have you not noticed? She's gone.'

'You get on a plane, you go after her.'

'Oh, Dad, come on. She wouldn't appreciate that. There's no point.'

'My God. I thought you weren't like me. I thought you had more sense. "No point"? Jesus Christ. Do anything but talk to her. Anything but say what needs to be said, to her face. Send her your essays every day if you like, but don't kid yourself that's talking.'

Eamonn walked to the edge of the terrace and looked out. 'I used to talk to her all the time. I told her everything. We'd talk all night. After we came here, I started waking in the nights. My heart hammering, difficulty breathing. Panic attacks, I suppose.' He turned to face Dermot. 'I could have just leaned over, reached out and held her hand, told her that I wasn't coping. But I didn't.

'She's very resilient, you know, Laura. Very strong. She took it all in her stride. She dealt with the disappointments here, the weirdnesses, and she still kept a purpose, was still funny. Still herself.

'She was everything to me. I know that's corny but it's true. And it's not good. To depend on someone like that. I mean, once we'd been everything to each other, but then suddenly we weren't equal, I was heavier, a big weight that she had to bear, and I didn't want her to feel it, to know it.' He rubbed his face with his hands. 'I just kept on and on and on until she was gone.'

He fell silent for a while.

'I know I need to speak to her.'

Dermot stood. 'So why don't you go and pack your bags?'

'I better book a flight first.'

'You don't need to. I've already done it.'

'You? On the Internet?'

'I got someone to help me.'

'Oh. OK. Am I on your flight?'

'You are.'

Eamonn was a little disoriented but headed to his room to start packing a bag. A moment later he returned.

'You haven't packed your shaving things.'

'I don't need to pack them.'

'You're leaving them here?'

'I am. I'll need them.'

Eamonn looked at him. 'I'm confused.'

'You're on my flight, son. On my ticket. I've changed the name. They let you do that. To be honest, I wouldn't have had a clue, but Inga sorted it all out for me.'

'You're not coming with me?'

'I thought I'd stay here.'

'Here?' Eamonn was aware of sounding stupid.

'I've got my pension. I've got savings. I've got more money than I can spend. I can keep up the payments. You go home, there's nothing to pay there, just the heating of the place.'

'That's insane.'

'Why is it? I like it here. Very much. Haven't I worked hard all my life? Don't I deserve a place in the sun?'

'That's not the point. This is my mess. I need to clear it up.'

'You've just told me how unhappy you've been here but you're insisting on staying. My God, Eamonn, your mother would have been proud. Maybe they'll make you a saint after you die.'

Eamonn looked at him. 'But you'd be on your own.'

'I'm on my own at home, aren't I? What's the difference? I like it here. There are good people around. I'll make friends. Remember, I've done it before – water off a duck's back to me.'

'You have it all worked out.'

'I have it all worked out.'

'What if you change your mind?'

'Then I'll go home.'

Eamonn dragged his fingers through his hair. 'I thought I'd be happy here.'

'Maybe you were happy enough at home.'

'I messed it all up.'

Dermot shrugged. 'You just took a wrong turning. Everyone's done that.'

Eamonn went to his room to resume packing. He had not spent a night away from Lomaverde since his mother's funeral. The idea that he could just get on a plane and leave seemed remarkable. The thought of being anywhere else unbelievable. He found it hard to imagine himself, the person he might be, away from there. It felt to him as if Lomaverde were inside him and he didn't know how he would feel on a busy street, in the rain, waiting for a bus. He found the prospect of even such prosaic moments exhilarating and faintly terrifying.

He packed an odd selection of clothes, found his passport and only at the last minute remembered his phone, recharging in the corner. There was a message.

Sorry it's taken so long. I've done a lot of thinking. I have something to tell you. Then you'll need to think too. Phone you this evening.

He stared at the message for a long time and finally he knew what it was.

46

One year later

He sat down carefully and she woke up. Her face instantly clouded with anguish and she began to cry. He stood up and she quietened and fell asleep once more. Her breathing slowed and steadied and he tried again, bending his knees almost imperceptibly, lowering himself gradually on to the chair. As he made contact with the seat, her eyelids flickered open again, revealing two dark blue irises, burning with betrayal and pain, and she let out a howl. He spoke in a low voice as he got up:

'It's OK. I'm sorry. I'm standing. No chair. No chair.'

He cradled the back of her head with his hand. She was asleep within seconds. He stood then for a long time, humming a tune from a long-forgotten advert, the tempo slowed down, a hidden mournfulness revealed in its melody. He swayed in a kind of trance, conscious only of the cycle of the notes, the heat of her head, the weight of her body. Eventually he took her back and laid her next to Laura on the bed. He put his lips to her forehead, placed her hand on her mother's, and left.

Outside the block he stood blinking for a moment, waiting to adjust to the light and the heat. He walked into the street wondering which way he might go when he caught a glimpse of movement high on the hill above him. He shielded his eyes with his hands and looked up towards the black shape. It was a human figure, picking its way slowly down the steep path. Eamonn's legs recognized him first. They started moving, seemingly independent of his will, up the slope. He called out: 'Hello there!' And was pleased to hear the surprise in his father's voice.

'Eamonn?'

He made his way quickly up the track until he stood smiling and out of breath before him.

'What's this?'

'Surprise.'

Dermot looked at him. 'But I've nothing ready. How long have you been here? Have you had a drink even?'

'It's fine. We let ourselves in. I was just coming out to find you.'

'I haven't even a cot set up. I could have had it all arranged.'

Eamonn reached out and touched him lightly on the arm. 'The best visits are unannounced, you used to say that.'

Dermot looked at him and then smiled.

'Well, then.'

'Well, then.'

Eamonn frowned. 'You look strange with a tan.'

'I always had some colour in my face.'

'That was Birmingham bus-driver colour. Now you're all Mediterranean. It makes you look . . .'

'Wealthy and handsome?'

'No. Like a labourer. You look like you've been out building a motorway.'

'Oh, I see.'

They walked down the hill together.

'I'm sorry I wasn't here. I was walking. Best time to do it, before it gets too hot.'

'You look well.'

'I feel fine.' He looked at Eamonn. 'And what about you? Are you all well?'

'We are.'

'You look like you've gained a little weight.'

'Takeaways. I missed them.'

'You're less skeletal now. More cadaverous, I'd say.'

'That's good.'

'And everything's OK, is it?'

Eamonn smiled. 'Yes. Everything's OK.'

'What's funny?'

'You sound like Mom.'

'Do I? I suppose I do. How is the little one?'

'She's good. A baby. You know. She doesn't sleep.'

'Do you know who she is yet?'

'What do you mean?'

'Your mother and I, we used to look in at you in your cot when you were sleeping, and ask: "Who are you?" You were a little stranger come to live with us. A mystery. We were waiting for you to reveal yourself to us.'

'No, I'm not sure she's done that yet.'

'Good for her.'

They left the hillside and walked along the street.

'I see the pool's been restored to its former glory.'

'It wasn't that big a job in the end. We found the right fellas to do it, and it didn't cost an arm and a leg. Just a crack in the lining. I like to sneak over there at night.'

'Why do you need to sneak?'

'I suppose I don't really. There's nobody to mind. I float on my back in the dark, looking up at the stars, thinking. A nocturnal fish, that's what Inga calls me. I can give the cats a rare fright when I sit up.'

They reached the apartment block. He hesitated as Dermot held the door open.

'Come in, come in, will you.'

Eamonn looked over at the pool.

'I'd love a swim now. Do you fancy it?'

'I do not. There's someone inside that I'm very keen to see.'

Eamonn nodded. 'She's asleep. She didn't sleep last night.'

'Well, it's no more than you deserve. You were the worst. She'll be a good girl now for her Granddad. I have a cupboard there in the kitchen with a few little things in that she'll like.'

'Dad, please don't stuff her with rubbish.'

'What? I'm not going to stuff her. She can have a little chocolate, can't she? My God, I bet you have her eating dried fruit and yoghurt.'

'She likes yoghurt.'

'Because she doesn't know any better.'

Eamonn shrugged. 'Try not to wake Laura. She's exhausted.'

Dermot smiled. 'Well, she can take it easy now for a few days. You both can. You just let me get on with it.'

Eamonn crossed over the road and let himself in through the turnstile. A few minutes later he heard the gate open again.

'Did he wake you up?'

'No. I was awake.'

'Is she still asleep?'

'He's watching her. I mean literally: watching her. Peering into her face. She'll get a shock when she wakes up.'

Something moved behind them and they turned to see a mottled cat emerging from the shadows under one of the sun loungers. It scampered away in panic at the sight of them.

Eamonn looked at her. 'How are you?'

'OK.' She pushed the hair out of her eyes. 'What about you?'

'Yeah. OK.'

They stripped and stood at the edge of the pool. It never failed to entice. The clean lines. The perfect contrast. The endless blue.

'It's strange to be back.'

'Maybe it's too soon.'

They held hands, experiencing the same desire to break the surface of the water. To feel the shock of the cold.

'No. It's OK, I think. A few days. It's finite.'

He smiled and they leaped together into the view.

Acknowledgements

Sincere thanks to Stan Nutt and Bill Ralph from the National Express Yardley Wood Bus Garage for sharing their time and experiences with me.

I'm grateful to Jim Hannah, Francisco Dominguez-Montero, Dr Kristin Ewins and James Yarker of Stan's Cafe, who all gave time, advice and/or assistance with research at various points.

Thanks also to Emer Carr, Oonagh O'Flynn, Mary Noonan, Frances Jones and Nicholas O'Flynn for help with questions about our parents and countless things past; and Damien Flynn for information about Uncle Tom and the Irish Citizens' League. In addition James Moran's book *Irish Birmingham* (Liverpool University Press) was fascinating and especially helpful.

Thanks to Lucy Luck, Venetia Butterfield, Sarah Bowlin and Sarah Coward.

Finally, the least adequate thank-you of all to Peter Fletcher.